Difficult Loves

ITALO CALVINO

Difficult Loves

Translated from the Italian by WILLIAM WEAVER,
ANN GOLDSTEIN, *and* ARCHIBALD COLQUHOUN

MARINER CLASSICS
New York   Boston

First Mariner Books edition 2017

Copyright © 1958, 1949 by Giulio Einaudi Editore, S.p.A., Torino

First published in Italy by Giulio Einaudi Editore, S.p.A. as *Gli Amori Difficili*

English translation copyright © 1984, 1983 by HarperCollins Publishers with the following exceptions:
   Translation of "The Adventure of a Crook," "The Adventure of a Wife," and "The Adventure of the Married Couple" copyright © 1983 by Martin Secker & Warburg Ltd.
   Translation of "The Adventure of a Skier" and "The Adventure of a Motorist" copyright © 2017 by The Estate of Italo Calvino
   Translation of "The Argentine Ant" copyright © 1957 by Harper Collins. First published in Italy in *I racconti*, by Giulio Einaudi Editore, S.p.A., Torino, 1958
   Translation of "Smog" copyright © 1971 by   HarperCollins I
First published in Italy in *I racconti*, by Giulio Einaudi Editore, S.p.A., Torino, 1958

Mariner Books
An Imprint of HarperCollins Publishers, registered in the United States of America and/or other jurisdictions.

www.marinerbooks.com

Library of Congress Cataloging-in-Publication Data is available.
ISBN 978-0-544-95912-5

Printed in the United States of America
24 25 26 27 28 LBC 11 10 9 8 7

Contents

Contents

Editor's Note

The stories in this collection were written during the 1950s and collected in the anthology *I racconti* (Turin: Einaudi, 1958). "The Adventure of a Skier" and "The Adventure of a Motorist" were translated by Ann Goldstein for this volume. "The Argentine Ant" was translated by Archibald Colquhoun for the volume *Adam, One Afternoon* (London: William Collins & Sons, 1957). The remaining stories were translated by William Weaver: "The Adventure of a Crook," "The Adventure of a Wife," and "The Adventure of the Married Couple" for the volume *Difficult Loves* (London: Secker & Warburg, 1983); "Smog" for the volume *The Watcher and Other Stories* (New York: Harcourt Brace, 1971); and all others for the volume *Difficult Loves* (New York: Harcourt Brace, 1984).

PART I

Difficult Loves

The Adventure of a Soldier

In the compartment, a lady came and sat down, tall and buxom, next to Private Tomagra. She must have been a widow from the provinces, to judge by her dress and her veil: the dress was black silk, appropriate for prolonged mourning, but with useless frills and furbelows; and the veil went all around her face, falling from the brim of a massive, old-fashioned hat. Other places were free, there in the compartment, Private Tomagra noticed, and he had assumed the widow would surely choose one of them. But, on the contrary, despite the vicinity of a coarse soldier like himself, she came and sat right there — no doubt for some reason connected with travel, the soldier quickly decided, a draft, or the direction of the train.

Her body was in full bloom, solid, indeed a bit square. If its upper curves had not been tempered by a matronly softness, you would have said she was no more than thirty; but when you looked at her face, at the complexion both marmoreal and relaxed, the unattainable gaze beneath the heavy eyelids and the thick black brows, at the sternly sealed lips, hastily colored with a jarring red, she seemed instead past forty.

Tomagra, a young infantryman on his first leave (it was Easter), huddled down in his seat for fear that the lady, so ample and shapely, might not fit; immediately he found himself in the aura of her perfume, a popular and perhaps cheap scent, but now, out of long wear, blended with natural human odors.

The lady sat down with a composed demeanor, revealing, there beside him, less majestic proportions than he had imagined when he had seen her standing. Her hands were plump, with tight, dark rings; she kept them folded in her lap, over a shiny purse and a jacket she had taken off to expose round white arms. At her first movement Tomagra had shifted to make space for a broad maneuvering of her arms; but she had remained almost motionless, slipping out of the sleeves with a few brief twitches of her shoulders and torso.

The railroad seat was therefore fairly comfortable for two, and Tomagra could feel the lady's extreme closeness, though without any fear of offending her by his contact. All the same, Tomagra reasoned, lady though she was, she had surely not shown any sign of repugnance toward him, toward his rough uniform; otherwise she would have sat farther away. And at these thoughts his muscles, till now contracted and tensed, relaxed freely, serenely; indeed, without his moving, they tried to expand to their greatest extension, and his leg—its tendons taut, at first detached even from the cloth of his trousers—settled more broadly, tightening the material that covered it, and the wool grazed the widow's black silk. And now, through this wool and that silk, the soldier's leg was adhering to her leg with a soft, fleeting motion, like one shark grazing another, and sending waves through its veins to those other veins.

It was still a very light contact, which every jolt of the train could break off and re-create; the lady had strong, fat knees, and Tomagra's bones could sense at every jerk the lazy bump of the kneecap. The calf had raised a silken cheek that, with an imperceptible thrust, had to be made to coincide with his own. This meeting of calves was precious, but it came at a price, a loss: in fact, the body's weight was shifted and the reciprocal support of the hips no longer occurred with the same docile abandon. In order to achieve a natural and satisfied position, it was necessary to move slightly on the seat, with the aid of a curve in the track, and also of the comprehensible need to shift position every so often.

The lady was impassive beneath her matronly hat, her gaze fixed, lidded, and her hands steady on the purse in her lap. And yet her body, for a very long stretch, rested against that stretch of man. Hadn't she realized this yet? Or was she preparing to flee? To rebel?

Tomagra decided to transmit, somehow, a message to her: he contracted the muscle of his calf into a kind of hard, square fist, and then with this calf-fist, as if a hand inside it wanted to open, he quickly knocked at the calf of the widow. To be sure, this was a very rapid movement, barely long enough for a flicker of the tendons; but in any case, she didn't draw back—at least not so far as he could tell, because immediately, needing to justify that covert movement, Tomagra extended his leg as if to get a kink out of it.

Now he had to begin all over again; that patient and prudently established contact had been lost. Tomagra decided to be more courageous; as if looking for something, he stuck his hand in his pocket, the pocket toward the woman, and then, as if absently, he left it there. It had been a rapid action, Tomagra didn't know whether he had touched her or not, an inconsequential gesture; yet he now realized what an important step forward he had made, and in what a risky game he was now involved. Against the back of his hand, the hip of the lady in black was now pressing; he felt it weighing on every finger, every knuckle; now any movement of his hand would have been an act of incredible intimacy toward the widow. Holding his breath, Tomagra turned his hand inside his pocket; in other words, he set the palm toward the lady, open against her, though still in that pocket. It was an impossible position, the wrist twisted. And yet at this point he might just as well attempt a decisive action: and so he ventured to move the fingers of that contorted hand. There could no longer be any possible doubt: the widow couldn't have helped noticing his maneuvering, and if she didn't draw back, but pretended to be impassive and absent, it meant that she wasn't rejecting his advances. When Tomagra thought about it, however, her paying no attention to his mobile right hand might mean that she really believed he was hunting for something in that pocket: a railroad ticket, a match . . . There: and if now the soldier's fingertips, the pads, seemingly endowed with a sudden clairvoyance, could sense through those different stuffs the hems of subterranean garments and even the very minute roughness of skin, pores and moles—if, as I said, his fingertips arrived at this, perhaps her flesh, marmoreal and lazy, was hardly aware that these were in fact fingertips and not, for example, nails or knuckles.

Then, with furtive steps, the hand emerged from the pocket, paused there undecided, and, with sudden haste to adjust the trouser along the side seam, proceeded all the way down to the knee. More precisely, it cleared a path: to go forward, it had to dig in between himself and the woman, a route that, even in its speed, was rich in anxieties and sweet emotions.

It must be said that Tomagra had thrown his head back against the seat, so one might also have thought he was sleeping. This was not so much an alibi for himself as it was a way of offering the lady, in the event that his insistence didn't irritate her, a reason to feel at ease, knowing that his actions were divorced from his consciousness, barely surfacing from the depths of sleep. And there, from this alert semblance of sleep, Tomagra's hand, clutching his knee, detached one finger, and sent it out to reconnoiter. The finger slid along her knee, which remained still and docile; Tomagra could perform diligent figures with the little finger on the silk of the stocking, which, through his half-closed eyes, he could barely glimpse, light and curving. But he realized that the risk of this game was without reward, because the little finger, scant of surface and awkward in movement, transmitted only partial hints of sensations and was incapable of conceiving the form and substance of what it was touching.

Then he reattached the little finger to the rest of the hand, not withdrawing it, but adding to it the ring finger, the middle finger, the forefinger: now his whole hand rested inert on that female knee, and the train cradled it in a rocking caress.

It was then that Tomagra thought of the others: if the lady, whether out of compliance or out of a mysterious intangibility, didn't react to his boldness, facing them were still seated other persons who might be scandalized by that nonsoldierly behavior of his, and by that possible silent complicity on the woman's part. Chiefly to spare the lady such suspicion, Tomagra withdrew his hand, or rather, he hid it, as if it were the only guilty party. But hiding it, he later thought, was only a hypocritical pretext: in abandoning it there on the seat he intended simply to move it closer to the lady, who occupied in fact such a large part of the space.

Indeed, the hand groped around. There: like a butterfly's lighting, the fingers already sensed her presence; and there: it was enough merely to thrust the whole palm forward gently, and the widow's gaze beneath the veil was impenetrable, the bosom only faintly stirred by her respiration. But no! Tomagra had already withdrawn his hand, like a mouse scurrying off.

She didn't move; he thought, Maybe she wants this. But he also thought, Another moment and it will be too late. Or maybe she's sitting there studying me, preparing to make a scene.

Then, for no reason except prudent verification, Tomagra slid his hand along the back of the seat and waited until the train's jolts, imperceptibly, made the lady slide over his fingers. To say he waited is not correct: actually, with the tips of his fingers wedgelike between the seat and her, he made an invisible push, which could also have been the effect of the train's speeding. If he stopped at a certain point, it wasn't because the lady had given any indication of disapproval, but, on the contrary, because Tomagra thought that if she did accept, it would be easy for her, with a half rotation of the muscles, to meet him halfway, to fall, as it were, on that expectant hand. To suggest to her the friendly nature of his attention, Tomagra, in that position beneath the lady, attempted a discreet wiggle of the fingers; the lady was looking out of the window, and her hand was idly toying with the purse clasp, opening and closing it. Was this a signal to him to stop? Was it a final concession she was granting him, a warning that her patience could be tried no longer? Was it this? Tomagra asked himself. Was it this?

He noticed that his hand, like a stubby octopus, was clasping her flesh. Now all was decided: he could no longer draw back, not Tomagra. But what about her? She was a sphinx.

With a crab's oblique scuttle, the soldier's hand now descended her thigh. Was it out in the open, before the eyes of the others? No, now the lady was adjusting the jacket she held folded on her lap, allowing it to spill to one side. To offer him cover, or to block his path? There: now the hand moved freely and unseen, it clasped her, it opened in fleeting caresses like brief puffs of wind. But the widow's face was still turned away, distant; Tomagra stared at a part of her, a zone of naked skin between the ear and the curve of her full chignon. And in that dimple beneath the ear a vein throbbed: this was the answer she was giving him, clear, heart-rending, and fleeting. She turned her face all of a sudden, proud and marmoreal; the veil hanging below the hat stirred like a curtain; the gaze was lost beneath the heavy lids. But that gaze had gone past him, Tomagra, perhaps had not even grazed him; she was looking beyond him, at something, or nothing, the pretext of some thought, but anyway something more important than he. This he decided later, because earlier, when he had barely seen that movement of hers, he had immediately thrown himself back and shut his eyes tight, as if he were asleep, trying to quell the flush spreading over his face, and thus perhaps losing the opportunity to catch in the first glint of her eyes an answer to his own extreme doubts.

His hand, hidden under the black jacket, had remained as if detached from him, numb, the fingers drawn back toward the wrist: no longer a real hand, now without sensitivity beyond that arboreal sensitivity of the bones. But as the truce the widow had granted to her own impassivity with that vague glance around soon ended, blood and courage flowed back into the hand. And it was then that, resuming contact with that soft saddle of leg, he realized he had reached a limit: the fingers were running along the hem of the skirt, beyond which there was the leap to the knee, and the void.

It was the end, Private Tomagra thought, of this secret spree. Thinking back, he found it truly a poor thing in his memory, though he had greedily blown it up while experiencing it: a clumsy feel of a silk dress, something that could in no way have been denied him simply because of his miserable position as a soldier, and something that the lady had discreetly condescended, without any show, to concede.

He was interrupted, however, in his desolate intention of withdrawing his hand when he noticed the way she was holding her jacket on her knees: no longer folded (though it had seemed so to him before) but flung carelessly, so that one edge fell in front of her legs. His hand was thus in a sealed den—perhaps a final proof of the trust the lady was giving him, confident that the disparity between her station and the soldier's was so great that he surely wouldn't take advantage of the opportunity. And the soldier recalled, with effort, what had happened so far between the widow and himself as he tried to discover something in her behavior that hinted at further condescension; now he considered whether his own actions had been insignificant and trivial, casual grazings and strokings, or, on the other hand, of a decisive intimacy, committing him not to withdraw again.

His hand surely agreed with this second consideration, because before he could reflect on the irreparable nature of the act, he was already passing the frontier. And the lady? She was asleep. She had rested her head, with the pompous hat, against a corner of the seat, and she was keeping her eyes closed. Should he, Tomagra, respect this sleep, genuine or false as it might be, and retire? Or was it a consenting woman's device, which he should already know, for which he should somehow indicate gratitude? The point he had now reached admitted no hesitation: he could only advance.

Private Tomagra's hand was small and plump, and its hard parts and calluses had become so blended with the muscle that it was uniform, flexible; the bones could not be felt, and its movement was made more with nerves, though gently, than with joints. And this little hand had constant and general and minuscule movements, to maintain the completeness of the contact alive and burning. But when, finally, a first stirring ran through the widow's softness, like the motion of distant marine currents through secret underwater channels, the soldier was so surprised by it that, as if he really supposed the widow had noticed nothing till then, had really been asleep, he drew his hand away in fright.

Now he sat there with his hands on his own knees, huddled in his seat as he had been when she came in. He was behaving absurdly; he realized that. With a scraping of heels, a stretching of hips, he seemed eager to reestablish the contacts, but this prudence of his was absurd too, as if he wanted to start his extremely patient operation again from the beginning, as if he were not sure now of the deep goals already gained. But had he really gained them? Or had it been only a dream?

A tunnel fell upon them. The darkness became denser and denser, and Tomagra, first with timid gestures, occasionally drawing back as if he were really at the first advances and amazed at his own temerity, then trying more and more to convince himself of the profound intimacy he had already reached with that woman, extended one hand, shy as a pullet, toward her bosom, large and somewhat abandoned to its own gravity, and with an eager groping he tried to explain to her the misery and the unbearable happiness of his condition, and his need of nothing else but for her to emerge from her reserve.

The widow did react, but with a sudden gesture of shielding herself and rejecting him. It was enough to send Tomagra crouching in his corner, wringing his hands. But it was, probably, a false alarm caused by a passing light in the corridor, which had made the widow fear the tunnel was suddenly going to end. Perhaps; or had he gone too far, had he committed some horrible rudeness toward her, who had already been so generous toward him? No, by now there could be nothing forbidden between them; and her action, on the contrary, was a sign that this was all real, that she accepted, participated. Tomagra approached again. To be sure, in these reflections a great deal of time had been wasted; the tunnel wouldn't last much longer, and it wasn't wise to allow oneself to be caught by the sudden light. Tomagra was already expecting the first grayness there on the wall; the more he expected it, the riskier it was to attempt anything. Of course, this was a long tunnel; he remembered it from other journeys as very, very long. And if he took advantage immediately, he would have a lot of time ahead of him. Now it was best to wait for the end, but it never ended, and so this had perhaps been his last chance. There: now the darkness was being dispelled, it was ending.

They were at the last stations of a provincial line. The train was emptying; some passengers in the compartment had already got out, and now the last ones were taking down their bags, leaving. Finally they were alone in the compartment, the soldier and the widow, very close and detached, their arms folded, silent, eyes staring into space. Tomagra still had to think, Now that all the seats are free, if she wanted to be nice and comfortable, if she were fed up with me, she would move . . .

Something restrained him and frightened him still, perhaps the presence of a group of smokers in the passage, or a light that had come on because it was evening. Then he thought to draw the curtains on the passage, like somebody wanting to get some sleep. He stood up with elephantine steps; with slow, meticulous care he began to unfasten the curtains, draw them, fasten them again. When he turned, he found her stretched out. As if she wanted to sleep: even though she had her eyes open and staring, she had slipped down, maintaining her matronly composure intact, with the majestic hat still on her head, which was resting on the seat arm.

Tomagra was standing over her. Still, to protect this image of sleep, he chose also to darken the outside window; and he stretched over her, to undo the curtain. But it was only a way of shifting his clumsy actions above the impassive widow. Then he stopped tormenting that curtain's snap and understood he had to do something else: show her all his own, compelling condition of desire, if only to explain to her the misunderstanding into which she had certainly fallen, as if to say to her, You see, you were kind to me because you believe we have a remote need for affection, we poor lonely soldiers, but here is what I really am, this is how I received your courtesy, this is the degree of impossible ambition I have reached, you see, here.

And since it was now evident that nothing could manage to surprise the lady, and indeed everything seemed somehow to have been foreseen by her, Private Tomagra could only make sure that no further doubts were possible; and finally the urgency of his madness managed also to grasp its mute object: her.

When Tomagra stood up and, beneath him, the widow remained with her clear, stern gaze (she had blue eyes), with her hat and veil still squarely on her head, and the train never stopped its shrill whistling through the fields, and outside those endless rows of grapevines went on, and the rain that throughout the journey had tirelessly streaked the panes now resumed with new violence, he had again a brief spurt of fear, thinking how he, Private Tomagra, had been so daring.

The Adventure of a Crook

The important thing was not to get himself arrested immediately. Gim flattened himself in the recess of a doorway; the police seemed to run straight past, but then, all at once, he heard their steps come back, turn into the alley. He darted off, in agile leaps.

"Stop or we'll shoot, Gim!"

Sure, sure, go ahead and shoot! he thought, and he was already out of their range, his feet thrusting him from the edge of the pebbled steps, down the slanting streets of the old city. Above the fountain, he jumped over the railing of the stairs, then he was under the archway, which amplified the pounding of his steps.

The whole circuit that came into his mind had to be rejected: Lola no, Nilde no, Renée no. Those guys would soon be all over the place, knocking at doors. It was a mild night, the clouds so pale they wouldn't have looked out of place in the daytime, above the arches set high over the alleyways.

On reaching the broad streets of the new city, Mario Albanesi alias Gim Bolero slowed his pace a little, tucked behind his ears the strings of hair that fell from his temples. Not a step was heard. Determined and discreet, he crossed over, reached Armanda's doorway, and climbed to her apartment. At this time of night she surely didn't have anybody with her; she would be sleeping. Gim knocked hard.

"Who's there?" a man's voice asked, irritated, after a moment. "At this time of night people get their sleep . . ." It was Lilin.

"Open up a minute, Armanda. It's me, it's Gim," he said, not loud, but firmly.

Armanda rolled over in bed. "Oh, Gim boy, just a minute, I'll open the door. Uh, it's Gim." She grabbed the wire at the head of the bed that opened the front door and pulled.

The door clicked, obedient; Gim went along the corridor, hands in his pockets; he entered the bedroom. In Armanda's huge bed, her body, in great mounds under the sheets, seemed to take up all the space. On the pillow, her face without makeup, under the black bangs, hung slack, baggy, and wrinkled. Beyond, as if in a fold of the blanket, on the far side of the bed, her husband, Lilin, was lying; and he seemed to want to bury his little bluish face in the pillow, to recover his interrupted sleep.

Lilin has to wait till the last customer has gone before he can get into bed and sleep off the weariness that accumulates during his lazy days. There is nothing in the world that Lilin knows how to do or wants to do; if he has his smokes, he's content. Armanda can't say Lilin costs her much, except for the packets of tobacco he consumes in the course of a day. He goes out with his packet in the morning, sits for a while at the cobbler's, at the junk dealer's, at the plumber's, rolls one paper after another and smokes, seated on those shop stools, his long, smooth, thief's hands on his knees, his gaze dull, listening like a spy to everyone, hardly ever contributing a word to the talk except for brief remarks and unexpected smiles, crooked and yellow. At evening, when the last shop has closed, he goes to the wine counter and drains a liter, burns up the cigarettes he has left, until they also pull down the shutters. He comes out; his wife is still on her beat along the Corso in her short dress, her swollen feet in her tight shoes. Lilin appears around a corner, gives her a low whistle, mutters a few words to tell her it's late now; she should come to bed. Without looking at him, on the step of the sidewalk as if on a stage, her bosom compressed in the armature of wire and elastic, her old woman's body in her young girl's dress, nervously twitching her purse in her hands, drawing circles on the pavement with her heels, suddenly humming, she tells him no, people are still around, he must go off and wait. They woo each other like this every night.

. . .

"Well then, Gim?" Armanda says, widening her eyes.

He has already found some cigarettes on the night table and lights one.

"I have to spend the night here. Tonight." And he is already taking off his jacket, undoing his tie.

"Sure, Gim, get into bed. You go onto the sofa, Lilin, go on, Lilin honey, clear out now, let Gim get to bed."

Lilin lies there a bit, like a stone; then he pulls himself up, emitting a complaint without distinct words; he gets down from the bed, takes his pillow, a blanket, the tobacco from the table, the cigarette papers, matches, ashtray. "Go on, Lilin honey, go on." Tiny and hunched, he goes off, under his load, toward the sofa in the corridor.

Gim smokes as he undresses, folds his trousers neatly and hangs them up, arranges his jacket around a chair by the head of the bed, brings the cigarettes from the dresser to the night table, matches, an ashtray, and climbs into bed. Armanda turns off the lamp and sighs. Gim smokes. Lilin sleeps in the corridor. Armanda rolls over. Gim stubs out his cigarette. There is a knocking at the door.

With one hand Gim is already touching the revolver in the pocket of his jacket; with the other he has taken Armanda by the elbow, warning her to be careful. Armanda's arm is fat and soft. They stay like that for a while.

"Ask who it is, Lilin," Armanda says in a low voice.

Lilin, in the hall, huffs impatiently. "Who is it?" he asks rudely.

"Hey, Armanda, it's me. Angelo."

"Angelo who?" she says.

"Angelo the sergeant, Armanda. I happened to be going by, and I thought I'd come up . . . Can you open the door a minute?"

Gim has got out of the bed and is signaling her to be quiet. He opens a door, looks into the toilet, takes the chair with his clothes and carries it inside.

"Nobody's seen me. Get rid of him fast," he says softly, and locks himself in the toilet.

"Come on, Lilin honey, get back into bed, come on, Lilin." From the bed Armanda directs the rearrangement.

"Armanda, you're keeping me waiting," the other man says, beyond the door.

Calmly Lilin collects blanket, pillow, tobacco, matches, papers, ashtray, and comes back to bed, gets in, and pulls the sheet to his eyes. Armanda grabs the wire and clicks open the door.

Sergeant Soddu comes in, with the rumpled look of an old policeman in civilian clothes, his mustache gray against his fat face.

"You're out late, Sergeant," Armanda says.

"Oh, I was just taking a walk," Soddu says, "and I thought I'd pay you a call."

"What was it you wanted?"

Soddu was at the head of the bed, wiping his sweaty face with his handkerchief.

"Nothing, just a little visit. What's new?"

"New how?"

"Have you seen Albanesi by any chance?"

"Gim? What's he done now?"

"Nothing. Kid stuff . . . We wanted to ask him something. Have you seen him?"

"Three days ago."

"I mean now."

"I've been asleep for two hours, Sarge. Why are you asking me? Go ask his girls: Rosy, Nilde, Lola . . ."

"No use. When he's in trouble, he stays away from them."

"He hasn't shown up here. Next time, Sarge."

"Well, Armanda, I was just asking. Anyway, I'm glad to pay you a visit."

"Goodnight, Sarge."

"Goodnight, eh."

Soddu turned but didn't leave.

"I was thinking . . . it's practically morning, and I don't have any other rounds to make. I don't feel like going back to that cot. So long as I'm here, I've half a mind to stay. What about it, Armanda?"

"Sergeant, you're always great, but to tell you the truth, at this time of night, I'm not receiving. That's how it is, Sarge. We all have our schedule."

"Armanda . . . an old friend like me." Soddu was already removing his jacket, his undershirt.

"You're a nice man, Sergeant. Why don't we get together tomorrow night?"

Soddu went on undressing. "It's to pass the night, you
understand, Armanda? Well, make some room for me."

"Lilin will go on the sofa then. Go on, Lilin honey, go
on out now."

Lilin groped with his long hands, found the tobacco
on the table, pulled himself up, grumbling, climbed from
the bed almost without opening his eyes, collected pillow,
blanket, papers, matches. "Go on, Lilin honey." He went
off, dragging the blanket along the hall. Soddu turned over
between the sheets.

Next door, Gim looked through the panes of the little
window at the sky, turning green. He had forgotten his
cigarettes on the table, that was the trouble. And now the
other man was getting into bed and Gim had to stay shut
up until daylight between that bidet and those boxes of
talcum powder, unable to smoke. He had dressed again in
silence, had combed his hair neatly, looking at himself in
the washstand mirror, above the fence of perfumes and
eye drops and syringes and medicines and insecticides that
adorned the shelf. He read some labels in the light from
the window, stole a box of tablets, then continued his tour
of the toilet. There weren't many discoveries to be made:
some clothes in a tub, others on a line. He tested the taps
of the bidet; the water spurted noisily. What if Soddu
heard? To hell with Soddu and with jail. Gim was bored;

he went back to the basin, sprinkled some cologne on his jacket, spread brilliantine on his hair. The fact was, if they didn't arrest him today, they would tomorrow, but they hadn't caught him red-handed, and if all went well, they'd turn him loose right away. To wait there another two or three hours, without cigarettes, in that cubbyhole—why did he bother? Of course they'd let him out right away. He opened a closet: it creaked. To hell with the closet and everything else. Inside it, Armanda's clothes were hanging. Gim stuck his revolver into the pocket of a fur coat. I'll come back and get it, he thought; she won't be wearing this till winter anyhow. He drew out his hand, white with naphthalene. All the better: the gun won't get moth-eaten. He laughed. He went to wash his hands again, but Armanda's towels turned his stomach and he wiped himself on a topcoat in the closet.

Lying in bed, Soddu had heard noises next door. He put one hand on Armanda. "Who's there?"

She turned, pressed to him, and put her big soft arm around his neck. "It's nothing . . . Who could it be?"

Soddu didn't want to free himself, but still he heard movements in there and he asked, as if playing, "What is it, eh? What's that?"

Gim opened the door. "Come on, Sarge, don't play dumb. Arrest me."

Soddu reached out one hand to the revolver in his jacket, hung on a peg, but he didn't let go of Armanda. "Who's that?"

"Gim Bolero."

"Hands up."

"I'm not armed, Sarge, don't be silly. I'm turning myself in." He was standing at the head of the bed, his jacket around his shoulders, his hands half raised.

"Oh, Gim," Armanda said.

"I'll come back to see you in a few days, 'Anda," Gim said.

Soddu got up, mumbling, and slipped on his trousers. "What a lousy job . . . Never a moment's peace . . ."

Gim took the cigarettes from the table, lighted one, slipped the pack into his pocket.

"Give me a smoke, Gim," Armanda said, and she leaned out, lifting her flabby bosom.

Gim put a cigarette in her mouth, lighted it for her, helped Soddu on with his jacket. "Let's go, Sarge."

"Another time, Armanda," Soddu said.

"So long, Angelo," she said.

"So long, eh? Armanda," Soddu said again.

"Bye, Gim."

They went out. In the corridor Lilin was sleeping, perched on the edge of the broken-down sofa; he didn't even move.

Armanda was smoking, seated on the big bed; she

turned off the lamp because a gray light was already coming into the room.

"Lilin," she called. "Come on, Lilin, come to bed, come on, Lilin honey, come."

Lilin was already gathering up the pillow, the ashtray.

The Adventure of a Bather

While enjoying a swim at the beach at ——, Signora Isotta Barbarino had an unfortunate mishap. She was swimming far out in the water, and when it seemed time to go back in and she turned toward the shore, she realized that an irreparable event had occurred. She had lost her bathing suit.

She couldn't tell whether it had slipped off just then or whether she had already been swimming without it for some time, but of the new two-piece suit she had been wearing, only the halter was left. At some twist of her hip, some buttons must have popped, and the bottom part, reduced to a shapeless rag, had slipped down her leg. Perhaps it was still sinking a few feet below her; she tried dropping down underwater to look for it, but she immediately lost her breath, and only vague green shadows flashed before her eyes.

Stifling the anxiety rising inside her, she tried to think in a calm, orderly fashion. It was noon; there were people around in the sea, in kayaks and in rowboats, or swimming. She didn't know anyone; she had arrived the day before with her husband, who had had to go back to the city at once. Now there was no other course, the signora thought (and she was the first to be surprised at her clear, serene reasoning), but to find among these people a beach attendant's boat, which there had to be, or the boat of some other person who inspired trust, hail it, or rather approach it, and manage to ask for both help and tact.

This is what Signora Isotta was thinking as she kept afloat, huddled almost into a ball, pawing the water, not daring to look around. Only her head emerged, and unconsciously she lowered her face toward the surface, not to delve into its secrecy, now held inviolable, but like someone rubbing eyelids and temples against the sheet or the pillow to stem tears provoked by some night-thought. And it was a genuine pressure of tears that she felt at the corners of her eyes, and perhaps that instinctive movement of her head was really meant to dry those tears in the sea: this is how distraught she was, this is what a gap there was in her between reason and feeling. She wasn't calm, then: she was desperate. Inside that motionless sea, wrinkled only at long intervals by the barely indicated hump of a wave, she also kept herself motionless, no longer with slow strokes but only by a pleading movement of the hands, half in the water; and the most alarming sign of her condition, though perhaps not even she realized it, was this usury of strength she was observing, as if she had a very long and exhausting time ahead of her.

She had put on her two-piece suit that morning for the

first time; and at the beach, in the midst of all those strangers, she realized it made her feel a bit ill at ease. But the moment she was in the water, she had felt content, freer in her movements, with a greater desire to swim. She liked to take long swims, well away from the shore, but her pleasure was not an athlete's, for she was actually rather plump and lazy; what meant most to her was the intimacy with the water, feeling herself a part of that peaceful sea. Her new suit gave her that very impression; indeed, the first thing she had thought as she swam was, It's like being naked. The only irksome thing was the recollection of that crowded beach. It was not unreasonable that her future beach acquaintances would perhaps form an idea of her that they would have to some extent to modify later: not so much an opinion about her behavior, since at the seaside all the women dressed like this, but a belief, for example, that she was athletic, or fashionable, whereas she was really a very simple, domestic person. It was perhaps because she was already feeling this sensation of herself as different from usual that she had noticed nothing when the mishap took place. Now that uneasiness she had felt on the beach, and that novelty of the water on her bare skin, and her vague concern at having to return among the other bathers: all had been enlarged and engulfed by her new and far more serious dismay.

What she would have preferred never to look at was the beach. And she looked at it. Bells were ringing noon; and on the beach the great umbrellas with black and yellow concentric circles were casting black shadows in which the bodies became flat, and the teeming of the bathers spilled into the sea; and none of the boats was on the shore now, and as soon as one returned it was seized even before it could touch bottom; and the black rim of the blue expanse was disturbed by constant explosions of white splashing, especially behind the ropes, where the horde of children was roiling; and at every bland wave a shouting arose, its notes immediately swallowed up by the blast. Just off that beach, she was naked.

Nobody would have suspected it, seeing only her head rising from the water, and occasionally her arms and her bosom, as she swam cautiously, never lifting her body to the surface. She could, then, carry out her search for help without exposing herself too much. And to check how much of her could be glimpsed by alien eyes, Signora Isotta now and then stopped and tried to look at herself, floating almost vertically. With anxiety she saw the sun's beams sway in the water in limpid underwater glints, and illuminate drifting seaweed and rapid schools of little striped fish, on the bottom the corrugated sand, and on top her body. In vain, twisting it with clenched legs, she tried to hide it from her own gaze: the skin of the pale belly gleamed revealingly, between the tan of the bosom and the thighs, and neither the motion of a wave nor the half-sunken drift of seaweed could merge the darkness and the pallor of her abdomen. The signora resumed swimming in that mongrel way of hers, keeping her body as low as she could, but, never stopping, she would turn to look over her shoulder, out of the corner of her eye: at every stroke, all the white breadth of her person appeared in the light of day, in its most identifiable and secret forms. She did everything possible to change the style and direction of her swimming — she turned in the water, she observed herself at every angle and in every light, she writhed upon herself — and always this offensive, naked body pursued her. It was a flight from her own body that she was attempting, as if from another person whom she, Signora Isotta, was unable to save at a difficult juncture and could only abandon to her fate. Yet this body, so rich and so impossible to conceal, had indeed been a glory of hers, a source of self-satisfaction; only a contradictory chain of circumstances, apparently sensible, could make it now a cause for shame. Or perhaps not; perhaps her life always consisted only of the clothed lady she had been all of her days, and her nakedness hardly belonged to her, was a rash state of nature revealed only every now and then, arousing wonder in human beings, foremost in her. Now Signora Isotta recalled that even when she was alone or in private with her husband she had always surrounded her being naked with an air of complicity, of irony, part embarrassed and part feline, as if she were temporarily putting on joyous but outrageous disguises, for a kind of secret carnival between husband and wife. She had become accustomed with some reluctance to owning a body, after the first disappointed, romantic years, and she had taken it on like someone who learns he can command a long-yearned-for property. Now the awareness of this right of hers disappeared again among the old fears, as that yelling beach loomed ahead.

When noon had passed, among the bathers scattered through the sea a reflux toward the shore began; it was the hour of lunch at the *pensioni,* of picnics outside the cabins, and also the hour in which the sand was to be enjoyed at its most searing, under the vertical sun. As the keels of boats and the pontoons of catamarans passed close to the signora, she studied the faces of the men on board, and sometimes she almost decided to move toward them; but each time a flash, a glance beneath their lashes, or the hint of an abrupt jerk of shoulder or elbow put her to flight, with false-casual strokes, whose calm masked an already burdensome weariness. The men in the boats, alone or in groups, boys all excited by the physical exercise or gentlemen with shrewd demands or insistent gaze, on encountering her — lost in the sea, her prim face unable to conceal a shy, pleading anxiety, with a cap that gave her a slightly peevish, doll-like expression, and with her soft shoulders heaving around, uncertain — immediately emerged from their self-centered or bustling nirvana. Those who were not alone pointed her out to their companions with a snap of the chin or a wink; and those who were alone, braking with one oar, swerved their prow deliberately to cross her path. Her need for trust was met by these rising barriers of slyness and double-entendre, a hedge of piercing pupils, of incisors bared in ambiguous laughter, of oars pausing, suddenly interrogatory, on the surface of the water; and the only thing she could do was flee. An occasional swimmer passed by, ducking his head blindly and puffing out spurts of water without raising his eyes; but the signora distrusted these men and evaded them. In fact, even though they passed at some distance from her, the swimmers, overcome by sudden fatigue, let themselves float and stretched their legs in a senseless splashing until she displayed her disdain by moving away. Thus this net of insistent hints was already spread around her, as if lying in ambush for her, as if each of those men had been daydreaming for years of a woman to whom what had happened to her would happen, and these men spent their summers at the sea hoping to be present at the right moment. There was no way out: the front of preordained male insinuations extended to all men, with no possible breach, and that savior she had stubbornly dreamed of as the most anonymous possible creature, almost angelic, a beach boy, a sailor, could not exist: she was now sure of that. The lifeguard she did see pass by, certainly the only one who would be out in a boat to prevent possible accidents, given this calm sea, had such fleshy lips and such tense muscles that she would never have had the courage to entrust herself to his hands, even if — she actually thought in the emotion of the moment — it were to have him unlock a cabin or set up an umbrella.

In her disappointed fantasies, the people to whom she had hoped to turn had always been men. She hadn't thought of women, and yet with them everything should

have been more simple; a kind of female solidarity would
certainly have gone into action in this serious crisis, in this
anxiety that only a fellow woman could completely understand. But possibilities of communication with members
of her own sex were rarer and more uncertain, unlike the
perilous ease of encounters with men; and a distrust—reciprocal this time—blocked such communication. Most
of the women went by in catamarans accompanied by
men, and they were jealous, inaccessible, seeking the open
sea, where the body, whose shame she suffered passively,
would for them be the weapon of an aggressive and calcu-
lable strategy. Now and then a boat came out packed with
chirping, overheated young girls, and the signora thought
of the distance between the profound vulgarity of her suffering and their volatile heedlessness; she thought of how
she would have to repeat her appeal to them, because they
surely wouldn't understand her the first time; she thought
of how their expression would change at the news, and she
couldn't bring herself to call out to them. A blonde also
went by in a catamaran, alone, tanned, full of smugness
and egoism; surely she was going far out to take the sun
completely naked, and it would never remotely occur to
her that nakedness could be a misfortune or a torment.
Signora Isotta realized then how alone a woman is, and
how rare, among her own kind, is solidarity, spontaneous
and good (destroyed perhaps by the pact made with man),
which would have foreseen her appeals and come to her

side at the merest hint in the moment of a secret misfortune no man would understand. Women would never save her; and her own man was away. She felt her strength abandoning her.

A little rust-colored buoy, till then fought over by a cluster of diving kids, was suddenly, at a general plunge, deserted. A seagull lighted on it, flapped its wings, then flew off as Signora Isotta grasped the buoy's rim. She would have drowned if she hadn't grabbed it in time. But not even death was possible, not even that indefensible, excessive remedy was left her: when she was about to faint and couldn't manage to keep her chin up, drawn down toward the water, she saw a rapid, tensed alertness among the men on the surrounding boats, all ready to dive in and come to her rescue. They were there only to save her, to carry her naked and unconscious among the questions and stares of a curious public; and her risk of death would have achieved only the ridiculous and vulgar result that she was trying in vain to evade.

From the buoy, looking at the swimmers and rowers, who seemed to be gradually reabsorbed by the shore, she remembered the marvelous weariness of those returns, and the cries from one boat to another—"See you on shore!" or "I'll race you there!"—filled her with a boundless envy. But then, when she noticed a thin man in long pants, the only person still out in the water, standing erect in a motionless motorboat, looking at something or other in the water, immediately her longing to go ashore burrowed down, hid within her fear of being seen, her anxious effort to conceal herself behind the buoy.

She no longer remembered how long she had been there: already the beach crowd was thinning out, boats were again lined up on the sand, the umbrellas, furled one after the other, were now only a cemetery of short poles, the gulls skimmed the water, and on the motionless motorboat the thin man had disappeared and in his place a dumbfounded boy's curly head peered from the side; and over the sun a cloud passed, driven by a just-wakened wind against a cumulus collected above the hills. The signora thought of that hour as seen from the land, the polite afternoons, the destiny of unassuming correctness and respectful joys she had thought was guaranteed her and of the contemptible incongruity that had occurred to contradict it, like the chastisement for a sin not committed. Not committed? But that abandonment of hers in bathing, that desire to swim all alone, that joy in her own body in the two-piece suit recklessly chosen: weren't these perhaps signs of a flight begun some time past, the defiance of an inclination to sin, the progressive stages of a mad race toward this state of nakedness that now appeared to her in all its wretched pallor? And the society of men, among whom she had thought to pass intact like a big butterfly, pretending a compliant, doll-like nonchalance, now revealed its basic cruelties, its doubly diabolical essence, the presence of an evil against which she had not sufficiently armed herself and at once the agent, the instrument of her sentence.

Clinging to the studs of the buoy with bloodless fingertips now with accentuated wrinkles from the prolonged stay in the water, the signora felt herself cast out by the whole world, and she couldn't understand why this nakedness that all people carry with themselves forever should banish her alone, as if she were the only one who was naked, the only being who could remain naked under heaven. And as she raised her eyes, she saw now the man and boy together on the motorboat, both standing, making signs to her as if to say she should remain there, that she shouldn't distress herself pointlessly. They were serious, the two of them, composed, unlike any of the other, earlier, ones, as if they were announcing a verdict to her: she was to resign herself; she alone had been chosen to pay for all. If, as they gesticulated, they tried to muster a kind of smile, it was without any hint of maliciousness: perhaps an invitation to accept her sentence good-naturedly, willingly.

Immediately the boat sped off, faster than one would have thought possible, and the two paid attention to the motor and the course and didn't turn again toward the signora, who tried to smile back at them, as if to show that if she were accused only of being made in this way so dear and prized by all, if she had only to expiate our somewhat clumsy tenderness of forms, well, she would take the whole burden on herself, content.

The boat, with its mysterious movements, and her own tangled reasoning had kept her in a state of such timorous bewilderment that it was a while before she became aware of the cold. A sweet plumpness allowed Signora Isotta to take long and icy swims that amazed her husband and family, all thin people. But now she had been in the water too long, and the sun was covered, and her smooth skin rose in grainy bumps, and ice was slowly taking possession of her blood. There, in this shivering that ran through her, Isotta realized she was alive, and in danger of death, and innocent. Because the nakedness that had suddenly seemed to grow on her body was something she had always accepted not as a guilt but as her anxious innocence, as her secret fraternity with others as flesh and root of her being in the world. And they, on the contrary, the smart men in the boats and the fearless women under the umbrellas, who did not accept it, who insinuated it was a crime, an accusation—only they were guilty. She didn't want to pay for them; and she wriggled, clinging to the buoy, her teeth chattering, tears on her cheeks . . . Over there, from the harbor, the motorboat was returning even faster than before, and at the prow the boy was holding up a narrow green sail: a skirt!

When the boat stopped near her and the thin man stretched out one hand to help her on board and covered his eyes with the other, smiling, the signora was already so far from any hope of being saved, and the train of her thoughts had traveled so far afield, that for a moment she couldn't connect her senses with her reasoning and action,

To get to the beach, the man took the boat past the docks and the harbor and the vegetable gardens along the sea; anyone who saw them from the shore no doubt believed that the three were a little family coming home in their boat as they did every evening during the fishing season. The gray fishermen's houses overlooked the dock; red nets were stretched across short stakes; and from the boats, already tied up, some youths lifted lead-colored fish and passed them to girls standing with square baskets, the low rims propped against their hips. Men with tiny gold earrings, seated on the ground with spread legs, were sewing endless nets, and in some tubs they were boiling tannin to dye the nets again. Little stone walls marked off tiny vegetable gardens on the sea, where the boats lay beside the canes of the seedbeds. Women with their mouths full of nails helped their husbands, lying under the keel, to patch holes. Every pink house had a low roof covered with tomatoes split in two and set out to dry with salt on a grill; and under the asparagus plants the kids were hunting for worms; and some old men with bellows were spraying insecticide on their loquats; and the yellow melons were growing under creeping leaves; and in flat pans the old women were frying squid and polyps or else pumpkin flowers dredged in flour; and the prows of fishing boats rose in the yards redolent of wood fresh from the plane; and a brawl among the boys caulking the hulls had broken out, with threats of brushes black with tar; and then the beach began, with the little sand castles and volcanoes abandoned by the children.

Signora Isotta, seated in the boat with that pair, in that excessive green-and-orange dress, would even have liked the trip to continue. But the boat was aiming its prow at the shore, and the beach attendants were carrying away the deck chairs, and the man had bent over the motor, turning his back: that brick-red back divided by the knobs of the spine, on which the hard, salty skin rippled as if moved by a sigh.

The Adventure of a Clerk

It so happened that Enrico Gnei, a clerk, spent a night with a beautiful lady. Coming out of her house, early, he felt the air and the colors of the spring morning open before him, cool and bracing and new, and it was as if he were walking to the sound of music.

It must be said that only a lucky conjunction of circumstances had rewarded Enrico Gnei with this adventure: a party at some friends' house, a special, fleeting mood of the lady's—a woman otherwise controlled and hardly prone to obeying whims—a slight alcoholic stimulation, whether real or feigned, and in addition a rather favorable logistic combination at the moment of goodbyes. All this, and not any personal charm of Gnei's—or, rather, none but his discreet and somewhat anonymous looks, which would mark him as an undemanding, unobtrusive companion—had produced the unexpected result of that night. He was well aware of all this, and, modest by nature, he considered his good luck all the more precious. He also knew that the event would have no sequel; nor did he complain of that, because a steady relationship would have created problems too awkward for his usual way of living. The perfection of the adventure lay in its having begun and ended in the space of a night. Therefore Enrico Gnei that morning was a man who has received what he could most desire in the world.

The lady's house was in the hill district. Gnei came down a green and fragrant boulevard. It was not yet the hour when he was accustomed to leave home for the office. The lady had made him slip out now so the servants wouldn't see. The fact that he hadn't slept didn't bother him; in fact, it gave him a kind of unnatural lucidity, an arousal no longer of the senses but of the intellect. A gust of wind, a buzzing, an odor of trees, seemed to him things he should somehow grasp and enjoy; he couldn't become accustomed again to humbler ways of savoring beauty.

Because he was a methodical sort of man, getting up in a strange house and dressing in haste without shaving left in him an impression of disturbed habits; for a moment he thought of dashing home to shave and tidy himself up before going to the office. He would have had the time, but Gnei immediately dismissed the idea; he preferred to convince himself it was too late, because he was seized by the fear that his house, the repetition of daily acts, would dispel the rich and extraordinary atmosphere in which he now moved.

He decided that his day would follow a calm and generous curve, to retain as far as possible the inheritance of that night. His memory, if he could patiently reconstruct the hours he had passed, second by second, promised him boundless Edens. And thus, letting his thoughts stray, Enrico Gnei went without haste to the beginning of the tramline.

The tram, almost empty, was waiting for the time when its schedule began. Some drivers were there, smoking. Gnei whistled as he climbed aboard, his overcoat open, flapping; he sat down, sprawling slightly, then immediately assumed a more citified position, pleased that he had thought to correct himself promptly but not displeased by the carefree attitude that had come to him naturally.

The neighborhood was sparsely inhabited, and the inhabitants were not early risers. On the tram there was an elderly housewife, two workmen having an argument, and himself, the contented man. Solid, morning people. He found them likable; he, Enrico Gnei, was for them a mysterious gentleman, mysterious and content, never seen before on this tram at this hour. Where could he come from? they were perhaps asking themselves now. And he gave them no clue: he was looking at the wisteria. He was a man who looks at the wisteria like a man who knows how wisteria should be looked at; he was aware of this, Enrico Gnei was. He was a passenger who hands the money for his ticket to the conductor, and between him and the conductor there is a perfect passenger-conductor relationship; it couldn't be better. The tram moved down toward the river; it was a great life.

Enrico Gnei got off downtown and went to a café. Not the usual one. A café with mosaic walls. It had just opened; the cashier hadn't arrived yet; the counterman was starting up the coffee machine. Gnei strode like a master right to the center of the place, went to the counter, ordered a coffee, chose a cake from the glass pastry case, and bit into it, first with hunger, then with the expression of a man with a bad taste in his mouth after a wild night.

A newspaper lay open on the counter; Gnei glanced at it. He hadn't bought the paper this morning—and to think that that was always the first thing he did on leaving his house. He was a habitual reader, meticulous; he kept up with the most trivial events, and there wasn't a page he skipped without reading. But that day his gaze ran over the headlines and his thoughts remained unconnected. Gnei couldn't manage to read: perhaps—who knows? —stirred by the food, by the hot coffee, or by the dulling of the morning air's effect, a wave of sensations from the night came over him. He shut his eyes, raised his chin, and smiled.

Attributing this pleased expression to the sports news in the paper, the counterman said to him, "Ah, you're glad Boccadasse will be playing again on Sunday?" and he pointed to the headline that announced the return of a center half.

Gnei read, recovered himself, and instead of exclaiming, as he would have liked to, "Oh, I've got something a lot better than Boccadasse to think about, my friend!" he confined himself to saying, "Hmm . . . right . . ." And, unwilling to let a conversation about the forthcoming match disrupt the flow of his feelings, he turned toward the cashier's desk, where in the meantime a young girl with a disenchanted look had installed herself.

"So," Gnei said, in a tone of intimacy, "I owe you for a coffee and a cake." The cashier yawned. "Sleepy? Too early for you?" Gnei asked. Without smiling, the cashier nodded. Gnei assumed an air of complicity: "Aha! Didn't get enough sleep last night, did you?" He thought for a moment, then, persuading himself he was with a person who would understand, added, "I still haven't gone to bed." Then he was silent, enigmatic, discreet. He paid, said good morning to all, and left. He went to the barber's.

"Good morning, sir. Have a seat, sir," the barber said in a professional falsetto that to Enrico Gnei was like a wink of the eye.

"Um-hum, give me a shave!" he replied with skeptical condescension, looking at himself in the mirror. His face, with the towel knotted around his neck, had the appearance of an independent object, and some trace of weariness, no longer corrected by the general bearing of his person, was beginning to show. It was still quite a normal face, like that of a traveler who had got off the train at dawn or a gambler who has spent the night over his cards; except there was a certain look that marked the special nature of his weariness, Gnei observed smugly — a certain relaxed, indulgent expression, that of a man who has had his share of things and is prepared to take the bad with the good.

Far different caresses, Gnei's cheeks seemed to say to the brush that encased them in warm foam, far different caresses from yours are what we're used to!

Scrape, razor, his skin seemed to say, you won't scrape off what I have felt and know!

It was, for Gnei, as if a conversation filled with allusions were taking place between him and the barber, who, however, was also silent, devoting himself to handling his implements. He was a young barber, somewhat taciturn more from lack of imagination than from a reserved character; and in fact, attempting to start a conversation, he said, "Some year, eh? The good weather's already here. Spring . . ."

The remark reached Gnei right in the middle of his imaginary conversation, and the word "spring" became charged with meanings and hidden references. "Aaah! Spring . . ." he said, a knowing smile on his foamy lips. And here the conversation died.

But Gnei felt the need to talk, to express, to communicate, and the barber didn't say anything further. Two or three times Gnei started to open his mouth when the young man lifted the razor, but he couldn't find any words, and the razor descended again over his lip and chin.

"What did you say?" the barber asked, having seen Gnei's lips move without producing any sound.

And Gnei, with all his warmth, said, "Sunday, Bocca-dasse'll be back with the team!"

He had almost shouted; the other customers turned toward him their half-lathered faces; the barber had remained with his razor suspended in air.

"Ah, you're a —— fan?" he said, a bit mortified. "I'm a follower of ——," and he named the city's other team.

"Oh, —— has an easy game Sunday. They can't lose . . ." But his warmth was already extinguished.

Shaven, he came outside. The city was loud and bustling; there were glints of gold on the windows, water flew over the fountains, the trams' poles struck sparks from the overhead wires. Enrico Gnei proceeded as if on the crest of a wave, bursts of vigor alternating in his heart with fits of lassitude.

"Why, it's Gnei!"

"Why, it's Bardetta!"

He ran into an old schoolmate he hadn't seen for ten years. They traded the usual remarks, how time had gone by, how they hadn't changed. Actually, Bardetta had somewhat faded, and the vulpine, slightly crafty expression of his face had become accentuated. Gnei knew that Bardetta was in business, but had a rather murky record and had been living abroad for some time.

"Still in Paris?"

"Venezuela. I'm about to go back. What about you?"

"Still here," and in spite of himself he smiled in embarrassment, as if he were ashamed of his sedentary life, and at the same time irked because he couldn't make it clear, at first sight, that his existence in reality was fuller and more satisfied than might be imagined.

"Are you married?" Bardetta asked.

To Gnei this seemed an opportunity to rectify the first impression. "Bachelor!" he said. "Still a bachelor, ha ha! We're a vanishing race!" Yes, Bardetta, a man without scruples, about to leave again for America, with no ties now to the city and its gossip, was the ideal person; with him Gnei could give free rein to his euphoria, to him alone Gnei could confide his secret. Indeed, he could even exaggerate a little, talk of last night's adventure as if it were for him something habitual. "That's right," he insisted. "The old guard of bachelorhood, us two, eh?" — meaning to refer to Bardetta's one-time reputation as a successful chaser of chorus girls. And he was already studying the remark he would make to arrive at the subject, something on the order of "Why, only last night, for example . . ."

"To tell the truth," Bardetta said, with a somewhat shy smile, "I'm married and have four children."

Gnei heard this as he was re-creating around himself the atmosphere of a completely heedless, epicurean world; and he was thrown a bit off-balance by it. He stared at Bardetta; only then did he notice the man's shabby, downtrodden look, his worried, tired manner. "Ah, four children . . ."

he said, in a dull voice. "Congratulations! And how are things going over there?"

"Hmph . . . not much doing . . . It's the same all over . . . Scraping by . . . feeding the family . . ." and he stretched out his arms in a gesture of defeat.

Gnei, with his instinctive humility, felt compassion and remorse: how could he have thought of trumpeting his own good luck to impress a wreck of a man like this? "Oh, here, too, I can tell you," he said quickly, changing his tone again, "we barely manage, living from day to day."

"Well, let's hope things will get better."

"Yes, we have to keep hoping."

They exchanged all best wishes, said goodbye, and went off in different directions. Immediately Gnei felt overwhelmed with regret: the possibility of confiding in Bardetta, that Bardetta he had first imagined, seemed to him an immense boon, now lost forever. Between the two of them, Gnei thought, a man-to-man conversation could have taken place, good-natured, a shade ironic, without any showing off, without boasting; his friend would have left for America bearing a memory that would remain unchangeable; and Gnei vaguely saw himself preserved in the thoughts of that imaginary Bardetta, there in his Venezuela, remembering old Europe—poor, but always faithful to the cult of beauty and pleasure—and thinking instinctively of his friend, the schoolmate seen again after so many years, always with that prudent appearance and

yet completely sure of himself: the man who hadn't abandoned Europe and virtually symbolized its ancient wisdom
of life, its wary passions . . . Gnei grew excited: thus the adventure of the previous night could have left a mark, taken
on a definitive meaning, instead of vanishing like sand in a
sea of empty days, all alike.

Perhaps he should have talked about it to Bardetta anyway, even if Bardetta was a poor wretch with other things
on his mind, even at the cost of humiliating him. Besides,
how could he be sure that Bardetta really was a failure?
Perhaps he just said that and he was still the old fox he
had been in the past . . . I'll overtake him, Gnei thought; I'll
start a conversation, and I'll tell him.

He ran ahead along the sidewalk, turned into the square,
proceeded under the arcade. Bardetta had disappeared.
Gnei looked at the time; he was late; he hurried toward
his job. To calm himself, he decided that this telling others about his affairs, like a schoolboy, was too alien to his
character, his ways; this was why he had refrained from
doing it. Thus reconciled with himself, his pride restored,
he punched the time clock at the office.

For his job, Gnei harbored that amorous passion that,
though unconfessed, makes clerks' hearts warm, once
they come to know the secret sweetness and the furious
fanaticism that can charge the most habitual bureaucratic
routine, the answering of indifferent correspondence, the
precise keeping of a ledger. Perhaps this morning his un-

conscious hope was that amorous stimulation and clerkish passion would become a single thing, merge one with the other, to go on burning and never be extinguished. But the sight of his desk, the familiar look of a pale-green folder with "Pending" written on it, sufficed to make him feel the sharp contrast between the dizzying beauty from which he had just parted and his usual days.

He walked around the desk several times without sitting down. He had been overwhelmed by a sudden, urgent love for the beautiful lady, and he could find no rest. He went into the next office, where the accountants, careful and dissatisfied, were tapping on their adding machines.

He began walking past each of them, saying hello, nervously cheery, sly, basking in the memory, without hopes for the present, mad with love among the accountants. As I move now in your midst, in your office, he was thinking, so I was turning in her blankets not long ago. "Yes, that's right, Marinotti!" he said, banging his fist on a fellow clerk's papers.

Marinotti raised his eyeglasses and asked slowly, "Say, did they take an extra four thousand lire out of your salary this month too, Gnei?"

"No, my friend, in February," Gnei began, and at the same time he recalled a movement the lady had made, late, in the morning hours, that to him had seemed a new revelation and opened immense, unknown possibilities of love. "No, they already deducted mine then," he went on, in a mild voice, and he moved his hand gently before him, in midair, pursing his lips. "They took the whole amount from my February pay, Marinotti." He would have liked to add further details and explanations, just to keep talking, but he wasn't able to.

This is the secret, he decided, going back to his office; at every moment, in everything I do or say, everything I have experienced must be implicit. But he was consumed by an anxiety that he could never live up to what he had been, could never succeed in expressing, with hints, or still less with explicit words, and perhaps not even with his thoughts, the fullness he knew he had reached.

The telephone rang. It was the general manager. He was asking for the background on the Giuseppieri complaint.

"It's like this, sir," Gnei explained over the telephone. "Giuseppieri and Company, on the sixth of March . . ." and he wanted to say, You see, when she slowly said, "Are you going?" I realized I shouldn't let go of her hand . . .

"Yes, sir, the complaint was in reference to goods previously billed . . ." and he thought to say, Until the door closed behind us, I still wasn't sure . . .

"No," he explained, "the claim wasn't made through the local office . . ." and he meant, But only then did I realize that she was entirely different from the way I had imagined her, so cold and haughty . . .

He hung up. His brow was beaded with sweat. He felt tired now, burdened with sleep. It had been a mistake not to go by the house and freshen up, change: even the clothes he was wearing irked him.

He went to the window. There was a large courtyard surrounded by high walls full of balconies, but it was like being in a desert. The sky could be seen above the roofs, no longer limpid but bleached, covered by an opaque patina, as in Gnei's memory an opaque whiteness was wiping out every memory of sensations, and the presence of the sun was marked by a vague, still patch of light, like a secret pang of grief.

The Adventure of a Photographer

When spring comes, the city's inhabitants, by the hundreds of thousands, go out on Sundays with leather cases over their shoulders. And they photograph one another. They come back as happy as hunters with bulging game bags; they spend days waiting, with sweet anxiety, to see the developed pictures (anxiety to which some add the subtle pleasure of alchemistic manipulations in the darkroom, forbidding any intrusion by members of the family, relishing the acid smell that is harsh to the nostrils). It is only when they have the photos before their eyes that they seem to take tangible possession of the day they spent, only then that the mountain stream, the movement of the child with his pail, the glint of the sun on the wife's legs, take on the irrevocability of what has been and can no longer be doubted. Everything else can drown in the unreliable shadow of memory.

Seeing a good deal of his friends and colleagues, Antonino Paraggi, a nonphotographer, sensed a growing isolation. Every week he discovered that the conversations

57

of those who praise the sensitivity of a filter or discourse on the number of DINs were swelled by the voice of yet another to whom he had confided until yesterday, convinced that they were shared, his sarcastic remarks about an activity that to him seemed so unexciting, so lacking in surprises.

Professionally, Antonino Paraggi occupied an executive position in the distribution department of a production firm, but his real passion was commenting to his friends on current events large and small, unraveling the thread of general causes from the tangle of details; in short, by mental attitude he was a philosopher, and he devoted all his thoroughness to grasping the significance of even the events most remote from his own experience. Now he felt that something in the essence of photographic man was eluding him, the secret appeal that made new adepts continue to join the ranks of the amateurs of the lens, some boasting of the progress of their technical and artistic skill, others, on the contrary, giving all the credit to the efficiency of the camera they had purchased, which was capable (according to them) of producing masterpieces even when operated by inept hands (as they declared their own to be, because wherever pride aimed at magnifying the virtues of mechanical devices, subjective talent accepted a proportionate humiliation). Antonino Paraggi understood that neither the one nor the other motive of satisfaction was decisive: the secret lay elsewhere.

It must be said that his examination of photography

to discover the causes of a private dissatisfaction—as of someone who feels excluded from something—was to a certain extent a trick Antonino played on himself, to avoid having to consider another, more evident process that was separating him from his friends. What was happening was this: his acquaintances of his age were all getting married, one after another, and starting families, while Antonino remained a bachelor. Yet between the two phenomena there was undoubtedly a connection, inasmuch as the passion for the lens often develops in a natural, virtually physiological way as a secondary effect of fatherhood. One of the first instincts of parents, after they have brought a child into the world, is to photograph it. Given the speed of growth, it becomes necessary to photograph the child often, because nothing is more fleeting and unmemorable than a six-month-old infant, soon deleted and replaced by one of eight months, and then one of a year; and all the perfection that, to the eyes of parents, a child of three may have reached cannot prevent its being destroyed by that of the four-year-old. The photograph album remains the only place where all these fleeting perfections are saved and juxtaposed, each aspiring to an incomparable absoluteness of its own. In the passion of new parents for framing their offspring in the sights to reduce them to the immobility of black-and-white or a full-color slide, the nonphotographer and nonprocreator Antonino saw chiefly a phase in the race toward madness lurking in that black instrument. But his reflections on the iconography-family-madness nexus

ening of his arm would make the lens veer to capture the masts of ships or the spires of steeples, or to decapitate grandparents, uncles, and aunts. He was accused of doing this on purpose, reproached for making a joke in poor taste. It wasn't true: his intention was to lend the use of his finger as docile instrument of the collective wish, but also to exploit his temporary position of privilege to admonish both photographers and their subjects as to the significance of their actions. As soon as the pad of his finger reached the desired condition of detachment from the rest of his person and personality, he was free to communicate his theories in well-reasoned discourse, framing at the same time well-composed little groups. (A few accidental successes had sufficed to give him nonchalance and assurance with viewfinders and light meters.)

". . . because once you've begun," he would preach, "there is no reason why you should stop. The line between the reality that is photographed because it seems beautiful to us and the reality that seems beautiful because it has been photographed is very narrow. If you take a picture of Pierluca because he's building a sand castle, there is no reason not to take his picture while he's crying because the castle has collapsed, and then while the nurse consoles him by helping him find a seashell in the sand. The minute you start saying something—'Ah, how beautiful! We must photograph it!'—you are already close to the view of the person who thinks that everything that is not photographed is lost, as if it had never existed, and that therefore, in order really to live, you must photograph as much as you can, and to photograph as much as you can you must either live in the most photographable way possible or else consider photographable every moment of your life. The first course leads to stupidity, the second to madness."

"You're the one who's mad and stupid," his friends would say to him, "and a pain in the ass into the bargain."

"For the person who wants to capture everything that passes before his eyes," Antonino would explain, even if nobody was listening to him anymore, "the only coherent way to act is to snap at least one picture a minute, from the instant he opens his eyes in the morning to when he goes to sleep. This is the only way that the rolls of exposed film will represent a faithful diary of our days, with nothing left out. If I were to start taking pictures, I'd see this thing through, even if it meant losing my mind. But the rest of you still insist on making a choice. What sort of choice? A choice in the idyllic sense, apologetic, consolatory, at peace with nature, the fatherland, the family. Your choice isn't only photographic; it is a choice of life, which leads you to exclude dramatic conflicts, the knots of contradiction, the great tensions of will, passion, aversion. So you think you are saving yourselves from madness, but you are falling into mediocrity, into hebetude."

A girl named Bice, someone's ex-sister-in-law, and another named Lydia, someone else's ex-secretary, asked him please to take a snapshot of them while they were playing ball among the waves. He consented, but since in the meanwhile he had worked out a theory in opposition to snapshots, he dutifully expressed it to the two friends.

"What drives you two girls to cut from the mobile continuum of your day these temporal slices, the thickness of a second? Tossing the ball back and forth, you are living in the present, but the moment the scansion of the frames is insinuated between your acts, it is no longer the pleasure of the game that motivates you but rather that of seeing yourselves again in the future, of rediscovering yourselves in twenty years' time, on a piece of yellowed cardboard (yellowed emotionally, even if modern printing procedures will preserve it unchanged). The taste for the spontaneous, natural, lifelike snapshot kills spontaneity, drives away the present. Photographed reality immediately takes on a nostalgic character, of joy fled on the wings of time, a commemorative quality, even if the picture was taken the day before yesterday. And the life that you live in order to photograph it is already, at the outset, a commemoration of itself. To believe that the snapshot is more *true* than the posed portrait is a prejudice . . ."

So saying, Antonino darted around the two girls in the water to focus on the movements of their game and cut out of the picture the dazzling glints of the sun on the water. In a scuffle for the ball, Bice, flinging herself on the other girl, who was submerged, was snapped with her behind in close-up, flying over the waves. Antonino, so as not to lose this angle, had flung himself back in the water while holding up the camera, nearly drowning.

"They all came out well, and this one's stupendous," they commented a few days later, snatching the proofs from each other. They had arranged to meet at the photography shop. "You're good; you must take some more of us."

Antonino had reached the conclusion that it was necessary to return to posed subjects, in attitudes denoting their social position and their character, as in the nineteenth century. His antiphotographic polemic could be fought only from within the black box, setting one kind of photography against another.

"I'd like to have one of those old box cameras," he said to his girlfriends, "the kind you put on a tripod. Do you think it's still possible to find one?"

"Hmm, maybe at some junk shop."

"Let's go see."

The girls found it amusing to hunt for this curious object; together they ransacked flea markets, interrogated old street photographers, followed them to their lairs. In those cemeteries of objects no longer serviceable lay wooden columns, screens, backdrops with faded landscapes; everything that suggested an old photographer's studio, Antonino bought. In the end he managed to get hold of a box camera, with a bulb to squeeze. It seemed in perfect working order. Antonino also bought an assortment of plates. With the girls helping him, he set up the studio in a room of his apartment, all fitted out with old-fashioned equipment, except for two modern spotlights.

Now he was content. "This is where to start," he explained to the girls. "In the way our grandparents assumed a pose, in the convention that decided how groups were to be arranged, there was a social meaning, a custom, a taste, a culture. An official photograph, or one of a marriage or a family or a school group, conveyed how serious and important each role or institution was, but also how far they were all false or forced, authoritarian, hierarchical. This is the point: to make explicit the relationship with the world that each of us bears within himself, and which today we tend to hide, to make unconscious, believing that in this way it disappears, whereas—"

"Who do you want to have pose for you?"

"You two come tomorrow, and I'll begin by taking some pictures of you in the way I mean."

"Say, what's in the back of your mind?" Lydia asked, suddenly suspicious. Only now, as the studio was all set up, did she see that everything about it had a sinister, threatening air. "If you think we're going to come and be your models, you're dreaming!"

Bice giggled with her, but the next day she came back to Antonino's apartment, alone.

She was wearing a white linen dress with colored embroidery on the edges of the sleeves and pockets. Her hair was parted and gathered over her temples. She laughed, a bit slyly, bending her head to one side. As he let her in, Antonino studied her manner — a bit coy, a bit ironic — to discover what were the traits that defined her true character.

He made her sit in a big armchair and stuck his head under the black cloth that came with his camera. It was one of those boxes whose rear wall was of glass, where the image is reflected as if already on the plate, ghostly, a bit milky, deprived of every link with space and time. To Antonino it was as if he had never seen Bice before. She had a docility in her somewhat heavy way of lowering her eyelids, of stretching her neck forward, that promised something hidden, as her smile seemed to hide behind the very act of smiling.

"There. Like that. No, head a bit farther; raise your eyes. No, lower them." Antonino was pursuing, within that box, something of Bice that all at once seemed most precious to him, absolute.

"Now you're casting a shadow; move into the light. No, it was better before."

There were many possible photographs of Bice and many Bices impossible to photograph, but what he was seeking was the unique photograph that would contain both the former and the latter.

"I can't get you" — his voice emerged, stifled and complaining from beneath the black hood — "I can't get you anymore; I can't manage to get you."

He freed himself from the cloth and straightened up again. He was going about it all wrong. That expression, that accent, that secret he seemed on the very point of capturing in her face, was something that drew him into the quicksands of moods, humors, psychology: he too was one of those who pursue life as it flees, a hunter of the unattainable, like the takers of snapshots.

He had to follow the opposite path: aim at a portrait completely on the surface, evident, unequivocal, that did not elude conventional appearance, the stereotype, the mask. The mask, being first of all a social, historical product, contains more truth than any image claiming to be "true"; it bears a quantity of meanings that will gradually be revealed. Wasn't this precisely Antonino's intention in setting up this fair booth of a studio?

He observed Bice. He should start with the exterior elements of her appearance. In Bice's way of dressing and fixing herself up, he thought, you could recognize the somewhat nostalgic, somewhat ironic intention, widespread in the mode of those years, to hark back to the fashions of thirty years earlier. The photograph should underline this intention: why hadn't he thought of that?

Antonino went to find a tennis racket; Bice should stand up in a three-quarter turn, the racket under her arm, her face in the pose of a sentimental postcard. To Antonino, from under the black drape, Bice's image — in its slimness and suitability to the pose, and in the unsuitable and almost incongruous aspects that the pose accentuated — seemed very interesting. He made her change position several times, studying the geometry of legs and arms in relation to the racket and to some element in the background. (In the ideal postcard in his mind there would have been the net of the tennis court, but you couldn't demand too much, and Antonino made do with a Ping-Pong table.)

But he still didn't feel on safe ground. Wasn't he perhaps trying to photograph memories — or rather, vague echoes of recollection surfacing in the memory? Wasn't his refusal to live the present as a future memory, as the Sunday photographers did, leading him to attempt an equally unreal operation, namely to give a body to recollection, to substitute it for the present before his very eyes?

"Move! Don't stand there like a stick! Raise the racket, damn it! Pretend you're playing tennis!" All of a sudden he was furious. He had realized that only by exaggerating the poses could he achieve an objective alienness; only by feigning a movement arrested halfway could he give the impression of the unmoving, the nonliving.

Bice obediently followed his orders even when they became vague and contradictory, with a passivity that was also a way of declaring herself out of the game, and yet somehow insinuating, in this game that was not hers, the unpredictable moves of a mysterious match of her own. What Antonino now was expecting of Bice, telling her to put her legs and arms this way and that way, was not so much the simple performance of a plan as her response to the violence he was doing her with his demands, an unforeseeable aggressive reply to this violence that he was being driven more and more to wreak on her.

It was like a dream, Antonino thought, contemplating

from the darkness in which he was buried that improbable tennis player filtered into the glass rectangle: like a dream when a presence coming from the depth of memory advances, is recognized, and then suddenly is transformed into something unexpected, something that even before the transformation is already frightening because there's no telling what it might be transformed into.

Did he want to photograph dreams? This suspicion struck him dumb, hidden in that ostrich refuge of his with the bulb in his hand, like an idiot; and meanwhile Bice, left to herself, continued a kind of grotesque dance, freezing in exaggerated tennis poses, backhand, drive, raising the racket high or lowering it to the ground as if the gaze coming from that glass eye were the ball she continued to slam back.

"Stop, what's this nonsense? This isn't what I had in mind." Antonino covered the camera with the cloth and began pacing up and down the room.

It was all the fault of that dress, with its tennis, prewar connotations . . . It had to be admitted that if she wore a street dress, the kind of photograph he described couldn't be taken. A certain solemnity was needed, a certain pomp, like the official photos of queens. Only in evening dress would Bice become a photographic subject, with the décolleté that marks a distinct line between the white of the skin and the darkness of the fabric, accentuated by the glitter of jewels, a boundary between an essence of woman, almost atemporal and almost impersonal in her nakedness, and the other abstraction, social this time, the dress, symbol of an equally impersonal role, like the drapery of an allegorical statue.

He approached Bice, began to unbutton the dress at the neck and over the bosom and slip it down over her shoulders. He had thought of certain nineteenth-century photographs of women in which from the white of the cardboard emerge the face, the neck, the line of the bared shoulders, while all the rest disappears into the whiteness.

This was the portrait outside of time and space that he now wanted; he wasn't quite sure how it was achieved, but he was determined to succeed. He set the spotlight on Bice, moved the camera closer, fiddled around under the cloth adjusting the aperture of the lens. He looked into it. Bice was naked.

She had made the dress slip down to her feet; she wasn't wearing anything underneath it; she had taken a step forward—no, a step backward, which was as if her whole body were advancing in the picture; she stood erect, tall before the camera, calm, looking straight ahead, as if she were alone.

Antonino felt the sight of her enter his eyes and occupy the whole visual field, removing it from the flux of casual and fragmentary images, concentrating time and space in a finite form. And as if this visual surprise and the impression of the plate were two reflexes connected among themselves, he immediately pressed the bulb, loaded the camera again, snapped, put in another plate, snapped, and went on changing plates and snapping, mumbling, stifled by the cloth, "There, that's right now, yes, again, I'm getting you fine now, another."

He had run out of plates. He emerged from the cloth. He was pleased. Bice was before him, naked, as if waiting.

"Now you can dress," he said, euphoric, but already in a hurry. "Let's go out."

She looked at him, bewildered.

"I've got you now," he said.

Bice burst into tears.

Antonino realized that he had fallen in love with her that same day. They started living together, and he bought the most modern cameras, telescopic lenses, the most advanced equipment; he installed a darkroom. He even had a setup for photographing her when she was asleep at night. Bice would wake at the flash, annoyed; Antonino went on taking snapshots of her disentangling herself from sleep, of her becoming furious with him, of her trying in vain to find sleep again by plunging her face into the pillow, of her making up with him, of her recognizing as acts of love these photographic rapes.

In Antonino's darkroom, strung with films and proofs, Bice peered from every frame, as thousands of bees peer out from the honeycomb of a hive, but always the same bee: Bice in every attitude, at every angle, in every guise, Bice posed or caught unaware, an identity fragmented into a powder of images.

"But what's this obsession with Bice? Can't you photograph anything else?" was the question he heard constantly from his friends, and also from her.

"It isn't just a matter of Bice," he answered. "It's a question of method. Whatever person you decide to photograph, or whatever thing, you must go on photographing it always, exclusively, at every hour of the day and night. Photography has a meaning only if it exhausts all possible images."

But he didn't say what meant most to him: to catch Bice in the street when she didn't know he was watching her, to keep her in the range of hidden lenses, to photograph her not only without letting himself be seen but without seeing her, to surprise her as she was in the absence of his gaze, of any gaze. Not that he wanted to discover any particular thing; he wasn't a jealous man in the usual sense of the word. It was an invisible Bice that he wanted to possess, a Bice absolutely alone, a Bice whose presence presupposed the absence of him and everyone else.

Whether or not it could be defined as jealousy, it was, in any case, a passion difficult to put up with. And soon Bice left him.

Antonino sank into deep depression. He began to keep a diary—a photographic diary, of course. With the camera slung around his neck, shut up in the house, slumped in an armchair, he compulsively snapped pictures as he stared into the void. He was photographing the absence of Bice.

He collected the photographs in an album: you could

see ashtrays brimming with cigarette butts, an unmade bed, a damp stain on the wall. He got the idea of composing a catalogue of everything in the world that resists photography, that is systematically omitted from the visual field not only by cameras but also by human beings. On every subject he spent days, using up whole rolls at intervals of hours, so as to follow the changes of light and shadow. One day he became obsessed with a completely empty corner of the room, containing a radiator pipe and nothing else: he was tempted to go on photographing that spot and only that till the end of his days.

The apartment was completely neglected; old newspapers, letters, lay crumpled on the floor, and he photographed them. The photographs in the papers were photographed as well, and an indirect bond was established between his lens and that of distant news photographers. To produce those black spots the lenses of other cameras had been aimed at police assaults, charred automobiles, running athletes, ministers, defendants.

Antonino now felt a special pleasure in portraying domestic objects framed by a mosaic of telephotos, violent patches of ink on white sheets. From his immobility he was surprised to find he envied the life of the news photographer, who moves following the movements of crowds, bloodshed, tears, feasts, crime, the conventions of fashion, the falsity of official ceremonies; the news photographer, who documents the extremes of society, the richest and the poorest, the exceptional moments that are nevertheless produced at every moment and in every place.

Does this mean that only the exceptional condition has a meaning? Antonino asked himself. Is the news photographer the true antagonist of the Sunday photographer? Are their worlds mutually exclusive? Or does the one give meaning to the other?

Reflecting like this, he began to tear up the photographs with Bice or without Bice that had accumulated during the months of his passion, ripping to pieces the strips of proofs hung on the walls, snipping up the celluloid of the negatives, jabbing the slides, and piling the remains of this methodical destruction on newspapers spread out on the floor.

Perhaps true, total photography, he thought, is a pile of fragments of private images against the creased background of massacres and coronations.

He folded the corners of the newspapers into a huge bundle to be thrown into the trash, but first he wanted to photograph it. He arranged the edges so that you could clearly see two halves of photographs from different newspapers that in the bundle happened, by chance, to fit together. In fact he reopened the package a little so that a bit of shiny pasteboard would stick out, the fragment of a torn enlargement. He turned on a spotlight; he wanted it to be possible to recognize in his photograph the half-crumpled and torn images, and at the same time to feel their unreality as casual, inky shadows, and also at the same time their concreteness as objects charged with meaning, the strength with which they clung to the attention that tried to drive them away.

To get all this into one photograph he had to acquire an extraordinary technical skill, but only then would Antonino quit taking pictures. Having exhausted every possibility, at the moment when he was coming full circle Antonino realized that photographing photographs was the only course that he had left — or, rather, the true course he had obscurely been seeking all this time.

The Adventure of a Traveler

Federico V., who lived in a northern Italian city, was in love with Cinzia U., a resident of Rome. Whenever his work permitted, he would take the train to the capital. Accustomed to budgeting his time strictly, at the job and in his pleasures, he always traveled at night: there was one train, the last, that was not crowded—except in the holiday season—and Federico could stretch out and sleep.

Federico's days in his own city went by nervously, like the hours of someone between trains who, as he goes about his business, cannot stop thinking of the schedule. But when the evening of his departure finally came and his tasks were done and he was walking with his suitcase toward the station, then, even in his haste to avoid missing his train, he began to feel a sense of inner calm pervade him. It was as if all the bustle around the station—now at its last gasp, given the late hour—were part of a natural movement, and he also belonged to it. Everything seemed to be there to encourage him, to give a spring to his steps like the rubberized pavement of the station, and even the obstacles—the wait, his minutes numbered, at the last ticket window still open, the difficulty of breaking a large bill, the lack of small change at the newsstand—seemed to exist for his pleasure in confronting and overcoming them.

Not that he betrayed any sign of this mood; a staid man, he liked being indistinguishable from the many travelers arriving and leaving, all in overcoats like him, a case in hand. And yet he felt as if he were borne on the crest of a wave, because he was rushing toward Cinzia.

The hand in his overcoat pocket toyed with a telephone token. Tomorrow morning, as soon as he landed at the Stazione Termini in Rome, he would run, token in hand, to the nearest public telephone, dial the number, and say, "Hello, darling, I'm here." And he clutched the token as if it were a most precious object, the only one in the world, the sole tangible proof of what awaited him on his arrival.

The trip was expensive, and Federico wasn't rich. If he saw a second-class coach with padded seats and empty compartments, Federico would buy a second-class ticket. Or rather, he always bought a second-class ticket, with the idea that if he found too many people there, he would move into first, paying the difference to the conductor. In this operation he enjoyed the pleasure of economy (besides, when the cost of first class was paid in two installments, and through necessity, it upset him less), the satisfaction of profiting by his own experience, and a sense of freedom and expansiveness in his actions and in his thoughts.

As sometimes happens with men whose lives are more

conditioned by others, exterior, poured out, Federico tended constantly to defend his own inner concentration, and actually it took very little — a hotel room, a train compartment all to himself — for him to adjust the world into harmony with his life; the world seemed created specially for him, as if the railroads that swathed the peninsula had been built deliberately to bear him triumphantly toward Cinzia. That evening, again, second class was almost empty. Every sign was favorable.

Federico V. chose an empty compartment, not over the wheels but not too far into the coach either, because he knew that as a rule people who board a train in haste tend to reject the first few compartments. The defense of the space necessary to stretch out and travel lying down is made up of tiny psychological devices; Federico knew them and employed them all. For example, he drew the curtains over the door, an act that, performed at this point, might even seem excessive; but it aimed in fact at a psychological effect. Seeing those drawn curtains, the traveler who arrives later is almost always overcome by an instinctive scruple and prefers, if he can find it, a compartment with perhaps two or three people in it already but with the curtains open. Federico strewed his bag, overcoat, newspapers on the seats opposite and beside him. Another elementary move, abused and apparently futile but actually of use. Not that he wanted to make people believe those places were occupied: such a subterfuge would have been contrary to his civic conscience and to his sincere nature.

He wanted only to create a rapid impression of a cluttered, not very inviting compartment, a simple, rapid impression.

He sat down and heaved a sigh of relief. He had learned that being in a setting where everything can only be in its place, the same as always, anonymous, without possible surprises, filled him with calm, with self-awareness, freedom of thought. His whole life rushed along in disorder, but now he found the perfect balance between interior stimulus and the impassive neutrality of material things.

It lasted an instant (if he was in second; a minute if he was in first); then he was immediately seized by a pang: the squalor of the compartment, the plush threadbare in places, the suspicion of dust all about, the faded texture of the curtains in the old-style coaches, gave him a sensation of sadness, the uneasy prospect of sleeping in his clothes, on a bunk not his, with no possible intimacy between him and what he touched. But he immediately recalled the reason he was traveling, and he felt caught up again in that natural rhythm, as of the sea or the wind, that festive, light impulse; he had only to seek it within himself, closing his eyes or clasping the telephone token in his hand, and that sense of squalor was defeated; only he existed, alone, facing the adventure of his journey.

But something was still missing: what? Ah: he heard the bass voice approaching under the marquee: "Pillows!" He had already stood up, was lowering the window, extending his hand with the two hundred-lire pieces, shouting, "I'll take one!" It was the pillow man who every time gave the journey its starting signal. He passed by the window a minute before departure, pushing in front of him the wheeled rack with pillows hanging from it. He was a tall old man, thin, with white mustache and large hands, long, thick fingers: hands that inspired trust. He was dressed all in black: military cap, uniform, overcoat, a scarf wound tight around his neck. A character from the times of King Umberto; perhaps an old colonel, or only a faithful quartermaster sergeant. Or a postman, an old rural messenger: with those big hands, when he extended the thin pillow to Federico, holding it with his fingertips, he seemed to be delivering a letter, or perhaps to be posting it through the window. The pillow now was in Federico's arms, square, flat, just like an envelope, and what's more, covered with postmarks: it was the daily letter to Cinzia, also departing this evening, and instead of the page of eager scrawl there was Federico in person to take the invisible path of the night mail, through the hand of the old winter messenger, the last incarnation of the rational, disciplined north before the incursion among the unruly passions of the center-south.

But still, and above all, it was a pillow, namely, a soft object (though pressed and compact) and white (though covered with postmarks) from the steam laundry. It contained in itself, as a concept is enclosed within an ideographic sign, the idea of the bed, the twisting and turning, the privacy; and Federico was already anticipating with pleasure the island of freshness it would be for him that night, amid that rough and treacherous plush. And further, that slender rectangle of comfort prefigured later comforts, later intimacy, later sweetnesses, whose enjoyment was the reason he was setting out on this journey; indeed, the very fact of departing, the hiring of the cushion, was a form of enjoying them, a way of entering the dimension where Cinzia reigned, the circle enclosed by her soft arms.

And it was with an amorous, caressing motion that the train began to glide among the columns of the marquees, snaking through the iron-clad fields of the switches, hurling itself into the darkness, and becoming one with the impulse that till then Federico had felt within himself. And as if the release of his tension in the speeding of the train had made him lighter, he began to accompany its race, humming the tune of a song that this speed brought to his mind: *"J'ai deux amours . . . Mon pays et Paris . . . Paris toujours . . ."*

A man entered; Federico fell silent. "Is this place free?" He sat down. Federico had already made a quick mental calculation: strictly speaking, if you want to make your journey lying down, it's best to have someone else in the compartment, one person stretched out on one side and the other on the other, for then nobody dares disturb you; but if, on the other hand, half the compartment remains free, when you least expect it a family of six boards the train, complete with children, all bound for Siracusa, and you're forced to sit up. Federico was quite aware, then, that the wisest thing to do on entering an uncrowded train was to take a seat not in an empty compartment but in a compartment where there was already one traveler. But he never did this: he preferred to aim at total solitude, and when, through no choice of his, he acquired a traveling companion, he could always console himself with the advantages of the new situation.

And so he did now. "Are you going to Rome?" he asked the newcomer, so that he could then add, Fine, let's draw the curtains, turn off the light, and nobody else will come in. But instead the man answered, "No, Genoa." It would be fine for him to get off at Genoa and leave Federico alone again, but for a few hours' journey he wouldn't want to stretch out, would probably remain awake, wouldn't allow the light to be turned off; and other people could come in at the stations along the way. Thus Federico had the disadvantages of traveling in company, with none of the corresponding advantages.

But he didn't dwell on this. His forte had always been his ability to dismiss from the area of his thoughts any aspect of reality that upset him or was of no use to him. He erased the man seated in the corner opposite his, reduced him to a shadow, a gray patch. The newspapers that both held open before their faces assisted the reciprocal impermeability. Federico could go on soaring in his amorous flight. *"Paris toujours . . ."* No one could imagine that in that sordid setting of people coming and going, driven by necessity and by forbearance, he was flying to the arms of a woman the like of Cinzia U. And to feed this sense of pride, Federico felt impelled to consider his traveling companion (at whom he had not even glanced so far) to compare, with the cruelty of the nouveau riche, his own fortunate state with the grayness of other existences.

The stranger, however, didn't look the least downcast. He was still a young man, sturdy, hefty; his manner was satisfied, active; he was reading a sports magazine and had a large suitcase at his side. He looked, in other words, like the agent for some firm, a commercial traveler. For a moment Federico V. was gripped by the feeling of envy always inspired in him by people who seemed more practical and vital than he; but it was the impression of a moment, which he immediately dismissed, thinking, He's a man who travels in corrugated iron, or paints, whereas I . . . And he was seized again by that desire to sing, in a release of euphoria, clearing his mind. *"Je voyage en amour!"* he warbled in his mind, to the earlier rhythm that he felt harmonized with the race of the train, adapting words specially invented to enrage the salesman, if he could have heard them. *"Je voyage en volupté!"* underlining as much as he could the lilt and the languor of the tune, *"Je voyage toujours . . . l'hiver et l'été . . ."* He was thus becoming more and more worked up — *"l'hiver et . . . l'été!"* — to such a degree that a smile of complete mental beatitude must have appeared on his lips. At that moment he realized the salesman was staring at him.

He promptly resumed his staid mien and concentrated on reading his paper, denying even to himself that he had been caught a moment before in such a childish mood.

Childish? Why? Nothing childish about it: his journey put him in a propitious condition of spirit, a condition characteristic in fact of the mature man, of the man who knows the good and the evil of life and is now preparing himself to enjoy, deservedly, the good. Serene, his conscience perfectly at peace, he leafed through the illustrated weeklies, shattered images of a fast, frantic life, in which he sought some of the same things that moved him. Soon he discovered that the magazines didn't interest him in the least, mere scribbles of immediacy, of the life that flows on the surface. His impatience was voyaging through loftier heavens. *"L'hiver et . . . l'été!"* Now it was time to settle down to sleep.

He received an unexpected satisfaction: the salesman had fallen asleep sitting up, without changing position, the newspaper on his lap. Federico considered people who were capable of sleeping in a seated position with a sense of estrangement that didn't even manage to be envy. For him, sleeping on the train involved an elaborate procedure, a detailed ritual, but this too was precisely the arduous pleasure of his journeys.

First he had to take off his good trousers and put on an old pair, so he wouldn't arrive all rumpled. The operation would take place in the WC, but before — to have greater freedom of movement — it was best to change his shoes for slippers. From his bag Federico took out his old trousers and the slipper bag, took off his shoes, put on the slippers, hid the shoes under the seat, went to the WC to change his trousers. *"Je voyage toujours!"* He came back, arranged his good trousers on the rack so they would keep their crease. *"Trallala-la-la!"* He placed the pillow at the end of the seat toward the corridor, because it was better to hear the sudden opening of the door above your head than to be struck by it visually as you suddenly opened your eyes. *"Du voyage, je sais tout!"* At the other end of the seat he put a newspaper, because he didn't lie down barefoot but kept his slippers on. He hung his jacket from a hook over the pillow, and in one pocket he put his change purse and his money clip, which would have pressed against his leg if left in his trouser pocket. But he kept his ticket in the little pocket below his belt. *"Je sais bien voyager . . ."* He replaced his good sweater, so as not to wrinkle it, with an old one; he would change his shirt in the morning.

The salesman, waking when Federico came back into the compartment, had followed his maneuvering as if not completely understanding what was going on. *"Jusqu'à mon amour . . ."* He took off his tie and hung it up, took the celluloid stiffeners from his shirt collar and put them in a pocket of his jacket, along with his money. *". . . j'arrive avec le train!"* He took off his suspenders (like all men devoted to an elegance not merely external, he wore suspenders) and his garters; he undid the top button of his trousers so they wouldn't be too tight over the belly. *"Trallala-la-la!"* He didn't put the jacket on again over his old pullover, but his overcoat instead, after having taken his house keys from the pocket; he left the precious token, though, with the heart-rending fetishism of a child who puts his favorite toy under the pillow. He buttoned up the overcoat completely, turned up the collar; if he was careful, he could sleep in it without leaving a wrinkle. *"Maintenant voilà!"* Sleeping on the train meant waking with your hair all disheveled and maybe finding yourself in the station without even the time to comb it, so he pulled a beret all the way down on his head. *"Je suis prêt, alors!"* He swayed across the compartment in the overcoat, which, worn without a jacket, hung on him like a priestly vestment; he drew the curtains across the door, pulling them until the metallic buttons reached the leather buttonholes. With a gesture toward his companion, he asked permission to turn off the light; the salesman was sleeping. He turned the light off; in the bluish penumbra of the little safety light, he moved just enough to close the curtains at the window, or rather to draw them almost closed; here he always left a crack open: in the morning he liked to have a day of sunshine in his bedroom. One more operation: wind his watch. There, now he could go to bed. With one bound he had flung himself horizontally on the seat, on his side, the overcoat smooth, his legs bent, hands in his pockets, token in his hand, his feet—still in his slippers—on the newspaper, nose against the pillow, beret over his eyes. Now, with a deliberate relaxation of all his feverish inner activity, a vague anticipation of tomorrow, he would fall asleep.

The conductor's curt intrusion (he opened the door with a yank, with confident hand unbuttoned both curtains in a single movement as he raised his other hand to turn on the light) was foreseen. Federico, however, preferred not to wait for it: if the man arrived before he had fallen asleep, fine; if his first sleep had already begun, a habitual and anonymous appearance like the conductor's interrupted it only for a few seconds, just as a sleeper in the country wakes at the cry of a nocturnal bird but then rolls over as if he hadn't waked at all. Federico had the ticket ready in his pocket and held it out, not getting up, almost not opening his eyes, his hand remaining open until he felt the ticket again between his fingers; he pocketed it and would immediately have fallen back to sleep if he hadn't been obliged to perform an operation that nullified all his earlier effort at immobility: namely, to get up and fasten the curtains again. On this trip he was still awake, and the ticket check lasted a bit longer than usual, because the salesman, caught in his sleep, took a while to get his bearings and find his ticket. He doesn't have prompt reflexes like mine, Federico thought, and took the opportunity to overwhelm him with new variations of his imaginary song. *"Je voyage l'amour . . ."* he crooned. The idea of using the verb *"voyager"* transitively gave him the sense of fullness that poetic inspiration, even the slightest, gives, and the satisfaction of having finally found an expression adequate to his spiritual state. *"Je voyage amour! Je voyage liberté! Jour et nuit je cours . . . par les chemins-de-fer . . ."*

The compartment was again in darkness. The train devoured its invisible road. Could Federico ask more of life?

From such bliss to sleep, the transition is brief. Federico dozed off as if sinking into a pit of feathers. Five or six minutes only: then he woke. He was hot, all in a sweat. The coaches were already heated, since it was well into autumn, but he, recalling the cold he had felt on his previous trip, had thought to lie down in his overcoat. He rose, took it off, flung it over himself like a blanket, leaving his shoulders and chest free but still trying to spread it out so as not to make ugly wrinkles. He turned onto his other side. The sweat had spread over his body a network of itching. He unbuttoned his shirt, scratched his chest, scratched one leg. The constricted condition of his body that he now felt evoked thoughts of physical freedom, the sea, nakedness, swimming, running, and all this culminated in the embracing of Cinzia, the sum of the good of existence. And there, half asleep, he could no longer distinguish present discomforts from the yearned-for good; he had everything at once; he writhed in an uneasiness that presupposed and almost contained every possible well-being. He fell asleep again.

The loudspeakers of the stations that woke him every so often are not as disagreeable as many people suppose. Waking and knowing at once where you are offers two different possibilities of satisfaction. You can think, if the station is farther along than you imagined, How much I've slept! How far I've gone without realizing it! Or, if the station is way behind, Good, now I have plenty of time to fall asleep again and continue sleeping without any concern.

Now he was in the second of these situations. The salesman was there, now also stretched out asleep, softly snoring. Federico was still warm. He rose, half sleeping, groped for the regulator of the electric heating system, found it on the wall opposite his, just above the head of his traveling companion, extended his hands, balancing on one foot because one of his slippers had come off, and angrily turned the dial to low. The salesman had to open his eyes at that moment and see that clawing hand over his head; he gulped, swallowed saliva, then sank back into his haze. Federico flung himself down. The electric regulator let out a hum; a red light came on, as if it were trying to explain, to start a dialogue. Federico impatiently waited for the heat to be dispelled; he rose to lower the window a crack, but since the train was now moving very fast, he felt cold and closed it again. He shifted the regulator toward automatic. His face on the amorous pillow, he lay for a while listening to the buzzes of the regulator like mysterious messages from ultra-terrestrial worlds. The train was traveling over the earth, surmounted by endless spaces, and in all the universe he and he alone was the man who was speeding toward Cinzia U.

The next awakening was at the cry of a coffee vendor in the Stazione Principe, Genoa. The salesman had vanished. Carefully Federico stopped up the gaps in the wall of curtains and listened with apprehension to every footstep approaching along the passage, to every opening of a door. No, nobody came in. But at Genoa-Brignole a hand opened a breach, groped, tried to part the curtains, failed; a human form appeared, crouching, and cried in dialect toward the corridor, "Come on! It's empty here!" A heavy shuffling of boots replied, with scattered voices, and four Alpine soldiers entered the darkness of the compartment and almost sat down on top of Federico. As they bent over him, as if over an unknown animal—"Oh! Who's this here?"—he pulled himself up abruptly on his arms and confronted them: "Aren't there any other compartments?" "No. All full," they answered, "but never mind. We'll all sit over on this side. Stay comfortable." They seemed intimidated, but actually they were simply accustomed to curt manners and paid no attention to anything; brawling, they flung themselves on the other seat. "Are you going far?" Federico asked, meeker now, from his pillow. No, they were getting off at one of the first stations. "And where are you going?" "To Rome." "Madonna! All the way to Rome!" Their tone of amazed compassion was transformed in Federico's heart into a heroic, melting pride.

And so the journey continued. "Could you turn off the light?" They turned it off, and remained faceless in the dark, noisy, cumbersome, shoulder to shoulder. One raised a curtain at the window and peered out: it was a moonlit night. Lying down, Federico saw only the sky and now and then the row of lights of a little station that dazzled his eyes and cast a rake of shadows on the ceiling. These *alpini* were rough country boys, going home on leave; they never stopped talking loudly and hailing one another, and at times in the darkness they punched and slapped one another, except one of them who was sleeping and another who coughed. They spoke a murky dialect. Federico could grasp words now and then—talk about the barracks, the brothel. For some reason, he felt he didn't hate them. Now he was with them, almost one of them, and he identified with them for the pleasure of then imagining himself tomorrow at the side of Cinzia U., feeling the dizzying, sudden shift of fate. But this was not to belittle them, as with the stranger earlier; now he remained obscurely on their side; their unaware blessing accompanied him toward Cinzia; in everything that was most remote from her lay the value of having her, the sense of his being the one who had her.

Now Federico's arm was numb. He lifted it, shook it; the numbness wouldn't go away, turned into pain; the pain turned into slow well-being as he flapped his bent arm in the air. The *alpini,* all four of them, sat there staring at him, mouths agape. "What's come over him? . . . He's dreaming . . . Hey, what are you doing?" Then, with youthful fickleness, they went back to teasing one another. Federico now tried to revive the circulation in one leg, putting his foot on the floor and stamping hard.

Between dozing and clowning, an hour went by. And he didn't feel he was their enemy; perhaps he was no one's enemy; perhaps he had become a good man. He didn't hate them even when, a little before their station, they went out, leaving the door and the curtains wide open. He got up, barricaded himself again, savored once more the pleasure of solitude, but with no bitterness toward anyone.

Now his legs were cold. He pushed the cuffs of his trousers inside his socks, but he was still cold. He wrapped the folds of his overcoat around his legs. Now his stomach and shoulders were cold. He turned the regulator up almost to high, tucked himself in again, pretended not to notice that the overcoat was getting ugly creases, though he felt them under him. Now he was ready to renounce everything for his immediate comfort; the awareness of being good to his neighbor drove him to be good to himself and, in this general indulgence, to find once more the road to sleep.

From now on the awakenings were intermittent and mechanical. The entrances of the conductor, with his practiced movement in opening the curtains, were easily distinguishable from the uncertain attempts of the night travelers who had got on at an intermediate station and were bewildered at finding a series of compartments with the curtains drawn. Equally professional but more brusque and grim was the appearance of the policeman, who abruptly turned on the light in the sleeper's face, examined him, turned it off, and went out in silence, leaving behind him a prison chill.

Then a man came in, at some station buried in the night. Federico became aware of him when he was already huddled in one corner, and from the damp odor of his coat realized that outside it was raining. When he woke again the man had vanished, at God knows what other invisible station, and for Federico he had been only a shadow smelling of rain, with heavy respiration.

He was cold; he turned the regulator all the way to high, then stuck his hand under the seat to feel the warmth rise. He felt nothing; he groped there; everything must have been cut off. He put his overcoat on again, then removed it; he hunted for his good sweater, took off the old one, put on the good one, put the old one on over it, put the overcoat on again, huddled down, and tried to achieve once more the sensation of fullness that earlier had led him to sleep; but he couldn't manage to recall anything, and when he remembered the song he was already sleeping, and that rhythm continued cradling him triumphantly in his sleep.

The first morning light came through the cracks like the cries of "Hot coffee!" and "Newspapers!" at a station perhaps still in Tuscany, or at the very beginning of Latium. It wasn't raining; beyond the damp windows the sky already displayed a southern indifference to autumn. The desire for something hot, and also the automatic reaction of the city man who begins all his mornings by glancing at the newspapers, acted on Federico's reflexes, and he felt that he should rush to the window and buy coffee or the paper or both. But he succeeded so well in convincing himself that he was still asleep and hadn't heard anything that this persuasion still held when the compartment was invaded by the usual people from Civitavecchia who take the early morning trains into Rome. And the best part of his sleep, that of the first hours of daylight, had almost no breaks.

When he really did wake up, he was dazzled by the light that came in through the panes, now without curtains. On the seat opposite him a row of people were lined up, including even a little boy on a fat woman's lap, and a man was seated on Federico's own seat, in the space left free by his bent legs. The men had various faces but all had something vaguely bureaucratic about them, with the one possible variant of an air force officer in a uniform laden with ribbons; it was also obvious that the women were going to call on relatives who worked in some government office. In any case, these were people going to Rome to deal with red tape for themselves or for others. And all of them, some looking up from the conservative newspaper *Il Tempo,* observed Federico stretched out there at the level of their knees, shapeless, bundled into that overcoat, without feet, like a seal; as he was detaching himself from the saliva-stained pillow, disheveled, the beret on the back of his head, one cheek marked by the wrinkles in the pillowcase; as he got up, stretched with awkward, seal-like movements, gradually rediscovering the use of his legs, slipping the slippers on the wrong feet, and now unbuttoning and scratching himself between the double sweaters and the rumpled shirt while running his still-sticky eyes over them and smiling.

At the window, the broad Roman *campagna* spread out. Federico sat there for a moment, his hands on his knees, still smiling; then, with a gesture, he asked permission to take the newspaper from the knees of the man facing him.

top of one rock to the next. Leaping in this way on his skinny legs, he crossed half the rocky shore, sometimes almost grazing the faces of half-hidden pairs of bathers stretched out on beach towels. Having gone past an outcrop of sandy rock, its surface porous and irregular, he came upon smooth stones with rounded corners; Amedeo took off his sandals, held them in his hand, and continued running barefoot, with the confidence of someone who can judge distances between rocks and whose soles nothing can hurt. He reached a spot directly above the sea; there was a kind of shelf running around the cliff at the halfway point. There Amedeo stopped. On a flat ledge he arranged his clothes, carefully folded, and set the sandals on them, soles up, so no gust of wind would carry everything off (in reality, only the faintest breath of air was stirring, from the sea, but this precaution was obviously a habit with him). A little bag he was carrying turned into a rubber cushion; he blew into it until it had filled out, then set it down; and below it, at a point slightly sloping from that rocky ledge, he spread out his towel. He flung himself on it supine, and already his hands were opening his book at the marked page. So he lay stretched out on the ledge, in that sun glaring on all sides, his skin dry (his tan was opaque, irregular, as of one who takes the sun without any method but doesn't burn); on the rubber cushion he set his head, sheathed in a white canvas cap, moistened (yes, he had also climbed down to a low rock, to dip his cap in the water), immobile except for his eyes (invisible behind his dark glasses), which followed along the black-and-white lines the horse of Fabrizio del Dongo. Below him opened a little cove of greenish blue water, transparent almost to the bottom. The rocks, according to their exposure, were bleached white or covered with algae. A little pebble beach was at their foot. Every now and then Amedeo raised his eyes to that broad view, lingered on a glinting of the surface, on the oblique dash of a crab; then he went back, gripped, to the page where Raskolnikov counted the steps that separated him from the old woman's door, or where Lucien de Rubempré, before sticking his head into the noose, gazed at the towers and roofs of the Conciergerie.

For some time Amedeo had tended to reduce his participation in active life to the minimum. Not that he didn't like action; on the contrary, love of action nourished his whole character, all his tastes. And yet from one year to the next, the yearning to be someone who did things declined, declined, until he wondered if he had ever really harbored that yearning. His interest in action survived, however, in his pleasure in reading; his passion was always the narration of events, the stories, the tangle of human situations —nineteenth-century novels especially, but also memoirs and biographies, and so on down to thrillers and science fiction, which he didn't disdain but which gave him less satisfaction because they were short. Amedeo loved thick tomes, and in tackling them he felt the physical pleasure of undertaking a great task. Weighing them in his hand, thick, closely printed, squat, he would consider with some apprehension the number of pages, the length of the chapters, then venture into them, a bit reluctant at the beginning, without any desire to perform the initial chore of remembering the names, catching the drift of the story; then he would entrust himself to it, running along the lines, crossing the grid of the uniform page, and beyond the leaden print the flame and fire of battle appeared, the cannonball that, whistling through the sky, fell at the feet of Prince Andrei, and the shop filled with engravings and statues where Frédéric Moreau, his heart in his mouth, was to meet the Arnoux family. Beyond the surface of the page you entered a world where life was more alive than here on this side: like the surface of the water that separates us from that blue-and-green world, rifts as far as the eye can see, expanses of fine, ribbed sand, creatures half animal and half vegetable.

The sun beat down hard, the rock was burning, and after a while Amedeo felt he was one with the rock. He reached the end of the chapter, closed the book, inserted an advertising coupon to mark his place, took off his canvas cap and his glasses, stood up half dazed, and with broad leaps went down to the far end of the rock, where a group of kids were constantly, at all hours, diving in and climbing out. Amedeo stood erect on a shelf over the sea, not too high, a couple of yards above the water; his eyes, still daz-

him but sky and water; for a while he would move close to the rocks scattered along the cape, not to overlook any of the possible itineraries of that little archipelago. But as he swam, he realized that the curiosity occupying more and more of his mind was to know the outcome, for example, of the story of Albertine. Would Marcel find her again, or not? He swam furiously or floated idly, but his heart was between the pages of the book left behind on shore. And so with rapid strokes he would regain his rock, seek the place for climbing up, and almost without realizing it he would be up there again, rubbing the Turkish towel on his back. Sticking the canvas cap on his head once more, he would lie in the sun again, to begin the next chapter.

He was not, however, a hasty, voracious reader. He had reached the age when rereading a book—for the second, third, or fourth time—affords more pleasure than a first reading. And yet he still had many continents to discover. Every summer, the most laborious packing before his departure for the sea involved the heavy suitcase to be filled with books. Following the whims and dictates of the months of city life, each year Amedeo would choose certain famous books to reread and certain authors to essay for the first time. And there on the rock he went through them, lingering over sentences, often raising his eyes from the page to ponder, to collect his thoughts. At a certain point, raising his eyes in this way, he saw that on the little pebble beach below, in the cove, a woman had appeared and was lying there.

She was deeply tanned, thin, not very young or particularly beautiful, but nakedness became her (she wore a very tiny two-piece, rolled up at the edges to get as much sun as she could), and Amedeo's eye was drawn to her. He realized that as he read he was raising his eyes more and more often from the book to gaze into the air, and this air was the air that lay between that woman and himself. Her face (she was stretched out on the sloping shore, on a rubber mattress, and at every flicker of his pupils Amedeo saw her legs, not shapely but harmonious, the excellently smooth belly, the bosom slim in a perhaps not unpleasant way but probably sagging a bit, the shoulders a bit too bony, and then the neck and the arms, and the face masked by the sunglasses and by the brim of the straw hat) was slightly lined, lively, aware, and ironic. Amedeo classified the type: the independent woman, on holiday by herself, who dislikes crowded beaches and prefers the more deserted rocks, and likes to lie there and become black as coal; he evaluated the amount of lazy sensuality and of chronic frustration there was in her; he thought fleetingly of the likelihood of a rapidly consummated fling, measured it against the prospect of a trite conversation, a program for the evening, probable logistic difficulties, the effort of concentration always required to become acquainted, even superficially, with a person; and he went on reading, convinced that this woman couldn't interest him at all.

But he had been lying on that stretch of rock for too long, or else those fleeting thoughts had left a wake of restlessness in him. Anyway, he felt an ache; the harshness of the rock under the towel that was his only pallet began to chafe him. He got up to look for another spot where he could stretch out. For a moment he hesitated between two places that seemed equally comfortable to him: one more distant from the little beach where the tanned lady was lying (actually behind an outcrop of rock that blocked the sight of her), the other closer. The thought of approaching, and of then perhaps being led by some unforeseeable circumstance to start a conversation, and thus perforce to interrupt his reading, made him immediately prefer the farther spot; but when he thought it over, it really would look as if the moment that lady had arrived he wanted to run off, and this might seem a bit rude; so he picked the closer spot, since his reading absorbed him so much anyway that the view of the lady—not specially beautiful, for that matter—could hardly distract him. He lay on one side, holding the book so that it blocked the sight of her, but it was awkward to keep his arm at that height, and in the end he lowered it. Now every time he had to start a new line the same gaze that ran along the lines encountered, just beyond the edge of the page, the legs of the solitary vacationer. She too had shifted slightly, looking for a more comfortable position, and the fact that she had raised her knees and crossed her legs precisely in Amedeo's direction allowed him to better observe her proportions, not at all unattractive. In short, Amedeo (though a shaft of rock was sawing at his hip) couldn't have found a finer position: the pleasure he could derive from the sight of the tanned lady — a marginal pleasure, something extra, but not for that reason to be discarded, since it could be enjoyed with no effort — did not mar the pleasure of reading but was inserted into its normal process, so that now he was sure he could go on reading without being tempted to look away.

Everything was calm; only the course of his reading flowed on, with the motionless landscape serving as frame; the tanned lady had become a necessary part of this landscape. Amedeo was naturally relying on his own ability to remain absolutely still for a long time, but he hadn't taken into account the woman's restlessness: now she rose, was standing, making her way among the stones toward the water. She had moved, Amedeo understood immediately, to get a closer look at a great medusa that a group of boys were bringing ashore, poking at it with lengths of reed. The tanned lady bent toward the overturned body of the medusa and was questioning the boys; her legs rose from wooden clogs with very high heels, unsuited to those rocks; her body, seen from behind as Amedeo now saw it, was that of a more attractive younger woman than she had first seemed to him. He thought that for a man seeking a romance, that dialogue between her and the fisher-boys would have been a classic opening: approach, also remark on the capture of the medusa, and in that way engage her in conversation. The very thing he wouldn't have done for all the gold in the world! he added to himself, plunging again into his reading.

To be sure, this rule of conduct of his also prevented him from satisfying a natural curiosity concerning the medusa, which seemed, as he saw it there, of unusual dimensions, and also of a strange hue between pink and violet. This curiosity about marine animals was in no way a sidetrack, either; it was coherent with the nature of his passion for reading. At that moment, in any case, his concentration on the page he was reading—a long descriptive passage —had been relaxing; in short, it was absurd that to protect himself against the danger of starting a conversation with that woman he should also deny himself spontaneous and quite legitimate impulses such as that of amusing himself for a few minutes by taking a close look at a medusa. He shut his book at the marked page and stood up. His decision couldn't have been more timely: at that same moment the lady moved away from the little group of boys, preparing to return to her mattress. Amedeo realized this as he was approaching and felt the need of immediately saying something in a loud voice. He shouted to the kids, "Watch out! It could be dangerous!"

The boys, crouched around the animal, didn't even look up: they continued, with the lengths of reed they held in their hands, to try to raise it and turn it over; but the lady turned abruptly and went back to the shore, with a half-questioning, half-fearful air. "Oh, how frightening! Does it bite?"

"If you touch it, it stings," he explained, and realized he was heading not toward the medusa but toward the lady, who for some reason covered her bosom with her arms in a useless shudder and cast almost furtive glances first at the supine animal, then at Amedeo. He reassured her, and so, predictably, they started conversing; but it didn't matter, because Amedeo would soon be going back to the book awaiting him: he only wanted to take a glance at the medusa. He led the tanned lady over to lean into the center of the circle of boys. The lady was now observing with revulsion, her knuckles against her teeth, and at a certain point, as she and he were side by side, their arms came into contact and they delayed a moment before separating them. Amedeo then started talking about medusas. His direct experience wasn't great, but he had read some books by famous fishermen and underwater explorers, so —skipping the smaller fauna—he began promptly talking about the famous manta. The lady listened to him, displaying great interest and interjecting something from time to time, always irrelevantly, the way women will. "You see this red spot on my arm? That wasn't a medusa, was it?" Amedeo touched the spot, just above the elbow, and said no. It was a bit red because she had been leaning on it while lying down.

With that, it was all over. They said goodbye; she went back to her place and he to his, where he resumed reading. It had been an interval lasting the right amount of time, neither more nor less, a human encounter, not unpleasant (the lady was polite, discreet, unassuming) precisely because it was barely adumbrated. In the book he now found a far fuller and more concrete attachment to reality, where everything had a meaning, an importance, a rhythm. Amedeo felt himself in a perfect situation: the printed page opened true life to him, profound and exciting, and raising his eyes, he found a pleasant but casual juxtaposition of colors and sensations, an accessory and decorative world that couldn't commit him to anything. The tanned lady, from her mattress, gave him a smile and a wave; he replied also with a smile and a vague gesture and immediately lowered his eyes. But the lady had said something.

"Eh?"

"You're reading. Do you read all the time?"

"Mmm . . ."

"Interesting?"

"Yes."

"Enjoy yourself!"

"Thank you."

He mustn't raise his eyes again. At least not until the end of the chapter. He read it in a flash. The lady now had a cigarette in her mouth and motioned to him as she pointed to it. Amedeo had the impression that for some time she had been trying to attract his attention. "I beg your pardon?"

". . . match. Forgive me . . ."

"Oh, I'm very sorry. I don't smoke."

The chapter was finished. Amedeo rapidly read the first

lines of the next one, which he found surprisingly attractive, but to begin the next chapter without anxiety he had
to resolve as quickly as possible the matter of the match.
"Wait!" He stood up, began leaping among the rocks, half
dazed by the sun, until he found a little group of people
smoking. He borrowed a box of matches, ran to the lady,
lit her cigarette, ran back to return the matches, and they
said to him, "Keep them, you can keep them." He ran
again to the lady to leave the matches with her, and she
thanked him; he waited a moment before leaving her, but
realized that after this delay he had to say something, and
so he said, "You aren't swimming?"

"In a little while," the lady said. "What about you?"

"I've already had my swim."

"And you're not going to take another dip?"

"Yes, I'll read one more chapter, then have a swim again."

"Me too. When I finish my cigarette, I'll dive in."

"See you later then."

"Later . . ."

This kind of appointment restored to Amedeo a calm
such as he—now he realized—had not known since the
moment he became aware of the solitary lady: now his
conscience was no longer oppressed by the thought of
having to have any sort of relationship with that lady; everything was postponed to the moment of their swim—a
swim he would have taken anyway, even if the lady hadn't
been there—and for now he could abandon himself with-

out remorse to the pleasure of reading. So thoroughly that he didn't notice when, at a certain point—before he had reached the end of the chapter—the lady finished her cigarette, stood up, and approached him to invite him to go swimming. He saw the clogs and the straight legs just beyond the book; his eyes moved up; he lowered them again to the page—the sun was dazzling—and read a few lines in haste, looked up again, and heard her say, "Isn't your head about to explode? I'm going to have a dip!" It was nice to stay there, to go on reading and look up every now and then. But since he could no longer put it off, Amedeo did something he never did: he skipped almost half a page, to the conclusion of the chapter, which he read, on the other hand, with great attention, and then he stood up. "Let's go. Shall we dive from the point there?"

After all the talk of diving, the lady cautiously slipped into the water from a ledge on a level with it. Amedeo plunged headlong from a higher rock than usual. It was the hour of the still slow inclining of the sun. The sea was golden. They swam in that gold, somewhat separated. Amedeo at times sank for a few strokes underwater and amused himself by frightening the lady, swimming beneath her. Amused himself, after a fashion: it was kid stuff, of course, but for that matter, what else was there to do, anyway? Swimming with another person was slightly more tiresome than swimming alone, but the difference was minimal. Beyond the gold glints, the water's blue deepened, as if from down below rose an inky darkness. It was useless: nothing equaled the savor of life found in books. Skimming over some bearded rocks in mid-water and leading her, frightened (to help her onto a sandbar, he also clasped her hips and bosom, but his hands, from the immersion, had become almost insensitive, with white, wrinkled pads), Amedeo turned his gaze more and more often toward land, where the colored jacket of his book stood out. There was no other story, no other possible expectation beyond what he had left suspended, between the pages where his bookmark was; all the rest was an empty interval.

However, returning to shore, giving her a hand, drying himself, then each rubbing the other's back, finally created a kind of intimacy, so that Amedeo felt it would have been impolite to go off on his own once more. "Well," he said, "I'll stretch out and read here; I'll go get my book and pillow." And *read:* he had taken care to warn her. She said, "Yes, fine. I'll smoke a cigarette and read *Annabella* a bit myself." She had one of those women's magazines with her, and so both of them could lie and read, each on his own. Her voice struck him like a drop of cold water on the nape of the neck, but she was only saying, "Why do you want to lie there on that hard rock? Come onto the mattress—I'll make room for you." The invitation was polite, the mattress was comfortable, and Amedeo gladly accepted. They lay there, he facing in one direction and she in the other. She didn't say another word; she leafed through those illustrated pages, and Amedeo managed to sink completely into his reading. It was a lingering sunset, when the heat and light hardly decline but remain only barely, sweetly attenuated. The novel Amedeo was reading had reached the point where the darkest secrets of characters and plot are revealed, and you move in a familiar world, and you achieve a kind of parity, an ease between author and reader: you proceed together, and you would like to go on forever.

On the rubber mattress it was possible to make those slight movements necessary to keep the limbs from going to sleep, and one of his legs, in one direction, came to graze a leg of hers, in the other. He didn't mind this, and kept his leg there, and obviously she didn't mind either, because she also refrained from moving. The sweetness of the contact mingled with the reading and, as far as Amedeo was concerned, made it the more complete; but for the lady it must have been different, because she rose, sat up, and said, "Really . . ."

Amedeo was forced to raise his head from the book. The woman was looking at him, and her eyes were bitter.

"Something wrong?" he asked.

"Don't you ever get tired of reading?" she asked. "You could hardly be called good company! Don't you know that with women, you're supposed to make conversation?" she added; her half smile was perhaps meant only to be ironic, though to Amedeo, who at that moment would have paid anything rather than give up his novel, it seemed downright threatening. What have I got myself into, moving down here? he thought. Now it was clear that with this woman beside him he wouldn't read a line.

I must make her realize she's made a mistake, he thought, that I'm not at all the type for a beach courtship, that I'm the sort it's best not to pay too much attention to. "Conversation," he said aloud, "what kind of conversation?" and he extended his hand toward her. There, now: if I lay a hand on her, she will surely be insulted by such an unsuitable action; maybe she'll give me a slap and go away. But whether it was his own natural reserve or there was a different, sweeter yearning that in reality he was pursuing, the caress, instead of being brutal and provocatory, was shy, melancholy, almost entreating: he grazed her throat with his fingers, lifted a little necklace she was wearing, and let it fall. The woman's reply consisted of a movement, first slow, as if resigned and a bit ironic—she lowered her chin to one side, to trap his hand—then rapid, as if in a calculated, aggressive spring: she bit the back of his hand. "Ow!" Amedeo cried. They moved apart.

"Is this how you make conversation?" the lady said.

There, Amedeo quickly reasoned, my way of making conversation doesn't suit her, so there won't be any conversing, and now I can read; he had already started a new paragraph. But he was trying to deceive himself: he understood clearly that by now they had gone too far, that between him and the tanned lady a tension had been created that could no longer be interrupted; he also understood that he was the first to wish not to interrupt it, since in any case he wouldn't be able to return to the single tension of his reading, all intimate and interior. He could, on the contrary, try to make this exterior tension follow, so to speak, a course parallel to the other, so that he would not be obliged to renounce either the lady or the book.

Since she had sat up, with her back propped against a rock, he sat beside her, put his arm around her shoulders, keeping his book on his knees. He turned toward her and kissed her. They moved apart, then kissed again. Then he lowered his head toward the book and resumed reading.

As long as he could, he wanted to continue reading. His fear was that he wouldn't be able to finish the novel: the beginning of a summer affair could be considered the end of his calm hours of solitude, for a completely different rhythm would dominate his days of vacation; and obviously, when you are completely lost in reading a book, if you have to interrupt it, then pick it up again some time later, most of the pleasure is lost—you forget so many details, you never manage to become immersed in it as before.

The sun was gradually setting behind the next promontory, and then the next, and the one after that, leaving remnants of color against the light. From the little coves of the cape, all the bathers had gone. Now the two of them were alone. Amedeo had his arm around the woman's shoulders, he was reading, he gave her kisses on the neck and on the ears—which it seemed to him she liked—and every now and then, when she turned, on the mouth; then he resumed reading. Perhaps this time he had found the ideal equilibrium: he could go on like this for a hundred pages or so. But once again it was she who wanted to change the situation. She began to stiffen, almost to reject him, and then said, "It's late. Let's go. I'm going to dress."

This abrupt decision opened up quite different prospects. Amedeo was a bit disoriented, but he didn't stop to weigh the pros and cons. He had reached a climax in the book, and her dimly heard words, "I'm going to dress," had in his mind immediately been translated into these others: While she dresses, I'll have time to read a few pages without being disturbed.

But she said, "Hold up the towel, please," addressing him as *tu* for perhaps the first time. "I don't want anyone to see me." The precaution was useless because the shore by now was deserted, but Amedeo consented amiably, since he could hold up the towel while remaining seated and so continue to read the book on his knees.

On the other side of the towel, the lady had undone her halter, paying no attention to whether he was looking at her or not. Amedeo didn't know whether to look at her, pretending to read, or to read, pretending to look at her.

He was interested in the one thing and the other, but looking at her seemed too indiscreet, while going on reading seemed too indifferent. The lady did not follow the usual method used by bathers who dress outdoors, first putting on clothes and then removing the bathing suit underneath them. No: now that her bosom was bared, she also took off the bottom of her suit. This was when, for the first time, she turned her face toward him, and it was a sad face, with a bitter curl to the mouth, and she shook her head, shook her head and looked at him.

Since it has to happen, it might as well happen immediately, Amedeo thought, diving forward, book in hand, one finger between the pages, but what he read in that gaze — reproach, commiseration, dejection, as if to say, Stupid, all right, we'll do it if it has to be done like this, but you don't understand a thing, any more than the others — or rather, what he did *not* read, since he didn't know how to read gazes, but only vaguely sensed, roused in him a moment of such transport toward the woman that, embracing her and falling onto the mattress with her, he only slightly turned his head toward the book to make sure it didn't fall into the sea.

It had fallen instead right beside the mattress, open, but a few pages had flipped over, and Amedeo, even in the ecstasy of his embraces, tried to free one hand to put the bookmark at the right page. Nothing is more irritating when you're eager to resume reading than to have to search through the book, unable to find your place.

Their lovemaking was a perfect match. It could perhaps have been extended a bit longer, but then, hadn't everything been lightning fast in their encounter?

Dusk was falling. Below, the rocks opened out, sloping, into a little harbor. Now she had gone down there and was halfway into the water. "Come down; we'll have a last swim . . ." Amedeo, biting his lip, was counting how many pages were left till the end.

The Adventure of a Nearsighted Man

Amilcare Carruga was still young, not lacking resources, without exaggerated material or spiritual ambitions: nothing, therefore, prevented him from enjoying life. And yet he came to realize that for a while now this life, for him, had imperceptibly been losing its savor. Trifles like, for example, looking at women in the street: there had been a time when he would cast his eyes on them greedily; now perhaps he would instinctively start to look at them, but it would immediately seem to him that they were speeding past like a wind, stirring no sensation, so he would lower his eyelids, indifferent. Once new cities had excited him —he traveled often, since he was a merchant—but now he felt only irritation, confusion, loss of bearings. Before, since he lived alone, he used to go to the movies every evening; he enjoyed himself no matter what the picture was. Anyone who goes all the time sees, as it were, one huge film, in endless installments; he knows all the actors, even the character players and the walk-ons, and this recognition of them every time is amusing in itself. Well, now even at the movies, all those faces seemed to have become colorless to him, flat, anonymous; he was bored.

He caught on, finally. The fact was that he was nearsighted. The oculist prescribed eyeglasses for him. After that moment his life changed, became a hundred times richer in interest than before.

Just slipping on the glasses was, every time, a thrill for him. He might be, for instance, at a tram stop, and he would be overcome by sadness because everything, people and objects around him, was so vague, banal, worn from being as it was, and him there, groping in the midst of a flabby world of nearly decayed forms and colors. He would put on his glasses to read the number of the arriving tram, and all would change: the most ordinary things, even lampposts, were etched with countless tiny details, with sharp lines, and the faces, the faces of strangers, each filled up with little marks, dots of beard, pimples, nuances of expression that there had been no hint of before; and he could understand what material clothes were made of, could guess the weave, could spot the fraying at the hem. Looking became an amusement, a spectacle—not looking at this thing or that, just looking. And so Amilcare Carruga forgot to note the tram number, missed one car after another or else climbed onto the wrong one. He saw such a quantity of things that it was as if he no longer saw anything. Little by little he had to become accustomed, learn all over again from the beginning what was pointless to look at and what was necessary.

The women he encountered in the street, who before had been reduced for him to impalpable, blurred shadows, he could now see in all the precise interplay of voids and solids that their bodies make as they move inside their dresses, and could judge the freshness of the skin and the warmth contained in their gaze, and it seemed to him he was not only seeing them but already actually possessing them. He might be walking along without his glasses (he didn't wear them all the time, to avoid tiring his eyes unnecessarily; only if he had to look into the distance) and there, ahead of him on the sidewalk, a bright-colored dress would be outlined. With a now automatic movement, Amilcare would promptly take his glasses from his pocket and slip them onto his nose. This indiscriminate covetousness of sensations was often punished: maybe the woman proved a hag. Amilcare Carruga became more cautious. And at times an approaching woman might seem to him, from her colors, her walk, too humble, insignificant, not worth taking into consideration, and he wouldn't put on his glasses, but then when they passed each other close, he realized that, on the contrary, there was something about her that attracted him strongly, God knows what, and at that moment he seemed to catch a look of hers, as if of expectation, perhaps a look that she had trained on him at his first appearance and he hadn't been aware of it. But by now it was too late: she had vanished at the intersection, climbed into the bus, was far away beyond the traffic light, and he wouldn't be able to recognize her another time. And so, through his need for eyeglasses, he was slowly learning how to live.

But the newest world his glasses opened up to him was that of the night. The night city, formerly shrouded in shapeless clouds of darkness and colored glows, now revealed precise divisions, prominences, perspectives; the lights had specific borders, the neon signs once immersed in a vague halo now could be read letter by letter. The beautiful thing about night was, however, that the margin of haziness his lenses dispelled in daylight here remained: Amilcare Carruga would feel impelled to put his glasses on, then realize he was already wearing them. The sense of fullness never equaled the drive of dissatisfaction; darkness was a bottomless humus in which he never tired of digging. In the streets, above the houses spotted with yellow windows, square at last, he raised his eyes toward the starry sky, and he discovered that the stars were not splattered against the ground of the sky like broken eggs but were very sharp jabs of light that opened up infinite distances around themselves.

This new concern with the reality of the external world was connected with his worries about what he himself was, also inspired by the use of eyeglasses. Amilcare Carruga didn't attach much importance to himself; however, as sometimes happens with the most unassuming of people, he was greatly attached to his way of being. Now, to pass from the category of men without glasses to that of men with glasses seems nothing, but it is a very big leap. For example, when someone who doesn't know you is trying to describe you, the first thing he says is, "He wears glasses," so that accessory detail, which two weeks earlier was completely unknown to you, becomes your prime attribute, is identified with your very existence. To Amilcare —foolishly, if you like—becoming all at once someone who "wears glasses" was a bit irritating. But that wasn't the real trouble: it was that once you begin to suspect that everything concerning you is purely casual, subject to transformation, and that you could be completely different and it wouldn't matter at all, then, following this line of reasoning, you come to think it's all the same whether you exist or don't exist, and from this notion to despair is only a brief step. Therefore Amilcare, when he had to select a kind of frame, instinctively chose some fine, very understated earpieces, just a pair of thin silver hooks, to hold the naked lenses and connect them over the nose with a little bridge. But after a while he realized he wasn't happy: if he inadvertently caught sight of himself in the mirror with his glasses on, he felt a keen dislike for his face, as if it were the typical face of a category of persons alien to him. It was precisely those glasses, so discreet, light, almost feminine, that made him look more than ever like "a man who wears glasses," one who had never done anything in his whole life but wear glasses, so that you now no longer even notice he wears them. They were becoming part of his physiognomy, those glasses, blending with his features, and so they were diminishing every natural contrast between what was his face—an ordinary face, but still a face—and what was an extraneous object, an industrial product.

He didn't love them, and so it wasn't long before they fell and broke. He bought another pair. This time his choice took the opposite direction: he selected a pair of black plastic frames an inch thick, with hinged corners that stuck out from the cheekbones like a horse's blinders, sidepieces heavy enough to bend the ear. They were a kind of mask that hid half his face, but behind them he felt like himself: there was no doubt that he was one thing and the glasses another, completely separate; it was clear that he was wearing glasses only incidentally and that without glasses he was an entirely different man. Once again—insofar as his nature allowed it—he was happy.

In that period he happened to go to V. on business. The city of V. was Amilcare Carruga's birthplace, and there he had spent all his youth. He had left it, however, ten years before, and his trips back had become more and more brief and sporadic; several years had gone by now since he last set foot there. You know how it is when you move away from a place where you've lived a long time: returning at long intervals, you feel disoriented; it seems that those sidewalks, those friends, those conversations in the café, either must be everything or can no longer be anything; either you follow them day by day or else you are no longer able to participate in them, and the thought of reappearing after too long a time inspires a kind of remorse, and you dismiss it. And so Amilcare had gradually stopped seeking occasions for going back to V.; then, if occasions did arise, he let them pass; and in the end he actually avoided them. But in recent times, in this negative attitude toward his native city, there had been, beyond the motive just defined, also that sense of general disaffection that had come over him, which he had subsequently identified with the worsening of his nearsightedness. So now, finding himself in a new frame of mind thanks to the glasses, the first time a chance to go to V. presented itself, he seized it promptly, and went.

V. appeared to him in a totally different light from the last few times he had been there. But not because of its changes. True, the city had changed a great deal, new buildings everywhere, shops and cafés and movie theaters all different from before, the younger generation all strangers, and the traffic twice what it had been. All this newness, however, only underlined and made more recognizable what was old; in short, Amilcare Carruga managed for the first time to see the city again with the eyes of his boyhood, as if he had left it the day before. Thanks to his glasses he saw a host of insignificant details—a certain window, for example, a certain railing; or rather he was conscious of seeing them, of distinguishing them from all the rest, whereas in the past he had merely seen them. To say nothing of the faces: a news vendor, a lawyer, some having aged, others still the same. Amilcare Carruga no longer had any real relatives in V., and his group of close friends had also dispersed long since. He did, however, have endless acquaintances: nothing else would have been possible in a city so small, as it had been in the days when he lived there, that, practically speaking, everybody knew everybody else, at least by sight. Now the population had grown a lot here too, as everywhere in the well-to-do cities of the north — there had been a certain influx of southerners, and the majority of the faces Amilcare encountered belonged to strangers. But for this very reason he enjoyed the satisfaction of recognizing at first glance the old inhabitants, and he recalled episodes, connections, nicknames.

V. was one of those provincial cities where the tradition of an evening stroll along the main street still obtained, and in that, nothing had changed from Amilcare's day to the present. As always happens in these cases, one of the sidewalks was crammed with a steady flow of people, the other sidewalk less so. In their day, Amilcare and his friends, out of a kind of nonconformity, had always walked on the less popular sidewalk, from there casting glances and greetings and quips at the girls going by on the other. Now he felt as he had then, indeed even more excited, and he set off along his old sidewalk, looking at all the people who passed. Encountering familiar people this time didn't make him uneasy; it amused him, and he hastened to greet them. With some of them he would also have liked to stop and exchange a few words, but the main street of V. had sidewalks so narrow that the crowd of people kept shoving you forward, and what's more, the traffic of vehicles was now so much increased that you could no longer, as in the past, walk a bit in the middle of the street and cross it whenever you chose. In short, the stroll proceeded either too rushed or too slow, with no freedom of movement. Amilcare had to follow the current or struggle against it, and when he saw a familiar face he barely had time to wave a greeting before it vanished, and he could never be sure whether he had been seen or not.

Thus he ran into Corrado Strazza, his classmate and billiards companion for many years. Amilcare smiled at him and waved broadly. Corrado Strazza came forward, his gaze on him, but it was as if that gaze went right through him, and Corrado continued on his way. Was it possible he hadn't recognized Amilcare? Time had gone by, but Amilcare Carruga knew very well he hadn't changed much; so far he had warded off a paunch, as he had baldness, and his features had not been greatly altered. Here came Professor Cavanna. Amilcare gave him a deferential greeting, a little bow. At first the professor started to respond to it, instinctively, but then he stopped and looked around, as if seeking someone else. Professor Cavanna, who was famous for his visual memory! Because of all his many classes, he remembered faces and first and last names and even semester grades. Finally Ciccio Corba, the coach of the football team, returned Amilcare's greeting. But immediately afterward he blinked and began to whistle, as if realizing he had intercepted by mistake the greeting of a stranger, addressed to God knows what other person.

Amilcare became aware that nobody would recognize him. The eyeglasses that made the rest of the world visible to him, those eyeglasses in their enormous black frames, made him invisible. Who would ever think that behind that sort of mask there was actually Amilcare Carruga, so long absent from V., whom no one was expecting to run into at any moment? He had barely managed to formulate these conclusions in his mind when Isa Maria Bietti appeared. She was with a girlfriend, strolling and looking in shop windows; Amilcare blocked her way and was about to cry "Isa Maria!" but his voice was paralyzed in his throat; Isa Maria Bietti pushed him aside with her elbow, said to her friend, "The way people behave nowadays ... ," and went on.

Not even Isa Maria Bietti had recognized him. He understood all of a sudden that it was only because of Isa Maria Bietti that he had come back, just as it was only because of Isa Maria Bietti that he had decided to leave V. and had stayed away so many years; everything, everything in his life and everything in the world, was only because of Isa Maria Bietti; and now finally he saw her again, their eyes met, and Isa Maria Bietti didn't recognize him. In his great emotion, he hadn't noticed if she had changed, grown fat, aged, if she was as attractive as ever or less or more — he had seen nothing except that she was Isa Maria Bietti and that Isa Maria Bietti hadn't seen him.

He had reached the end of the stretch of the street frequented in the evening stroll. Here, at the corner with the ice cream parlor, or a block farther on, at the newsstand, the people turned around and headed back along the sidewalk in the opposite direction. Amilcare Carruga also turned. He had taken off his glasses. Now the world had become once more that insipid cloud, and he groped, groped with his eyes widened, and could bring nothing to the surface. Not that he didn't succeed in recognizing anyone: in the better-lighted places he was always within a hair's-breadth of identifying a face or two, but a shadow of doubt that perhaps this wasn't the person he thought always remained, and anyway, who it was or wasn't mattered little to him after all. Someone nodded, waved; this greeting might actually have been for him, but Amilcare couldn't quite tell who the person was. Another pair too greeted him as they went by; he was about to respond but had no idea who they were. From the opposite sidewalk, one shouted a *"Ciao, Carrù!"* to him. To judge by the voice, it might have been a man named Stelvi. To his satisfaction, Amilcare realized they recognized him, they remembered him. The satisfaction was relative, because he couldn't even see them, or else couldn't manage to recognize them; they were persons who became confused in his memory, one with another, persons who basically were of little importance to him. "Good evening!" he said every so often, when he noticed a wave, a movement of the head. There, the one who had just greeted him must have been Bellintusi or Carretti, or Strazza. If it was Strazza, Amilcare would have liked perhaps to stop a moment with him and talk. But by now he had returned the greeting rather hastily, and when he thought about it, it seemed natural that their relations should be like this, conventional and hurried greetings.

His looking around, however, clearly had one purpose: to track down Isa Maria Bietti. She was wearing a red coat, so she could be sighted at a distance. For a while Amilcare followed a red coat, but when he managed to pass it he saw that it wasn't she, and meanwhile those other two red coats had gone past in the other direction. That year medium-weight red coats were all the fashion. Earlier, for example, in the same coat, he had seen Gigina, the one from the tobacco shop. Now he began to suspect that it hadn't been Gigina from the tobacco shop but had really been Isa Maria Bietti! But how was it possible to mistake Isa Maria for Gigina? Amilcare retraced his steps to make sure. He came upon Gigina; this was she, no doubt about it. But if she was now coming this way, she couldn't have covered the whole distance; or had she made a shorter circuit? He was completely at sea. If Isa Maria had greeted him and he had responded coldly, his whole journey, all his waiting, all those years, had gone by in vain. Amilcare went back and forth along those sidewalks, sometimes putting on his glasses, sometimes taking them off, sometimes greeting everyone and sometimes receiving the greetings of foggy, anonymous ghosts.

Beyond the other extreme of the stroll, the street continued and was soon beyond the city limits. There was a row of trees, a ditch, a hedge, and the fields. In his day you came out here in the evening with your girl on your arm, if you had a girl, or else, if you were alone, you came here to be even more alone, to sit on a bench and listen to the crickets sing. Amilcare Carruga went on in that direction; now the city extended a bit farther, but not much. There was the bench, the ditch, the crickets, as before. Amilcare Carruga sat down. Of that whole landscape the night left only some great swaths of shadow. Whether he put on or took off his eyeglasses here, it was really all the same. Amilcare Carruga realized that perhaps the thrill of his new glasses had been the last of his life, and now it was over.

rather, she should have remembered earlier that she didn't have the key; but she hadn't, it was as if she had acted deliberately. She had left the house in the afternoon without the key because she had thought she would be coming back for supper; instead she had let those girlfriends she hadn't seen for ages, and those boys, those friends of theirs, a whole party, drag her first to supper, then to drink and dance at one boy's house, then at another's. Obviously at two in the morning it was late to remember that she was without her key. It was all because she had fallen a bit in love with that boy Fornero. Fallen in love? Fallen a *bit*. Things should be seen as they are: neither more nor less. She had spent the night with him, true, but that expression was too strong, it really wasn't the right way to put it; she had waited in the company of that boy until it was time for the door of her building to be opened. That was all. She thought they opened up at six, and at six she had hastened to go home. Also because the cleaning woman came at seven and Stefania didn't want her to notice that she had spent the night out. And today, besides, her husband was coming home.

Now she found the door still locked, and she was alone there in the deserted street, in that early morning light, more transparent than at any other hour of the day, in which everything appeared to be seen through a magnifying glass. She felt a twinge of dismay, and the desire to be in her bed, sleeping there for hours, in the deep sleep of every morning; the desire too of her husband's nearness, his protection. But it was the matter of a moment, perhaps less:

perhaps she had only expected to feel that dismay but in reality hadn't felt it. The fact that the concierge hadn't opened
up yet was a bore, a great bore, but there was something
about that early morning air, about being alone here at this
hour, that made her blood race not at all unpleasantly. She
didn't even feel regret at having sent Fornero away: with
him she would have been a bit nervous; alone, on the other
hand, she felt a different agitation, a bit like when she was
a girl, but quite different.

She really had to admit it: she felt no remorse at all for
having spent the night out. Her conscience was easy. But
was it easy because by now she had taken the plunge, because she had finally set aside her conjugal duties, or, on
the contrary, because she had resisted, because in spite of
everything she had kept herself faithful? Stefania asked
herself this, and it was this uncertainty, this unsureness as
to how things really stood, along with the coolness of the
morning, that made her shudder briefly. In a word, was
she to consider herself an adulteress at this point or not?
She paced back and forth briefly, her hands thrust into the
pockets of her long coat. Stefania R. had been married for a
couple of years and had never thought of being unfaithful
to her husband. To be sure, in her life as a married woman
there was a kind of expectation, the awareness that something was still lacking for her. It was like a continuation of
her expectations as a girl, as if for her the complete emer-
gence from her minority had not yet occurred, or rather, as
if she had to emerge from a new minority, a minority with

regard to her husband, and finally become his equal before the world. Was it adultery she had been awaiting? And was Fornero adultery?

She saw that a couple of blocks farther on, on the opposite sidewalk, the bar had pulled up its shutters. She needed a hot coffee, at once. She started toward it. Fornero was a boy. You couldn't think of using big words for him. He had driven her around in his little car all night; they had covered the hills, backward and forward, the river road, until they had seen dawn breaking. They had run out of gas at a certain point; they had had to push the car, wake up a sleeping filling-station attendant. It had been a kids' night on the town. Three or four times Fornero's tries had been more dangerous, and once he had even taken her to the door of the *pensione* where he lived and had dug his feet in, stubbornly: "Now you're going to stop making a fuss and come upstairs with me." Stefania hadn't gone upstairs. Was it right to behave like that? And afterward? She didn't want to think about it now, she had spent a sleepless night, she was tired. Or rather, she didn't yet realize she was sleepy because she was in this extraordinary state, but once she got to bed she would go out like a light. She would write on the kitchen slate, telling the maid not to wake her. Maybe her husband would wake her later, when he arrived. Did she still love her husband? Of course she loved him. And then what? She would ask herself nothing. She was a little bit in love with that Fornero. A little bit. And when were they going to open that damn front door?

The chairs were piled up in the bar, sawdust scattered on the floor. There was only the barman, at the counter. Stefania came in; she didn't feel the least ill at ease, being there at that unlikely hour. Who had to know anything? She could have just gotten up, she could be heading for the station, or arriving at that moment. Anyway, she didn't owe explanations to anybody. She realized she enjoyed this feeling.

"Black, double, very hot," she said to the man. She had acquired a confident, self-assured tone, as if there were a familiarity between her and the man in this bar, where actually she never came.

"Yes, Signora, just another minute for the machine to warm up and it'll be ready," the barman said. And he added, "It takes me longer to warm up than the machine, in the morning."

Stefania smiled, huddled into her collar, and said, "Brrr . . ." There was another man in the bar, a customer, off to one side, standing, looking out the window. He turned at Stefania's shiver and she noticed him only then, and as if the presence of two men suddenly recalled her to self-awareness, she looked carefully at her reflection in the glass behind the bar. No, it wasn't obvious that she had spent the night out; she was only a bit pale. She took her compact from her bag and powdered her nose.

The man had come to the counter. He was wearing a dark overcoat with a white silk scarf, and a blue suit underneath. "At this hour of the morning," he said, addressing nobody in particular, "people who are awake fall into two categories: the still and the already."

Stefania smiled briefly, without letting her eyes rest on him. She had already seen him clearly in any case: he had a somewhat pathetic, somewhat ordinary face, one of those men who, accepting themselves and the world, have arrived, without being old, at a condition between wisdom and imbecility.

"And, when you see a pretty woman, after you've wished her a good morning!" And he bowed toward Stefania, taking the cigarette from his mouth.

"Good morning," Stefania said, a bit ironic, but not sharp.

"You ask yourself: Still? Already? Already? Still? There's the mystery."

"What?" Stefania said, with the air of someone who had caught on but doesn't want to play the game. The man examined her, indiscreetly, but Stefania didn't care at all even if he realized she was "still" awake.

"And you?" she asked slyly; she had understood that this gentleman was the self-styled night-owl type and not recognizing him as such at first glance would distress him.

"Me? Still! Always still!" Then he thought about it a moment. "Why? Hadn't you realized that?" And he smiled at her, but he wanted only to mock himself at this point. He stayed there a moment, swallowing, as if his saliva had an unpleasant taste. "Daylight drives me off, makes me return to my lair like a bat," he said absently, as if playing a part.

"Here's your milk. The signora's coffee," the barman said.

The man began blowing on the glass, then sipping slowly.

"Is it good?" Stefania asked.

"Revolting," he said. Then: "It drives out the poisons, they say. But how can it do anything for me at this point? If a poisonous snake bites me, it'll drop dead."

"As long as you've got your health . . ." Stefania said. Perhaps she was joking a bit too much.

And in fact he said, "The only antidote, I know, if you want me to tell you . . ." God knows what he was getting at.

"What do I owe you?" Stefania asked the barman.

"That woman I've been looking for always . . ." the night owl continued.

Stefania went outside, to see if they had opened the door. She took a few steps on the sidewalk. No, the door was still closed. Meanwhile the man had also come out of the bar, as if he meant to follow her. Stefania retraced her steps, reentered the bar. The man, who hadn't expected this, hesitated for a moment, started to go back too, then, overcome by an excess of resignation, he continued, coughing a bit, on his way.

"Do you sell cigarettes?" Stefania asked the barman. She

had run out, and wanted to smoke one the moment she was inside her house. The tobacconists were still closed.

The barman pulled out a pack. Stefania took it and paid him.

She went to the doorway of the bar again. A dog almost bumped into her, tugging violently on a leash and pulling after him a hunter, with gun, cartridge belt, and game bag.

"Down, Frisette! Down!" the hunter cried. And, into the bar, "Coffee!"

"Handsome!" Stefania said, petting the dog. "Is he a setter?"

"*Épagneul breton,*" the hunter said. "Female." He was young, somewhat blunt, but more out of shyness than anything else.

"How old is she?"

"About ten months. Down, Frisette. Behave yourself."

"Well? Where are the partridges?" the barman said.

"Oh, I just go out to exercise the dog," the hunter said.

"You go far?" Stefania asked.

The hunter mentioned the name of a locality not very distant. "It's nothing with the car. So I'm back by ten. The job . . ."

"It's nice up there," Stefania said. She didn't feel like letting the conversation die, even if they weren't talking about anything much.

"There's a deserted valley, clean, all bushes, heath, and in the morning there's no mist, you can see clearly. If the dog flushes something . . ."

"I wish I could go to work at ten. I'd sleep till nine forty-five," the barman said.

"Well, I like to sleep too," the hunter said. "All the same, being up there, while everybody else is still sleeping . . . I don't know, I like it. It's a passion with me."

Stefania felt that behind his apparent self-justification this young man concealed a sharp pride, a contempt for the sleeping city all around, a determination to feel different.

"Don't take offense, but in my opinion you hunters are all crazy," the barman said. "I mean, this business of getting up in the middle of the night."

"No," Stefania said, "I understand them."

"Hm, who knows?" the hunter said. "It's a passion like any other." Now he had taken to looking at Stefania, and that bit of conviction he had instilled earlier in his talk about hunting now seemed gone, and Stefania's presence seemed to make him suspect that his whole attitude was mistaken, that perhaps happiness was something different from what he was seeking.

"Really, I do understand you, a morning like this . . ." Stefania said.

The hunter remained for a moment like someone who wants to talk but doesn't know what to say. "In weather like this, dry, and cool, the dog can walk well," he said. He had finished his coffee, paid for it, the dog was pulling him to go outside, and he remained there still, hesitant. He said awkwardly, "Why don't you come along too, Signora?"

Stefania smiled. "Oh, if we run into each other again, we'll fix something, eh?"

The hunter said, "Mmm," moved around a bit to see if he could find another conversational ploy. "Well, I'll be going. Good morning." They waved and he let the dog pull him outside.

A worker had come in. He ordered a shot of grappa. "To the health of everybody who wakes up early," he said, raising his glass. "Beautiful ladies specially." He was a man not young but jolly-looking.

"Your health," Stefania said politely.

"First thing in the morning, you feel like you own the world," the worker said.

"And not in the evening?" Stefania asked.

"In the evening you're too sleepy," he said, "and you don't think of anything. If you do, it means trouble."

"Me, in the morning I think of every kind of problem, one after the other," the barman said.

"Because before you start working you need a nice ride. You should do like me: I go to the factory on my motorbike, with the cold air on my face."

"The air drives out thoughts," Stefania said.

"There, the lady understands me," the worker said. "And if she understands me, she should drink a little grappa with me."

"No, thanks, really, I don't drink."

"In the morning it's just what you need. Two grappas, chief."

"I really never drink. You drink to my health and you'll make me happy."

"You never drink?"

"Well, occasionally, in the evening."

"You see? There's your mistake."

"Oh, a person makes plenty of mistakes."

"Your health." And the worker drained one glass, then the other. "One and one makes two. You see, I'll explain . . ."

Stefania was alone, there in the midst of those men, those different men, and she was talking with them. She was calm, sure of herself, there was nothing that upset her. This was the new event of that morning.

She came out of the bar to see if they had opened the door. The worker also came out, straddled his motorbike, slipped on his driving gloves. "Aren't you cold?" Stefania asked. The worker slapped himself on the chest; there was a rustle of newspapers. "I'm armored." And then, in dialect, he said, "Goodbye, Signora." Stefania also said goodbye to him in dialect, and he rode off.

Stefania realized that something had happened from which she could not now turn back. This new way of hers of being among men — the night owl, the hunter, the worker — made her different. This had been her adultery, this being alone among them, like this, their equal. She didn't even remember Fornero anymore.

The front door was open. Stefania R. hurried home. The concierge didn't see her.

The Adventure of the Married Couple

The factory worker Arturo Massolari was on the night shift, the one that ends at six. To reach home he had to go a long way, which he covered on his bicycle in fine weather and on the tram during the rainy winter months. He got home between six forty-five and seven; in other words, sometimes before and sometimes after the alarm clock rang to wake Elide, his wife.

Often the two noises—the sound of the clock and his tread as he came in—merged in Elide's mind, reaching her in the depths of her sleep, the compact early morning sleep that she tried to squeeze out for a few more seconds, her face buried in the pillow. Then she pulled herself from the bed with a yank and was already blindly slipping her arms into her robe, her hair over her eyes. She appeared to him like that, in the kitchen, where Arturo was taking the empty receptacles from the bag that he carried with him to work: the lunchbox, the thermos. He set them in the sink. He had already lighted the stove and started the coffee. As soon as he looked at her, Elide instinctively ran one hand through her hair, forced her eyes wide open, as if every time she were ashamed of that first sight her husband had of her on coming home, always such a mess, her face half asleep. When two people have slept together it's different; in the morning both are surfacing from the same sleep, and they're on a par.

Sometimes, on the other hand, it was he who came into the bedroom to wake her, with the little cup of coffee, a moment before the alarm rang; then everything was more natural—the grimace on emerging from sleep took on a kind of lazy sweetness, the arms that were lifted to stretch, naked, ended by clasping his neck. They embraced. Arturo was wearing his rain-proof windbreaker; feeling him close, she could understand what the weather was like: whether it was raining or foggy or if it had snowed, according to how damp and cold he was. But she would ask him anyway, "What's the weather like?" and he would start his usual grumbling, half ironic, reviewing all the troubles he had encountered, beginning at the end: the trip on his bike, the weather he had found on coming out of the factory, different from when he had entered it the previous evening, and the problems on the job, the rumors going around his section, and so on.

At that hour the house was always scantily heated, but Elide had completely undressed and was washing in the little bathroom. Afterward he came in, more calmly, and also undressed and washed, slowly, removing the dust and grease of the shop. And so, as both of them stood at the same basin, half naked, a bit numbed, shoving each other now and then, taking the soap from each other, the toothpaste, and continuing to tell each other the things they had to tell, the moment of intimacy came, and at times, maybe when they were helpfully taking turns scrubbing each other's back, a caress slipped in, and they found themselves embracing.

But all of a sudden Elide would cry, "My God! Look at the time!" and she would run to pull on her garter belt, skirt, all in haste, on her feet, still brushing her hair, and stretching her face to the mirror over the dresser, hairpins held between her lips. Arturo would come in after her; he had a cigarette going, and would look at her, standing, smoking, and every time he seemed a bit embarrassed, having to stay there unable to do anything. Elide was ready, she slipped on her coat in the corridor, they exchanged a kiss, she opened the door and could already be heard running down the stairs.

Arturo remained alone. He followed the sound of Elide's heels down the steps, and when he couldn't hear her anymore he still followed her in his thoughts, that quick little trot through the courtyard, out of the door of the building, the sidewalk, as far as the tram stop. The tram, on the contrary, could be heard clearly: shrieking, stopping, the slam of the step as each passenger boarded. There, she's caught it, he thought, and could see his wife clinging in the midst of the crowd of workers, men and women, on the number 11 that took her to the factory as it did every day.

He stubbed out the butt, closed the shutters at the window, darkening the room, and got into bed.

The bed was as Elide had left it on getting up, but on his side, Arturo's, it was almost intact, as if it had just been made. He lay on his own half, properly, but later he stretched a leg over there, where his wife's warmth had remained, then he also stretched out the other leg, and so little by little he moved entirely over to Elide's side, into that niche of warmth that still retained the form of her body, and he dug his face into her pillow, into her perfume, and he fell asleep.

When Elide came back, in the evening, Arturo had been stirring around the rooms for a while already: he had lighted the stove, put something on to cook. There were certain jobs he did in those hours before supper, like making the bed, sweeping a little, even soaking the dirty laundry. Elide criticized everything, but to tell the truth he didn't then go to greater pains; what he did was only a kind of ritual in order to wait for her, like meeting her halfway while still remaining within the walls of the house, as outside the lights were coming on and she was going past the shops in the midst of the belated bustle of those neighborhoods where many of the women have to do their shopping in the evening.

Finally he heard her footsteps on the stairs, quite different from the morning, heavier now, because Elide was climbing up, tired from the day of work and loaded down with the shopping. Arturo went out on the landing, took the shopping bag from her hands, and they went inside, talking. She sank down on a chair in the kitchen, without taking off her coat, while he removed the things from the bag. Then she would say, "Well, let's pull ourselves together" and would stand up, take off her coat, put on her housecoat. They would begin to prepare the food: supper for both of them, plus the lunch he would take to the factory for his one a.m. break, and the snack to be left ready for when he would wake up the next day.

She would potter a bit, then sit for a bit on the straw chair and tell him what he should do. For him, on the contrary, this was the time when he was rested; he worked with a will, indeed he wanted to do everything, but always a bit absently, his mind already on other things. At those moments, there were occasions when they got on each other's nerves, said nasty things, because she would like him to pay more attention to what he was doing, take it more seriously, or else to be more attached to her, to be closer, comfort her more. But after the first enthusiasm when she came home, his mind was already out of the house, obsessed with the idea that he should hurry because he would soon have to be going.

When the table was set, when everything that had been prepared was placed within reach so they wouldn't have to get up afterward, then came the moment of yearning that overwhelmed them both, the thought that they had so little time to be together, and they could hardly raise the spoon to their mouth in their longing just to sit there and hold hands.

But even before the coffee had finished rising in the pot, he was already at his bike, to make sure everything was in order. They hugged. Arturo seemed only then to realize how soft and warm his wife was. But he hoisted the bike to his shoulder and carefully went down the stairs.

Elide washed the dishes, went over the house thoroughly, redoing the things her husband had done, shaking her head. Now he was speeding through the dark streets, among the sparse lamps; perhaps he had already passed the gasometer. Elide went to bed, turned off the light. From her own half, lying there, she would slide one foot toward her husband's place, looking for his warmth, but each time she realized it was warmer where she slept, a sign that Arturo had slept there too, and she would feel a great tenderness.

The Adventure of a Poet

The little island had a high, rocky shoreline. On it grew the thick, low scrub, the vegetation that survives by the sea. Gulls flew in the sky. It was a small island near the coast, deserted, uncultivated; in half an hour you could circle it in a rowboat, or in a rubber dinghy like the one the approaching couple had, the man calmly paddling, the woman stretched out, taking the sun. As they came nearer, the man listened intently.

"What do you hear?" she asked.

"Silence," he said. "Islands have a silence you can hear."

In fact every silence consists of the network of minuscule sounds that enfolds it: the silence of the island was distinct from that of the calm sea surrounding it because it was pervaded by a vegetable rustling, the calls of birds, or a sudden whir of wings.

Down below the rock, the water, without a ripple these days, was a sharp, limpid blue, penetrated to its depths by the sun's rays. In the cliff faces the mouths of grottoes opened, and the couple in the rubber boat were going lazily to explore them.

It was a coast in the south, still hardly affected by tourism, and these two were bathers who came from elsewhere. He was one Usnelli, a fairly well-known poet; she, Delia H., a very beautiful woman.

Delia was an admirer of the south, passionate, even fanatical, and, lying in the boat, she talked with constant ecstasy about everything she was seeing, and perhaps also with a hint of hostility toward Usnelli, who was new to those places and it seemed to her did not share her enthusiasm as much as he should have.

"Wait," Usnelli said, "wait."

"Wait for what?" she said. "What could be more beautiful than this?"

He, distrustful (by nature and through his literary education) of emotions and words already the property of others, accustomed more to discovering hidden and spurious beauties than those that were evident and indisputable, was still nervous and tense. Happiness for Usnelli was a suspended condition, to be lived holding your breath. Ever since he began loving Delia, he had seen his cautious, sparing relationship with the world endangered; but he wished to renounce nothing, either of himself or of the happiness that opened before him. Now he was on guard, as if every degree of perfection that nature achieved around him — a decanting of the blue of the water, a languishing of the coast's green into gray, the glint of a fish's fin at the very spot where the sea's expanse was smoothest—were only heralding another, higher degree, and so on to the point where the invisible line of the horizon would part like an oyster, revealing all of a sudden a different planet or a new word.

They entered a grotto. It began spaciously, like an interior lake of pale green, under a broad vault of rock. Farther on, it narrowed to a dark passage. The man with the paddle turned the dinghy around to enjoy the various effects of the light. The light from outside, through the jagged aperture, dazzled with colors made more vivid by the contrast. The water there sparkled, and the shafts of light ricocheted upward, in conflict with the soft shadows that spread from the rear. Reflections and flashes communicated to the rock walls and the vault the instability of the water.

"Here you understand the gods," the woman said.

"Hmm," Usnelli said. He was nervous. His mind, accustomed to translating sensations into words, was now helpless, unable to formulate a single one.

They went farther in. The dinghy passed a shoal, a hump of rock at the level of the water; now the dinghy floated among rare glints that appeared and disappeared at every stroke of the paddle, the rest was dense shadow; the paddle now and then struck a wall. Delia, looking back, saw the blue orb of the open sky constantly change outline.

"A crab! Huge! Over there!" she cried, sitting up.

". . . ab! . . . ere!" the echo sounded.

"The echo!" she said, pleased, and started shouting words under those grim vaults: invocations, lines of verse.

"You too! You shout too! Make a wish!" she said to Usnelli.

"Hoooo . . ." Usnelli shouted. "Heeey . . . Echoooo . . ."

Now and then the boat scraped. The darkness was deeper.

"I'm afraid. God knows what animals . . ."

"We can still get through."

Usnelli realized that he was heading for the darkness like a fish of the depths who flees sunlit water.

"I'm afraid. Let's go back," she insisted.

To him too, basically, any taste for the horrid was alien. He paddled backward. As they returned to where the cavern broadened, the sea became cobalt.

"Are there any octopuses?" Delia asked.

"You'd see them. The water's so clear."

"I'll have a swim, then."

She slipped over the side of the dinghy, let go, swam in that underground lake, and her body at times seemed white (as if that light stripped it of any color of its own) and at times as blue as that screen of water.

Usnelli had stopped rowing; he was still holding his breath. For him, being in love with Delia had always been like this, as in the mirror of this cavern: in a world beyond words. For that matter, in all his poems he had never written a verse of love—not one.

"Come closer," Delia said. As she swam, she had taken off the scrap of clothing covering her bosom; she threw it into the dinghy. "Just a minute." She also undid the piece of cloth tied at her hips and handed it to Usnelli.

Now she was naked. The whiter skin of her bosom and hips was hardly distinct, because her whole person gave off that pale-blue glow, like a medusa. She was swimming on one side, with a lazy movement, her head (the expression firm, almost ironic, a statue's) just out of the water, and at times the curve of a shoulder and the soft line of an extended arm. The other arm, in caressing strokes, covered and revealed the high bosom, taut at its tips. Her legs barely struck the water, supporting the smooth belly, marked by the navel like a faint print on the sand, and the star as of some mollusk. The sun's rays, reflected underwater, grazed her, making a kind of garment for her, or stripping her all over again.

Her swimming turned into a kind of dance movement; suspended in the water, smiling at him, she stretched out her arms in a soft rolling of the shoulders and wrists, or with a thrust of the knee she brought to the surface an arched foot, like a little fish.

Usnelli, in the boat, was all eyes. He understood that what life was now giving him was something not everyone has the privilege of looking at open-eyed, as if at the most dazzling core of the sun. And in the core of this sun was silence. Nothing that was there at this moment could be translated into anything else, perhaps not even into a memory.

Now Delia was swimming on her back, surfacing toward the sun, at the mouth of the cavern, proceeding with a light movement of her arms toward the open; and beneath her the water was changing its shade of blue, becoming paler and paler, more and more luminous.

"Watch out! Put something on! The boats come close out there!"

Delia was already among the rocks, beneath the sky. She slipped underwater, held out her arm. Usnelli handed her those skimpy bits of garment; she fastened them on, still swimming, and climbed back into the dinghy.

The approaching boats were fishermen's. Usnelli recognized them, part of that group of poor men who spent the fishing season on that beach, sleeping against certain rocks. He moved toward them. The man at the oars was the young one, grim with a toothache, a white sailor's cap pulled over his narrowed eyes, rowing in jerks as if every effort helped him feel the pain less; father of five children; a desperate case. The old man was at the poop; his Mexican-style straw hat crowned his whole lanky figure with a fringed halo; his round eyes, once perhaps widened in arrogant pride, now in drunkard's clowning; his mouth open beneath the still-black, drooping mustache. With a knife he was cleaning the mullet they had caught.

"Caught much?" Delia cried.

"What little there is," they answered. "Bad year."

Delia liked to talk with the local inhabitants. Not Usnelli. ("With them," he said, "I don't have an easy conscience." He would shrug, and leave it at that.)

Now the dinghy was alongside the boat, where the faded paint was streaked with cracks, curling in short segments. The oar tied with a length of rope to the peg oarlock creaked at every turn against the worn wood of the side, and a little rusty anchor with four hooks had got tangled, under the narrow plank seat, in one of the wicker-basket traps, bearded with reddish seaweed, dried out God knows how long before; over the pile of nets dyed with tannin and dotted at the edge with round slices of cork, the gasping fish glinted in their pungent dress of scales, dull gray or pale blue; the gills, still throbbing, displayed, below, a red triangle of blood.

Usnelli remained silent, but this anguish of the human world was the contrary of what the beauty of nature had been communicating to him a little earlier. There every word failed, while here there was a turmoil of words that crowded into his mind: words to describe every wart, every hair on the thin, ill-shaven face of the old fisherman, every silver scale of the mullet.

Onshore, another boat had been pulled in, overturned, propped up on sawhorses, and below, from the shadow, emerged the soles of the bare feet of the sleeping men, those who had fished during the night; nearby, a woman, all in black clothing, faceless, was setting a pot over a sea-weed fire, and a long trail of smoke was coming from it. The shore of that cove was of gray stones; those patches of faded, printed colors were the smocks of the playing children, the smaller watched over by older, whining sisters, while the bigger and livelier boys, wearing only shorts made from hand-me-down grownups' trousers, were running up and down between rocks and water. Farther on, a straight stretch of sandy beach began, white and deserted, which at one side disappeared into a sparse canebrake and untilled fields. A young man in his Sunday clothes—all black, even his hat—with a stick over his shoulder and a bundle hanging from it, was walking by the sea the length of that beach, the nails of his shoes marking the friable crust of sand: certainly a peasant or a shepherd from an inland village who had come down to the coast for some market or other and had taken the seaside path for the soothing breeze. The railroad showed its wires, its embankment, its poles and fence, then vanished into the tunnel, to begin again farther on, vanish once more, and once more emerge, like stitches in uneven sewing. Above the white-and-black highway markers, squat olive groves began to climb, and higher still, the mountains were bare, grazing land or shrubs or only stones. A village set in a cleft among those heights extended upward, the houses one on top of the other, separated by cobbled stair-streets, concave in the middle so that the trickle of mule refuse could flow down. And on the doorsteps of all those houses were numerous women, elderly or aged, and on the parapets, seated in a row, numerous men old and young, all in white shirts; in the middle of those streets like stairways, the babies were playing on the ground and an older boy was lying across the path, his cheek against the step, sleeping there because it was a bit cooler and less smelly than inside the house; and everywhere, lighting or circling, were clouds of flies, and on every wall and every festoon of newspaper around the fireplaces was the infinite spatter of fly excrement; and into Usnelli's mind came words and words, thick, woven one into another, with no space between the lines, until little by little they could no longer be distinguished; it was a tangle from which even the tiniest white spaces were vanishing and only the black remained, the most total black, impenetrable, desperate as a scream.

The Adventure of a Skier

There was a line at the ski lift. The group of boys who had come on the bus had joined it, pulling up side by side, skis parallel, and every time it advanced—it was long and, instead of going straight, as in fact it could have, zigzagged randomly, sometimes upward, sometimes down—they stepped up or slid down sideways, depending on where they were, and immediately propped themselves on their poles again, often resting their weight on the neighbor below, or trying to free the poles from under the skis of the neighbor above: stumbling on their skis, which had gotten twisted, leaning over to adjust the bindings and bringing the whole line to a halt, pulling off windbreakers or sweaters or putting them back on as the sun appeared or disappeared, tucking strands of hair under their woolen headbands or the billowing tails of their checked shirts into their belts, digging in their pockets for handkerchiefs and blowing their red, frozen noses, and for all these operations taking off and putting on the big gloves that sometimes fell in the snow and had to be picked up with the tip of a pole: that flurry of small disjointed gestures coursed through the line and became frenzied at its end, where the skier had to unzip every pocket to find where he'd stuck the ticket money or the badge, and hand it to the lift operator, who punched it, and then he had to put it back in the pocket, and readjust the gloves, and join the two poles together, the tip of one stuck in the basket of the other so they could be held with one hand—all this while climbing up the small slope of the little open space where he had to be ready to position the T-bar under his bottom and let it tug him jerkily upward.

The boy in the green goggles was at the midway point of the line, numb with cold, and next to him was a fat boy who kept pushing. And as they stood there the girl in the sky-blue hood passed. She didn't get in line; she kept going, up, on the path. And she moved uphill on her skis as lightly as if she were walking.

"What's that girl doing? She's going to walk up?" the fat boy who was pushing asked.

"She's got climbing skins," said the boy in the green goggles.

"Well, I'd like to see her up where it gets steep," said the fat boy.

"She's not as smart as she thinks, you can bet on that."

The girl moved easily, her high knees—she had very long legs, in close-fitting pants, snug at the ankles—moving rhythmically, in time with the raising and lowering of the shiny poles. In that frozen white air the sun looked like a precise yellow drawing, with all its rays: on the expanses of snow where there was no shadow, only its glint indicated humps and crevices and the trampled course of the trails. Framed by the hood of the sky-blue windbreaker, the blond girl's face was a shade of pink that on her cheeks turned red against the white plush lining of her hood. She laughed at the sun, squinting slightly. She moved lightly on her climbing skins. The boys in the group from the bus, with their frozen ears, chapped lips, sniffling noses, couldn't take their eyes off her and began shoving each other in the line, until she climbed over a ledge and disappeared.

Gradually, as their turn came, the boys in the group, after many initial stumbles and false starts, began to ascend, two by two, pulled along the almost vertical track. The boy in the green goggles ended up on the same lift as the fat boy who kept pushing. And there, halfway up, they saw her again.

"How did that girl get up here?"

At that point the lift skirted a sort of hollow, where a packed-down trail advanced between high dunes of snow and occasional fir trees fringed with embroideries of ice. The sky-blue girl was proceeding effortlessly, with that precise stride of hers and that push forward of her gloved hands, gripping the handles of the poles.

"Oooh!" the boys on the lift shouted, holding their legs stiff as they ascended. "She might even beat the rest of us!"

She had that delicate smile on her lips, and the boy in

the green goggles was confused, and didn't dare to keep up the banter, because she lowered her eyelids and he felt as if he'd been erased.

As soon as he reached the top, he started down the slope, behind the fat boy, both of them heavy as sacks of potatoes. But what he was looking for, as he made his way along the trail, was a glimpse of the sky-blue windbreaker, and he hurtled straight down, so that he'd appear bold and at the same time hide his clumsiness on the turns. "Look out! Look out!" he shouted, in vain, because the fat boy too and all the boys in the group were descending at breakneck speed, shouting "Look out! Look out!" and one by one they fell, backward or forward, and he alone was cutting through the air, bent double over his skis, until he saw her. The girl was still going up, off the trail, in the fresh snow. The boy in the green goggles grazed her, passing by like an arrow, rammed the fresh snow, and disappeared into it, face forward.

But at the bottom of the slope, breathless, dusted in snow from head to foot, c'mon, there he was again with all the others in line for the lift, and then up, up again to the top. This time when he met her, she too was going down. How did she go? For them, a champion was someone who sped straight down like a lunatic. "Well, she's no great champion, the blonde," the fat boy said quickly, relieved. The sky-blue girl was coming down in no hurry, making her turns with precision, or, rather, until the last moment they couldn't tell if she would turn or what she would do, and suddenly they'd see her descending in the opposite direction. She was taking her time, one would have said, stopping every so often to study the trail, upright on her long legs; meanwhile, though, the boys from the bus couldn't keep up. Until even the fat boy admitted, "No kidding! She's incredible!"

They wouldn't have been able to explain why, but this was what held them spellbound: all her movements were as simple as possible and perfectly suited to her person; she never exaggerated by a centimeter, never showed a hint of agitation or effort, or determination to do a thing at all costs, but did it naturally; and depending on the state of the trail, she even made a few uncertain moves, like someone walking on tiptoe, which was her way of overcoming the difficulties without revealing whether she was taking them seriously or not—in other words, not with the confident air of one who does things as they should be done but with a trace of reluctance, as if she were trying to imitate an expert but always ended up skiing better. This was the way the sky-blue girl moved on her skis.

Then, one after the other, awkward, heavy, snapping the christies, forcing snowplow turns into a slalom, the boys from the bus plunged down after her, trying to follow her, to pass her, shouting, making fun of each other, but everything they did was a jumbled downhill tumble, with disjointed shoulder movements, arms holding poles out straight, skis that crossed, bindings that broke off boots, and wherever they passed the snow was gouged by crashing bottoms, hips, head-over-heels dives.

After every fall, they raised their heads and immediately looked for her. Passing through the avalanche of boys, the sky-blue girl went along lightly; the straight creases of her close-fitting pants scarcely angled as her knees bent rhythmically, and you couldn't tell if her smile was in sympathy with the exploits and mishaps of her downhill companions or was instead a sign that she didn't even see them.

Meanwhile, the sun, instead of getting stronger as midday approached, grew numb, until it disappeared, as if soaked up by blotting paper. The air was full of light colorless crystals flying slantwise. It was sleet: you couldn't see from here to there. The boys skied blindly, shouting and calling to each other, and they were continually going off the trail and, c'mon, falling. Air and snow were now the same color, opaque white, but peering intently into it, so that it almost became less dense, they could make out the sky-blue shadow, suspended in the midst of it, flying this way and that as if on a violin string.

The sleet had scattered the crowd at the lift. The boy in the green goggles found himself, without realizing it, near the hut at the lift station. There was no sign of his companions. The girl in the sky-blue hood was already there. She was waiting for the T-bar, which was now making its turn. "Quick!" the lift man shouted to him, grabbing the T-bar and holding it so that the girl wouldn't set off alone.

With limping herringbones, he managed to position himself next to the girl just in time to depart with her, but he nearly caused her to fall as he grabbed hold of the bar. She kept them both balanced until he was able to right himself, muttering reproaches, to which she responded with a low laugh like the *glu-glu* of a guinea hen, muffled by the windbreaker drawn up over her mouth. Now the sky-blue hood, like the helmet of a suit of armor, left uncovered only her nose, her eyes, a few curls on her forehead, and her cheekbones. So he saw her, in profile, the boy in the green goggles, and didn't know whether to be happy to find himself on the same T-bar or to be ashamed of being there, all covered with snow, the hair pasted to his temples, the shirt puffing out between sweater and belt, and not daring to tuck it in, so as not to lose his balance by moving his arms; and partly he was glancing sideways at her, partly keeping an eye on the position of his skis, so that they wouldn't go off the trail at moments of traction too slow or too taut, and it was always she who kept them balanced, laughing her guinea-hen *glu-glu*, while he didn't know what to say.

The snow had stopped. Now there was a break in the fog, and in the break the sky appeared, blue at last, and the shining sun and, one by one, the clear, frozen mountains, their peaks feathered here and there by soft shreds of the snow cloud. The mouth and chin of the hooded girl reappeared.

"It's nice again," she said. "I said so."

"Yes," said the boy in the green goggles, "nice. Then the snow will be good."

"A little soft."

"Oh, yes."

"But I like it," she said, "and going down in the fog isn't bad."

"As long as you know the trail," he said.

"No, like this," she said, "guessing."

"I've already done it three times," said the boy.

"Good for you. I've done it once, but I went up without the lift."

"I saw you. You'd put on climbing skins."

"Yes. Now that the sun's out I'll go up to the pass."

"To the pass where?"

"Farther up from where the lift goes. Up to the top."

"What's up there?"

"The glacier seems so close it's as if you could touch it. And the white hares."

"The what?"

"The hares. At this altitude mountain hares put on a white coat. Also the partridges."

"Up there?"

"White partridges. Their feathers are all white. While in summer their feathers are pale brown. Where are you from?"

"Italy."

"I'm Swiss."

They had arrived. At the end they pulled away from

the lift, he clumsily, she holding the bar with her hand through the whole turn. She took off her skis, stood them upright, took the climbing skins out of the bag she wore at her waist, and fastened them to the bottoms of the skis. He watched, rubbing his cold fingers in the gloves. Then, when she began to climb, he followed.

The ascent from the lift to the summit of the pass was difficult.

The boy in the green goggles worked hard, sometimes herringboning, sometimes stepping, sometimes trudging up and sliding back, holding on to his poles like a lame man his crutches. And already she was up where he couldn't see her.

He reached the pass in a sweat, tongue out, half blinded by the glittering radiance all around. There the world of ice began. The blond girl had taken off her sky-blue windbreaker and tied it around her waist. She too had put on a pair of goggles. "There! Did you see? Did you see?"

"What is it?" he said, dazed. Had a white hare leaped out? A partridge?

"It's not there anymore," she said.

Below, over the valley, cawing blackbirds fluttered as usual at two thousand meters. Midday had turned perfectly clear, and from up there you could see the trails, the open slopes thronged with skiers, children sledding, the lift station and the line that had immediately re-formed, the hotel, the parked buses, the road that wove in and out of the black forest of fir trees.

The girl had set off on the descent, going back and
forth in her tranquil zigzags, and had already reached the
point where the trails were more trafficked by skiers, yet
her figure, faintly sketched, like an oscillating parenthesis,
didn't get lost in the confusion of darting interchangeable
profiles: it remained the only one that could be picked out
and followed, removed from chance and disorder. The air
was so clear that the boy in the green goggles could divine
on the snow the dense network of ski tracks, straight and
oblique, of abrasions, mounds, holes, pole marks, and it
seemed to him that there, in the shapeless jumble of life,
was hidden the secret line, the harmony, traceable only to
the sky-blue girl, and this was the miracle of her, that at
every instant in the chaos of innumerable possible movements she chose the only one that was right and clear and
light and necessary, the only gesture that, among an infinity of wasted gestures, counted.

The Adventure of a Motorist

As soon as I leave the city I realize it's dark. I turn on the headlights. I'm driving from A to B, on a three-lane highway whose middle lane is for passing, in both directions. When you drive at night your eyes too in a sense have to disconnect one interior mechanism and turn on another, because you no longer have to struggle to distinguish the specks of distant cars moving toward you or ahead of you amid the dim shadows and colors of the evening land- scape but, rather, have to check a kind of blackboard that demands a different reading, more precise but simplified, since the darkness erases all the details of the picture that might distract you, highlighting only the indispensable elements — white stripes on the asphalt, yellow rays of headlights, and red pinpoints of light. It's a process that happens automatically, and if tonight I'm led to reflect on it, that's because now that the external possibilities of dis- traction are diminished, the internal ones take over, and my thoughts run of their own accord, in a circuit of alternatives and doubts that I can't switch off, so I have to make a particular effort to concentrate on the driving.

I got in the car suddenly, after a fight on the phone with Y. I live in A, Y lives in B. I wasn't expecting to go and see her tonight. But in our daily phone call we said serious words to each other; in the end, driven by resentment, I said to Y that I wanted to break off our relationship; Y answered that it didn't matter to her and that she would immediately telephone Z, my rival. At that point one of us — I don't remember if it was she or I myself — hung up. Not a minute had passed before I realized that the occasion of our quarrel was a small thing in comparison to its consequences. Calling Y back on the phone would be a mistake; the only way to resolve the issue was to hurry to B and have it out with Y face-to-face. So here I am on this highway that I've traveled hundreds of times, at all hours and in all seasons, but which has never felt so long.

To be more precise, it seems to me that I've lost the sense of space and the sense of time: the cones of light projected by the headlights blur the outlines of places into indistinctness; the numbers of the kilometers on the road signs and those which leap into view on the dashboard are data that say nothing to me, that don't respond to the urgency of my questions about what Y is doing at this moment, what she's thinking. Did she really intend to call Z or was it only a threat, flung out in spite? And if she was serious, would she have called him immediately after our phone call, or would she have thought about it for a moment, let the an-

ger cool before deciding? Like me, Z lives in A; he's loved
Y for years in vain; if she called and summoned him, he
certainly jumped in his car and hurried to B. So he too is
racing along this highway; every car that passes me could
be his, and, similarly, every car that I pass. It's hard to con-
firm this: the cars that go in the same direction as me are
two red lights when they are ahead and two yellow eyes
when I see them behind me in the rearview mirror. At the
moment of passing I can distinguish at most the make of
car and how many people are inside, but the great majority
have just a driver, and as for the model, I don't think that
Z's vehicle is especially recognizable.

As if that weren't enough, it starts raining. The visual
field is reduced to the semicircle of glass swept by the
windshield wiper; all the rest is streaked or opaque darkness, and the only information that arrives from outside is
red and yellow flashes distorted by a swirl of drops. All I
can do about Z is try to pass him and not let him pass me,
whatever car he's in, but I have no way of knowing if he's
there or what it is. All the cars going in the direction of
B feel like enemies: every car that, faster than mine, fran-
tically flashes its turn signal in the mirror, asking me to
get over, provokes a pang of jealousy; and every time the
distance that separates me from the taillights of a rival di-
minishes, I accelerate triumphantly into the center lane so
that I'll get to Y before him.

All I need is a few minutes' advantage: seeing how
quickly I hurried to her, Y will immediately forget the rea-

sons for the fight; everything between us will go back to the way it was; Z, upon arriving, will understand that he's been drawn in only because of a sort of game between us, and he'll feel like an intruder. In fact, maybe at this moment Y has already regretted everything she said to me and tried to call me back, or she too, like me, thought that the best thing was to come in person, so she got in her car and is speeding along this highway in the opposite direction.

Now I've stopped paying attention to the cars that are going in the same direction as me and look at the ones that are coming toward me and that for me consist only of the double star of headlights that spreads until it sweeps the darkness from my field of vision and abruptly disappears behind me, trailing a kind of underwater luminescence. Y has a very common make of car—like mine, in fact. Each of these luminous apparitions could be her speeding toward me, and at each one something stirs in my blood, as if through an intimacy fated to remain secret: the message of love addressed exclusively to me is mixed up with all the other messages that run along the wire of the highway, and yet I couldn't wish from her a message different from that.

I realize that as I'm speeding toward Y, what I most desire is not to find Y at the end of my drive: I want Y to be speeding toward me, this is the response I need; that is, I need her to know that I am speeding toward her but at the same time I need to know that she is speeding toward me. The only thought that comforts me is the same that most torments me: the thought that if at this moment Y is speeding toward A, each time she sees the lights of a car heading toward B she'll wonder if it's I who am speeding toward her, and she'll hope that it's me but can never be sure. Now, two cars going in opposite directions found themselves side by side for an instant, a flare illuminated the raindrops, and the sound of the engines fused, as in a sharp gust of wind: maybe it was us, or rather, certainly I was I, if that means something, and the other might be her, that is, what I hope is her, the sign in which I want to recognize her, although it's precisely the sign itself that makes her unrecognizable to me. Driving along the highway is the only means that remains to us, to me and to her, to express what we have to say to each other, but as long as we're driving we can neither give nor receive the communication.

Of course, the reason I got in my car was to reach her as soon as possible, but the farther I go, the more clearly I realize that the arrival is not the true end of my journey. Our meeting, with all the inessential details that the scene of a meeting includes, the minute network of sensations and meanings and memories that would unfold before me —the room with the philodendron, the glass-shaded lamp, the earrings—and the things I would say, some of them surely wrong or misunderstood, and the things she would say, to some degree certainly jarring or anyway not those which I expect, and the whole progression of unpredictable consequences that every gesture and every word entails: all this would raise a cloud of noise around the things we have to say to each other, or rather that we wish to hear each other say, so that the communication that is already difficult on the telephone would be even more obstructed, suffocated, buried as if under an avalanche of sand. That's why, rather than continue to talk, I felt the need to transform the things to say into a cone of light launched at a hundred and forty kilometers an hour, to transform myself into this cone of light moving along the highway, because certainly a signal like that can be received and understood by her without getting lost in the ambiguous disorder of secondary vibrations, just as, in order to receive and understand the things that she has to tell me, I would like them not to be other (rather, I would like her not to be other) than this cone of light that I see advancing along the highway at a speed (I would say, roughly) of a hundred and ten or a hundred and twenty. What counts is to communicate the indispensable, leaving aside the superfluous, to reduce ourselves to essential communication, to a luminous signal that moves in a given direction, abolishing the complexity of our persons and situations and facial expressions, leaving them in the shadow box that the headlights carry along and conceal. The Y whom I love is in reality that bundle of luminous rays in motion, and all the rest of her can remain implicit; and the me whom she can love, the me who has the power to enter that circuit of exaltation which is her emotional life, is the flash of this pass that I, for love of her and not without some risk, am attempting.

And yet with Z (I haven't forgotten Z in the least) I can

establish the correct relationship only if he is merely the flash and dazzle that follows me, or the taillights that I follow: because if I begin to take his person into consideration, which is, let's say, somewhat pathetic but also undeniably disagreeable, yet also — I have to admit — excusable, with that whole boring story of his unhappy love, and his slightly equivocal behavior . . . well, who knows where it would end. Instead, as long as everything continues like this it's fine: Z who tries to overtake me or lets himself be overtaken by me (but I don't know if it's him), Y who accelerates toward me (but I don't know if it's her) remorseful and again in love, I who race toward her jealous and anxious (but I can't let her know, not her or anyone).

Of course, if I were absolutely alone on the highway, if I didn't see other cars driving in both directions, then everything would be much clearer: I would be certain that Z had made no move to supplant me and that Y had made no move to reconcile with me, facts that I could mark on the credit or the debit side in my accounts but that wouldn't leave any room for doubt. And yet if I were permitted to replace my present state of uncertainty with that negative certainty, I would certainly refuse to make the exchange. The ideal condition for excluding doubt would be for only three cars to exist in this entire part of the world: mine, Y's, and Z's. Then no other car could be going in my direction except Z's, and the only car headed in the opposite direction would certainly be Y's. Instead, among the hundreds of cars that darkness and rain reduce to anonymous flashes, only a motionless observer situated in a favorable position could distinguish one car from the other and maybe recognize who is in it. This is the contradiction I find myself in: if I want to receive a message, I would have to give up being a message myself, but the message I'd like to receive from Y — that is, that Y has become a message herself — has value only if I in turn am a message; and yet the message that I have become has meaning only if Y receives it not as an ordinary receiver of messages but as the message that I expect to receive from her.

By now, arriving in B, going to Y's house, finding that she stayed there, with her headache, pondering the reasons for the quarrel, would give me no satisfaction. If then Z too arrived, the result would be an odious and melodramatic scene; and if instead I discovered that Z had refrained from coming or that Y hadn't carried out her threat to call him, I would feel that I had played the role of the fool. On the other hand, if I had stayed in A and Y had come there to apologize, I would find myself in an embarrassing situation: I would see Y with different eyes, as a weak woman who is clinging to me, and something between us would change. The only situation I can accept is this transformation of ourselves into the message of ourselves. And Z? He can't escape our fate either; he too has to be transformed into the message of himself — it would be terrible if I drive to Y, jealous of Z, and Y drives to me, remorseful, in order to escape Z, whereas Z, meanwhile, hasn't even dreamed of leaving the house . . .

Halfway along the highway there's a service station. I stop, hurry to the bar, buy a handful of telephone tokens, dial the code for B, then Y's number. No one answers. Joyfully I drop the tokens: obviously Y couldn't stand her impatience, she got in her car and is driving toward A. Now I've returned to the highway, on the other side, and I too am driving toward A. All the cars I pass could be Y, or all the cars that pass me. All the cars in the opposite lane, advancing in the opposite direction, could be the deluded Z. Or: Y too stopped at a gas station, telephoned my house in A, and, not finding me, realized that I was going to B and reversed direction. Now we are driving in opposite directions, moving farther and farther apart, and the car that I pass or that passes me belongs to Z, who also, halfway along the highway, tried to telephone Y . . .

Everything is still more uncertain, but I feel I have now reached a state of inner tranquility. As long as we can try our telephone numbers and no one answers, all three of us will continue to flow forward and back along these white lines, without places of departure or arrival that, packed with sensations and meanings, loom over the univocality of our journey: finally liberated from the cumbersome materiality of our persons and voices and states of mind, reduced to luminous signals, the only mode of existence fitting for we who wish to be identical to what we say without the distorting buzz that our presence or that of others transmits to what is said.

Of course, the price to pay is high, but we have to accept

PART II

Difficult Lives

The Argentine Ant

When we came to settle here we did not know about the ants. We'd be all right here, it seemed that day; the sky and green looked bright, too bright, perhaps, for the worries we had, my wife and I — how could we have guessed about the ants? Thinking it over, though, Uncle Augusto may have hinted at this once: "You should see the ants over there . . . they're not like the ones here, those ants . . ." but that was just said while talking of something else, a remark of no importance, thrown in perhaps because as we talked we happened to notice some ants. Ants, did I say? No, just one single lost ant, one of those fat ants we have at home (they seem fat to me, now, the ants from my part of the country). Anyway, Uncle Augusto's hint did not seem to detract from the description he gave us of a region where, for some reason which he was unable to explain, life was easier and jobs were not too difficult to find, judging by all those who had set themselves up there — though not, apparently, Uncle Augusto himself.

On our first evening here, noticing the twilight still in the air after supper, realizing how pleasant it was to stroll along those lanes toward the country and sit on the low walls of a bridge, we began to understand why Uncle Augusto liked it. We understood it even more when we found a little inn which he used to frequent, with a garden behind, and squat, elderly characters like himself, though rather more blustering and noisy, who said they had been his friends; they too were men without a trade, I think, workers by the hour, though one said he was a clock-maker, but that may have been bragging; and we found they remembered Uncle Augusto by a nickname, which they all repeated among general guffaws; we noticed too rather stifled laughter from a woman in a knitted white sweater who was fat and no longer young, standing be-hind the bar.

And my wife and I understood what all this must have meant to Uncle Augusto — to have a nickname and spend light evenings joking on the bridges and watch for that knitted sweater to come from the kitchen and go out into the orchard, then spend an hour or two next day unloading sacks for the spaghetti factory; yes, we realized why he al-ways regretted this place when he was back home.

I would have been able to appreciate all this too, if I'd been a youth and had no worries, or been well settled with the family. But as we were, with the baby only just recov-ered from his illness and work still to find, we could do no more than notice the things that had made Uncle Augusto call himself happy; and just noticing them was perhaps rather sad, for it made us feel the difference between our own wretched state and the contented world around. Little things, often of no importance, worried us lest they should suddenly make matters worse (before we knew anything about the ants); the endless instructions given us by the owner, Signora Mauro, while showing us over the rooms increased this feeling we had of entering troubled waters. I remember a long talk she gave us about the gas meter, and how carefully we listened to what she said.

"Yes, Signora Mauro . . . We'll be very careful, Signora Mauro . . . Let's hope not, Signora Mauro . . ."

So that we did not take any notice when (though we remember it clearly now) she gave a quick glance all over the wall as if reading something there, then passed the tip of her finger over it and brushed it afterward as if she had touched something wet, sandy, or dusty. She did not mention the word "ants," though, I'm certain of that; perhaps she considered it natural for ants to be there in the walls and roof; but my wife and I think now that she was trying to hide them from us as long as possible and that all her chatter and instructions were just a smokescreen to make other things seem important and so direct our attention away from the ants.

When Signora Mauro had gone, I carried the mattresses inside. My wife wasn't able to move the cupboard by herself and called me to help. Then she wanted to begin cleaning out the little kitchen at once and got down on her knees to start, but I said, "What's the point, at this hour? We'll see to that tomorrow; let's just arrange things as best we can for tonight." The baby was whimpering and very sleepy, and the first thing to do was get his basket ready and put him to bed. At home we use a long basket for babies, and had brought one with us here; we emptied out the linen with which we'd filled it, and found a good place on the window ledge, where it wasn't damp or too far off the ground should it fall.

Our son soon went to sleep, and my wife and I began looking over our new home (one room divided in two by a partition—four walls and a roof), which was already showing signs of our occupation. "Yes, yes, whitewash it, of course we must whitewash it," I replied to my wife, glancing at the ceiling and at the same time taking her outside by an elbow. She wanted to have another good look at the toilet, which was in a little shack to the left, but I wanted to take a turn over the surrounding plot, for our house stood on a piece of land consisting of two large flower- or rather rough seedbeds, with a path down the middle covered with an iron trellis, now bare and made perhaps for some dried-up climbing plant of gourds or vines. Signora Mauro had said she would let me have this plot to cultivate as a kitchen garden, without asking any rent, as it had been abandoned for so long; she had not mentioned this to us today, however, and we had not said anything, as there were already too many other irons in the fire.

My intention now, by this first evening's walk of ours around the plot, was to acquire a sense of familiarity with the place, even of ownership in a way; for the first time in our lives the idea of continuity seemed possible, of walking evening after evening among beds of seeds as our circumstances gradually improved. Of course I didn't speak of those things to my wife, but I was anxious to see whether she felt them too, and that stroll of ours did in fact seem to have the effect on her which I had hoped. We began talking quietly, between long pauses, and we linked arms—a gesture symbolic of happier times.

Strolling along like this we came to the end of the plot, and over the hedge saw our neighbor, Signor Reginaudo, busy spraying around the outside of his house with a pair of bellows. I had met Signor Reginaudo a few months earlier when I had come to discuss my tenancy with Signora Mauro. I went up to greet him and introduce him to my wife. "Good evening, Signor Reginaudo," I said. "D'you remember me?"

"Of course I do," he said. "Good evening! So you are our new neighbor now?" He was a short man with spectacles, in pajamas and a straw hat.

"Yes, neighbors, and among neighbors . . ." My wife began producing a few vague pleasant phrases, to be polite: it was a long time since I'd heard her talk like that; I didn't particularly like it, but it was better than hearing her complain.

"Claudia," called our neighbor, "come here. Here are the new tenants of the Casa Laureri!" I had never heard our new home called that (Laureri, I learned later, was a previous owner), and the name made it sound strange. Signora Reginaudo, a big woman, now came out, drying her hands on her apron; they were an easygoing couple and very friendly.

"And what are you doing there with those bellows, Signor Reginaudo?" I asked him.

"Oh . . . the ants . . . these ants . . ." he said, and laughed as if not wanting to make it sound important.

"Ants?" repeated my wife in the polite detached tone she used with strangers to give the impression she was paying attention to what they were saying—a tone she never used with me, not even, as far as I can remember, when we first met.

We then took a ceremonious leave of our neighbors. But we did not seem to be enjoying really fully the fact of having neighbors, and such affable and friendly ones with whom we could chat so pleasantly.

On getting home we decided to go to bed at once. "D'you hear?" said my wife. I listened and could still hear the squeak of Signor Reginaudo's bellows. My wife went to the washbasin for a glass of water. "Bring me one too," I called, and took off my shirt.

"Oh!" she screamed. "Come here!" She had seen ants on the faucet and a stream of them coming up the wall.

We put on the light, a single bulb for the two rooms. The stream of ants on the wall was very thick; they were coming from the top of the door, and might originate any-where. Our hands were now covered with them, and we held them out open in front of our eyes, trying to see ex-actly what they were like, these ants, moving our wrists all the time to prevent them from crawling up our arms. They were tiny wisps of ants, in ceaseless movement, as if urged along by the same little itch they gave us. It was only then that a name came to my mind: "Argentine ants," or rather, "the Argentine ant," that's what they called them; and now I came to think of it, I must have heard someone saying that this was the country of "the Argentine ant." It was only now that I connected the name with a sensation, this irritating tickle spreading in every direction, which one couldn't get rid of by clenching one's fists or rubbing one's hands together, as there always seemed to be some stray ant running up one's arm or on one's clothes. When the ants were crushed, they became little black dots that fell like sand, leaving a strong acid smell on one's fingers.

"It's the Argentine ant, you know," I said to my wife. "It comes from South America . . ." Unconsciously my voice had taken on the inflection I used when wanting to teach her something; as soon as I'd realized this I was sorry, for I knew that she could not bear that tone in my voice and always reacted sharply, perhaps sensing that I was never very sure of myself when using it.

But instead she scarcely seemed to have heard me; she was frenziedly trying to destroy or disperse that stream of ants on the wall, but all she managed to do was get numbers of them on herself and scatter others around. Then she put her hand under the faucet and tried to squirt water at them, but the ants went on walking over the wet surface; she couldn't even get them off by washing her hands.

"There, we've got ants in the house!" she repeated. "They were here before too, and we didn't see them!" — as if things would have been very different if we had seen them before.

I said to her, "Oh, come, just a few ants! Let's go to bed now and think about it tomorrow!" And it occurred to me also to add, "There, just a few Argentine ants!" because by calling them by the exact name I wanted to suggest that their presence was already expected, and in a certain sense normal.

But the expansive feeling by which my wife had let herself be carried away during that stroll around the garden had now completely vanished; she had become distrustful of everything again and made her usual face. Nor was going to bed in our new home what I had hoped; we hadn't the pleasure now of feeling we were starting a new life, only a sense of dragging on into a future full of new troubles.

"All for a couple of ants," was what I was thinking —what I thought I was thinking, rather, for everything seemed different now for me too.

Exhaustion finally overcame our agitation, and we dozed off. But in the middle of the night the baby cried. At first we lay there in bed, always hoping it might stop and go to sleep again; this, however, never happened, and we began asking ourselves, "What can be the matter? What's wrong with him?" Since he was better he had stopped crying at night.

"He's covered with ants!" cried my wife, who had gone and taken him in her arms. I got out of bed too. We turned the whole basket upside down and undressed the baby completely. To get enough light for picking the ants off, half blind as we were from sleep, we had to stand under the bulb in the draft coming from the door. My wife was saying, "Now he'll catch cold." It was pitiable looking for ants on that skin, which reddened as soon as it was rubbed. There was a stream of ants going along the windowsill. We searched all the sheets until we could not find another ant and then said, "Where shall we put him to sleep now?" In our bed we were so squeezed up against each other we would have crushed him. I inspected the chest of drawers and, as the ants had not got into that, pulled it away from the wall, opened a drawer, and prepared a bed for the baby there. When we put him in he had already gone to sleep. If we had only thrown ourselves on the bed we would have soon dozed off again, but my wife wanted to look at our provisions.

"Come here, come here! God! Full of 'em! Everything's black! Help!"

What was to be done? I took her by the shoulders. "Come along, we'll think about that tomorrow, we can't even see now, tomorrow we'll arrange everything, we'll put it all in a safe place, now come back to bed!"

"But the food. It'll be ruined!"

"It can go to the devil! What can we do now? Tomorrow we'll destroy the ants' nest. Don't worry."

But we could no longer find peace in bed, with the thought of those insects everywhere, in the food, in all our things; perhaps by now they had crawled up the legs of the chest of drawers and reached the baby . . . We got off to sleep as the cocks were crowing, but before long we had again started moving about and scratching ourselves and feeling we had ants in the bed; perhaps they had climbed up there, or stayed on us after all our handling of them. And so even the early morning hours were no refreshment, and we were very soon up, nagged by the thought of the things we had to do, and of the nuisance too of having to start an immediate battle against the persistent imperceptible enemy which had taken over our home.

The first thing my wife did was see to the baby: examine him for any bites (luckily, there did not seem to be any), dress and feed him—all this while moving around in the ant-infested house. I knew the effort of self-control she was making not to let out a scream every time she saw, for example, ants going around the rims of the cups left in the sink, and the baby's bib, and the fruit. She did scream, though, when she uncovered the milk: "It's black!" On top there was a veil of drowned or swimming ants. "It's all on the surface," I said. "One can skim them off with a spoon." But even so we did not enjoy the milk; it seemed to taste of ants.

I followed the stream of ants on the walls to see where they came from. My wife was combing and dressing herself, with occasional little cries of hastily suppressed anger. "We can't arrange the furniture till we've got rid of the ants," she said.

"Keep calm. I'll see that everything is all right. I'm just going to Signor Reginaudo, who has that powder, and ask him for a little of it. We'll put the powder at the mouth of the ants' nest. I've already seen where it is, and we'll soon be rid of them. But let's wait till a little later, as we may be disturbing the Reginaudos at this hour."

My wife calmed down a little, but I didn't. I had said I'd seen the entrance to the ants' nest to console her, but the more I looked, the more new ways I discovered by which the ants came and went. Our new home, although it looked so smooth and solid on the surface, was in fact porous and honeycombed with cracks and holes.

I consoled myself by standing on the threshold and

gazing at the plants with the sun pouring down on them; even the brushwood covering the ground cheered me, as it made me long to get to work on it: to clean everything up thoroughly, then hoe and sow and transplant. "Come," I said to my son. "You're getting moldy here." I took him in my arms and went out into the "garden." Just for the pleasure of starting the habit of calling it that, I said to my wife, "I'm taking the baby into the garden for a moment," then corrected myself: "Into our garden," as that seemed even more possessive and familiar.

The baby was happy in the sunshine and I told him, "This is a carob tree, this is a persimmon," and lifted him up onto the branches. "Now Papa will teach you to climb." He burst out crying. "What's the matter? Are you frightened?" But I saw the ants; the sticky tree was covered with them. I pulled the baby down at once. "Oh, lots of dear little ants . . ." I said to him, but meanwhile, deep in thought, I was following the line of ants down the trunk, and saw that the silent and almost invisible swarm continued along the ground in every direction between the weeds. How, I was beginning to wonder, shall we ever be able to get the ants out of the house when over this piece of ground, which had seemed so small yesterday but now appeared enormous in relation to the ants, the insects formed an uninterrupted veil, issuing from what must be thousands of underground nests and feeding on the thick sticky soil and the low vegetation? Wherever I looked I'd see nothing at first glance and would be giving a sigh of relief when I'd look closer and discover an ant approaching and find it formed part of a long procession, and was meeting others, often carrying crumbs and tiny bits of material much larger than themselves. In certain places, where they had perhaps collected some plant juice or animal remains, there was a guarding crust of ants stuck together like the black scab of a wound.

I returned to my wife with the baby at my neck, almost at a run, feeling the ants climbing up from my feet. And she said, "Look, you've made the baby cry. What's the matter?"

"Nothing, nothing," I said hurriedly. "He saw a couple of ants on a tree and is still affected by last night, and thinks he's itching."

"Oh, to have this to put up with too!" my wife cried. She was following a line of ants on the wall and trying to kill them by pressing the ends of her fingers on each one.

I could still see the millions of ants surrounding us on that plot of ground, which now seemed immeasurable to me, and found myself shouting at her angrily, "What're you doing? Are you mad? You won't get anywhere that way."

She burst out in a flash of rage too. "But Uncle Augusto! Uncle Augusto never said a word to us! What a couple of fools we were! To pay any attention to that old liar!" In fact, what could Uncle Augusto have told us? The word "ants" for us then could never have even suggested the horror of our present situation. If he had mentioned ants, as perhaps he had—I won't exclude the possibility—we would have imagined ourselves up against a concrete enemy that could be numbered, weighed, crushed. Actually, now I think about the ants in our own parts, I remember them as reasonable little creatures, which could be touched and moved like cats or rabbits. Here we were face-to-face with an enemy like fog or sand, against which force was useless.

Our neighbor, Signor Reginaudo, was in his kitchen pouring liquid through a funnel. I called him from outside, and reached the kitchen window panting hard.

"Ah, our neighbor!" exclaimed Reginaudo. "Come in, come in. Forgive this mess! Claudia, a chair for our neighbor."

I said to him quickly, "I've come . . . please forgive the intrusion, but you know, I saw that you had some of that powder . . . all last night, the ants . . ."

"Oh, oh . . . the ants!" Signora Reginaudo burst out laughing as she came in, and her husband echoed her with a slight delay, it seemed to me, though his guffaws were noisier when they came. "Ha, ha, ha! You have ants too! Ha, ha, ha!"

Without wanting to, I found myself giving a modest smile, as if realizing how ridiculous my situation was, but now I could do nothing about it; this was in point of fact true, as I'd had to come and ask for help.

"Ants! You don't say so, my dear neighbor!" exclaimed Signor Reginaudo, raising his hands.

"You don't say so, dear neighbor, you don't say so!" exclaimed his wife, pressing her hands to her breast but still laughing with her husband.

"But you have a remedy, haven't you?" I asked, and the quiver in my voice could perhaps have been taken for a longing to laugh, and not for the despair I could feel coming over me.

"A remedy, ha, ha, ha!" The Reginaudos laughed louder than ever. "Have we a remedy? We've twenty remedies! A hundred . . . each, ha, ha, ha, each better than the other!"

They led me into a room lined with dozens of cartons and tins with brilliant-colored labels.

"D'you want some Profosfan? Or Mirminec? Or perhaps Tiobroflit? Or Arsopan in powder or liquid form?" And still roaring with laughter, he passed his hand over sprinklers with pistons, brushes, sprays, raising clouds of yellow dust, tiny beads of moisture, and a smell that was a mixture of a pharmacy and an agricultural depot.

"Have you really something that does the job?" I asked.

They stopped laughing. "No, nothing," he replied.

Signor Reginaudo patted me on the shoulder; the signora opened the blinds to let the sun in. Then they took me around the house.

He was wearing pink-striped pajama trousers tied over his fat little stomach and a straw hat on his bald head. She wore a faded dressing gown, which opened every now and then to reveal the shoulder straps of her undershirt; the hair around her big red face was fair, dry, curly, and disheveled. They both talked loudly and expansively; every corner of their house had a story, which they recounted, repeating and interrupting each other with gestures and exclamations as if each episode had been a huge joke. In one place they had put down Arfanax diluted two to a thousand and the ants had vanished for two days but returned on the third day; then he had used a concentrate of ten to a thousand, but the ants had simply avoided that part and circled around by the doorframe; they had isolated another corner with Crisotan powder, but the wind blew it away and they used three kilos a day; on the stairs they had tried Petrocid, which seemed at first to kill them at one blow, but instead it had only sent them to sleep; in another corner they put down Formikill and the ants went on passing over it, then one morning they found a mouse poisoned there; in one spot they had put down liquid Zimofosf, which had acted as a definite blockade, but his wife had put Italmac powder on top, which had acted as an antidote and completely nullified the effect.

Our neighbors used their house and garden as a battlefield, and their passion was to trace lines beyond which the ants could not pass, to discover the new detours they made, and to try out new mixtures and powders, each of which was linked to the memory of some strange episode or comic occurrence, so that one of them only had to pronounce a name—"Arsepit! Mirxidol!"—for them both to burst out laughing with winks and comments. As for the actual killing of the ants, that, if they had ever attempted it, they seemed to have given up, seeing that their efforts were useless; all they tried to do was bar them from certain passages and turn them aside, frighten them or keep them at bay. They always had a new labyrinth traced out with different substances which they prepared from day to day, and for this game ants were a necessary element.

"There's nothing else to be done with the creatures, nothing," they said, "unless one deals with them like the captain . . .

"Ah, yes, we certainly spend a lot of money on these insecticides," they said. "The captain's system is much more economical, you know.

"Of course, we can't say we've defeated the Argentine ant yet," they added, "but d'you really think that captain is on the right road? I doubt it."

"Excuse me," I asked, "but who is the captain?"

"Captain Brauni—don't you know him? Oh, of course, you only arrived yesterday! He's our neighbor there on the right, in that little white villa . . . an inventor." They laughed. "He's invented a system to exterminate the Argentine ant—lots of systems, in fact. And he's still perfecting them. Go and see him."

The Reginaudos stood there, plump and sly among their few square yards of garden, which was daubed all over with streaks and splashes of dark liquids, sprinkled with greenish powder, encumbered with watering cans, fumigators, masonry basins filled with some indigo-colored preparation; in the disordered flowerbeds were a few little rosebushes covered with insecticide from the tips of the leaves to the roots. The Reginaudos raised contented and amused eyes to the limpid sky. Talking to them, I found myself slightly heartened; although the ants were not just something to laugh at, as they seemed to think, neither were they so terribly serious, anything to lose heart about. Oh, the ants! I now thought. Just ants, after all! What harm can a few ants do? Now I'd go back to my wife and tease her a bit: "What on earth d'you think you've seen, with those ants?"

I was mentally preparing a talk in this tone while returning across our piece of ground with my arms full of cartons and tins lent by our neighbors for us to choose the ones that wouldn't harm the baby, who put everything in his mouth. But when I saw my wife outside the house holding the baby, her eyes glassy and her cheeks hollow, and realized the battle she must have fought, I lost all desire to smile and joke.

"At last you've come back," she said, and her quiet tone impressed me more painfully than the angry accent I had expected. "I didn't know what to do here anymore . . . if you saw . . . I really didn't know . . ."

"Look, now we can try this," I said to her, "and this and this and this . . ." and I put down my cans on the step in front of the house and at once began hurriedly explaining how they were to be used, almost afraid of seeing too much hope rising in her eyes, not wanting either to deceive or to undeceive her. Now I had another idea: I wanted to go at once and see that Captain Brauni.

"Do it the way I've explained; I'll be back in a minute."

"You're going away again? Where are you off to?"

"To another neighbor's. He has a system. You'll see soon."

And I ran off toward a metal fence covered with ramblers bounding our land to the right. The sun was behind a cloud. I looked through the fence and saw a little white villa surrounded by a tiny neat garden, with gravel paths encircling flowerbeds, bordered by wrought iron painted green as in public gardens, and in the middle of every flowerbed a little black orange or lemon tree.

Everything was quiet, shady, and still. I was standing there, uncertain whether to go away, when, bending over a well-clipped hedge, I saw a head covered with a shapeless white linen beach hat, pulled forward to a wavy brim above a pair of steel-framed glasses on a spongy nose, and then a sharp flashing smile of false teeth, also made of steel. He was a thin, shriveled man in a pullover, with trousers clamped at the ankles by bicycle clips, and sandals on his feet. He went up to examine the trunk of one of the orange trees, looking silent and circumspect, still with his tight-lipped smile. I looked out from behind the rambler and called, "Good day, Captain." The man raised his head with a start, no longer smiling, and gave me a cold stare.

"Excuse me, are you Captain Brauni?" I asked him. The man nodded. "I'm the new neighbor, you know, who's rented the Casa Laureri. May I trouble you for a moment, since I've heard that your system . . ."

The captain raised a finger and beckoned me to come nearer; I jumped through a gap in the iron fence. The captain was still holding up his finger, while pointing with the other hand to the spot he was observing. I saw that hanging from the tree, perpendicular to the trunk, was a short iron wire. At the end of the wire hung a piece — it seemed to me — of fish remains, and in the middle was a bulge at an acute angle pointing downward. A stream of ants was going to and fro on the trunk and the wire. Underneath the end of the wire was hanging a sort of meat can.

"The ants," explained the captain, "attracted by the smell of fish, run across the piece of wire; as you see, they can go to and fro on it without bumping into each other. But it's that *V* turn that is dangerous; when an ant going up meets one coming down on the turn of the *V*, they both stop, and the smell of the gasoline in this can stuns them; they try to go on their way but bump into each other, fall, and are drowned in the gasoline. Tic, tic." (This "tic, tic" accompanied the fall of two ants.) "Tic, tic, tic . . ." continued the captain with his steely, stiff smile, and every "tic" accompanied the fall of an ant into the can, where, on the surface of an inch of gasoline, lay a black crust of shapeless insect bodies.

"An average of forty ants are killed per minute," said Captain Brauni, "twenty-four hundred per hour. Naturally, the gasoline must be kept clean, otherwise the dead ants cover it and the ones that fall in afterward can save themselves."

I could not take my eyes off that thin but regular trickle of ants dropping off; many of them got over the dangerous point and returned dragging bits of fish back with them by the teeth, but there was always one which stopped at that point, waved its antennae, and then plunged into the depths. Captain Brauni, with a fixed stare behind his lenses, did not miss the slightest movement of the insects; at every fall he gave a tiny uncontrollable start and the tightly stretched corners of his almost lipless mouth twitched. Often he could not resist putting out his hands, either to correct the angle of the wire or to stir the gasoline around the crust of dead ants on the sides, or even to give his instruments a little shake to accelerate the victims' fall. But this last gesture must have seemed to him almost like breaking the rules, for he quickly drew back his hand and looked at me as if to justify his action.

"This is an improved model," he said, leading me to another tree, from which hung a wire with a horsehair tied to the top of the *V*: the ants thought they could save themselves on the horsehair, but the smell of the gasoline and the unexpectedly tenuous support confused them to the point of making the fatal drop. This expedient of the horsehair or bristle was applied to many other traps that the captain showed me: a third piece of wire would suddenly end in a piece of thin horsehair, and the ants would be confused by the change and lose their balance; he had even constructed a trap by which the corner was reached over a bridge made of a half-broken bristle, which opened under the weight of the ant and let it fall in the gasoline.

Applied with mathematical precision to every tree, every piece of tubing, every balustrade and column in this silent and neat garden were wire contraptions with cans of gasoline underneath, and the standard-trained rosebushes and latticework of ramblers seemed only a careful camouflage for this parade of executions.

"Aglaura!" cried the captain, going up to the kitchen door, and to me, "Now I'll show you our catch for the last few days."

Out of the door came a tall, thin, pale woman with frightened, malevolent eyes and a handkerchief knotted down over her forehead.

"Show our neighbor the sack," said Brauni, and I realized she was not a servant but the captain's wife, and greeted her with a nod and a murmur, but she did not reply. She went into the house and came out again dragging a heavy sack along the ground, her muscular arms showing a greater strength than I had attributed to her at first glance. Through the half-closed door I could see a pile of sacks like this one stacked about; the woman had disappeared, still without saying a word.

The captain opened the mouth of the sack; it looked as if it contained garden loam or chemical manure, but he put his arm in and brought out a handful of what seemed to be coffee grounds and let this trickle into his other hand; they were dead ants, a soft red-black sand of dead ants all rolled up in tight little balls, reduced to spots in which one could no longer distinguish the head from the legs. They gave out a pungent acid smell. In the house there were hundredweights, pyramids of sacks like this one, all full.

"It's incredible," I said. "You've exterminated all of these, so . . ."

"No," said the captain calmly. "It's no use killing the worker ants. There are ants' nests everywhere with queen ants that breed millions of others."

"What then?"

I squatted down beside the sack; he was seated on a step below me and to speak to me had to raise his head; the shapeless brim of his white hat covered the whole of his forehead and part of his round spectacles.

"The queens must be starved. If you reduce to a minimum the number of workers taking food to the ants' nests, the queens will be left without enough to eat. And I tell you that one day we'll see the queens come out of their ants' nests in high summer and crawl around searching for food with their own claws. That'll be the end of them all, and then . . ."

He shut the mouth of the sack with an excited gesture and got up. I got up too. "But some people think they can solve it by letting the ants escape." He threw a glance toward the Reginaudos' little house and showed his steel teeth in a contemptuous laugh. "And there are even those who prefer fattening them up. That's one way of dealing with them, isn't it?"

I did not understand his second allusion.

"Who?" I asked. "Why should anyone want to fatten them up?"

"Hasn't the ant man been to you?"

What man did he mean? "I don't know," I said. "I don't think so . . ."

"Don't worry, he'll come to you too. He usually comes on Thursdays, so if he wasn't here this morning, he will be in the afternoon. To give the ants a tonic, ha, ha!"

I smiled to please him but did not follow. Then, as I had come to him with a purpose, I said, "I'm sure yours is the best possible system. D'you think I could try it at my place too?"

"Just tell me which model you prefer," said Brauni, and led me back into the garden. There were numbers of his inventions that I had not yet seen. Swinging wire which when loaded with ants made contact with a battery that electrocuted the lot; anvils and hammers covered with honey which clashed together at the release of a spring and squashed all the ants left in between; wheels with teeth which the ants themselves put in motion, tearing their brethren to pieces until they in their turn were churned up by the pressure of those coming after. I couldn't get used to the idea of so much art and perseverance being needed to carry out such a simple operation as catching ants, but I realized that the important thing was to carry on continually and methodically. Then I felt discouraged, as no one, it seemed to me, could ever equal this neighbor of ours in terrible determination.

"Perhaps one of the simpler models would be best for us," I said, and Brauni snorted, I didn't know whether from approval or from sympathy with the modesty of my ambition.

"I must think a bit about it," he said. "I'll make some sketches."

There was nothing else left for me to do but thank him and take my leave. I jumped back over the hedge; my house, infested as it was, I felt for the first time to be really my home, a place where one returned saying, "Here I am at last."

But at home the baby had eaten the insecticide and my wife was in despair.

"Don't worry, it's not poisonous!" I quickly said.

No, it wasn't poisonous, but it wasn't good to eat either;

our son was screaming with pain. He had to be made to vomit; he vomited in the kitchen, which at once filled with ants again, and my wife had just cleaned it up. We washed the floor, calmed the baby, and put him to sleep in the basket, isolated him all around with insect powder, and covered him with a mosquito net tied tight, so that if he awoke he couldn't get up and eat any more of the stuff.

My wife had done the shopping but had not been able to save the basket from the ants, so everything had to be washed first, even the sardines in oil and the cheese, and each ant sticking to them picked off one by one. I helped her, chopped the wood, tidied the kitchen, and fixed the stove while she cleaned the vegetables. But it was impossible to stand still in one place; every minute either she or I jumped and said, "Ouch! They're biting," and we had to scratch ourselves and rub off the ants or put our arms and legs under the faucet. We did not know where to set the table; inside it would attract more ants, outside we'd be covered with ants in no time. We ate standing up, moving about, and everything tasted of ants, partly from the ones still left in the food and partly because our hands were impregnated with their smell.

After eating I made a tour of the piece of land, smoking a cigarette. From the Reginaudos' came a tinkling of knives and forks; I went over and saw them sitting at table under an umbrella, looking shiny and calm, with checked napkins tied around their necks, eating a custard and drinking glasses of clear wine. I wished them a good appetite and they invited me to join them. But around the table I saw sacks and cans of insecticide, and everything covered with nets sprinkled with yellowish or whitish powder, and that smell of chemicals rose to my nostrils. I thanked them and said I no longer had any appetite, which was true. The Reginaudos' radio was playing softly and they were chattering in high voices, pretending to celebrate.

From the steps which I'd gone up to greet them I could also see a piece of the Braunis' garden; the captain must already have finished eating; he was coming out of his house with his cup of coffee, sipping and glancing around, obviously to see if all his instruments of torture were in action and if the ants' death agonies were continuing with their usual regularity. Suspended between two trees I saw a white hammock and realized that the bony, disagreeable-looking Signora Aglaura must be lying in it, though I could see only a wrist and a hand waving a ribbed fan. The hammock ropes were suspended in a system of strange rings, which must certainly have been some sort of defense against the ants; or perhaps the hammock itself was a trap for the ants, with the captain's wife put there as bait.

I did not want to discuss my visit to the Braunis with the Reginaudos, as I knew they would only have made the ironic comments that seemed usual in the relations between our neighbors. I looked up at Signora Mauro's garden above us on the crest of the hills, and at her villa surmounted by a revolving weathercock. "I wonder if Signora Mauro has ants up there too," I said.

The Reginaudos' gaiety seemed rather more subdued during their meal; they only gave a little quiet laugh or two and said no more than "Ha, ha, she must have them too. Ha, ha, yes, she must have them, lots of them."

My wife called me back to the house, as she wanted to put a mattress on the table and try to get a little sleep. With the mattresses on the floor it was impossible to prevent the ants from crawling up, but with the table we just had to isolate the four legs to keep them off, for a bit at least. She lay down to rest and I went out, with the thought of looking for some people who might know of some job for me, but in fact because I longed to move about and get out of the rut of my thoughts.

But as I went along the road, things all around seemed different from yesterday; in every kitchen garden, in every house I sensed streams of ants climbing the walls, covering the fruit trees, wriggling their antennae toward everything sweet or greasy; and my newly trained eyes now noticed at once mattresses put outside houses to beat because the ants had got into them, a spray of insecticide in an old woman's hand, a saucerful of poison, and then, straining my eyes, the rows of ants marching imperturbably around the doorframes.

Yet this had been Uncle Augusto's ideal countryside. Unloading sacks, an hour for one employer and an hour for another, eating on the benches at the inn, going around in the evening in search of gaiety and a harmonica, sleeping wherever he happened to be, wherever it was cool and soft — what bother could the ants have been to him?

As I walked along I tried to imagine myself as Uncle Augusto and to move along the road as he would have done on an afternoon like this. Of course, being like Uncle Augusto meant first being like him physically: squat and sturdy, that is, with rather monkeylike arms that opened and remained suspended in midair in an extravagant gesture, and short legs that stumbled when he turned to look at a girl, and a voice which when he got excited repeated the local slang all out of tune with his own accent. In him body and soul were all one; how nice it would have been, gloomy and worried as I was, to have been able to move and joke like Uncle Augusto. I could always pretend to be him mentally, though, and say to myself, "What a sleep I'll have in that hayloft! What a bellyful of sausage and wine I'll have at the inn!" I imagined myself pretending to stroke the cats I saw, then shouting "Booo!" to frighten them unexpectedly, and calling out to the servant girls, "Hey, would you like me to come and give you a hand, Signorina?" But the game wasn't much fun; the more I tried to imagine how simple life was for Uncle Augusto here, the more I realized he was a different type, a man who never had my worries: a home to set up, a permanent job to find, an ailing baby, a long-faced wife, and a bed and kitchen full of ants.

I entered the inn where we had already been and asked the girl in the white sweater if the men I'd talked to the day before had come yet. It was shady and cool in there; perhaps it wasn't a place for ants. I sat down to wait for those men, as she suggested, and asked, looking as casual as I could, "So you haven't any ants here, then?"

She was passing a duster over the counter. "Oh, people come and go here, no one's ever paid any attention."

"But what about you who live here all the time?"

The girl shrugged her shoulders. "I'm grown up — why should I be frightened of ants?"

Her air of dismissing the ants, as if they were something to be ashamed of, irritated me more and more, and I insisted, "But don't you put any poison down?"

"The best poison against ants," said a man sitting at another table, who, I noted now, was one of those friends of Uncle Augusto's to whom I'd spoken the evening before, "is this," and he raised his glass and drank it in one gulp.

Others came in and wanted to buy me a drink, as they hadn't been able to put me on to any jobs. We talked about Uncle Augusto and one of them asked, "And what's that old *lingera* up to?" "*Lingera*" is a local word meaning vagabond and scamp, and they all seemed to approve of this definition of him and to hold my uncle in great esteem as a *lingera*. I was a little confused at this reputation being attributed to a man whom I knew to be in fact considerate and modest, in spite of his disorganized way of life. But perhaps this was part of the boasting, exaggerated attitude common to all these people, and it occurred to me in a confused sort of way that this was somehow linked with the ants, that pretending they lived in a world of great movement and adventure was a way of insulating themselves from petty annoyances.

What prevented me from entering their state of mind, I was thinking on my way home, was my wife, who had always been opposed to any fantasy. And I thought what an influence she had had on my life, and how nowadays I could never get drunk on words and ideas anymore.

She met me on the doorstep looking rather alarmed, and said, "Listen, there's a surveyor here."

I, who still had in my ears the sound of superiority of those blusterers at the inn, said almost without listening, "What now, a surveyor . . . Well, I'll just . . ."

She went on: "A surveyor's come to take measurements."

I did not understand and went in. "Ah, now I see. It's the captain!"

It was Captain Brauni who was taking measurements with a yellow tape measure, to set up one of his traps in our house. I introduced him to my wife and thanked him for his kindness.

"I wanted to have a look at the possibilities here," he said. "Everything must be done in a strictly mathematical way." He even measured the basket where the baby was sleeping, and woke it up. The child was frightened at seeing the yellow yardstick leveled over his head and began to cry. My wife tried to put him to sleep again. The baby's crying made the captain nervous, though I tried to distract him. Luckily, he heard his wife calling him and went out.

Signora Aglaura was leaning over the hedge and shouting, "Come here! Come here! There's a visitor! Yes, the ant man!"

Brauni gave me a glance and a meaningful smile from his thin lips and excused himself for having to return to his house so soon. "Now, he'll come to you too," he said, pointing toward the place where this mysterious ant man was to be found. "You'll soon see," and he went away.

I did not want to find myself face-to-face with this ant man without knowing exactly who he was and what he had come to do. I went to the steps that led to Reginaudo's land; our neighbor was just at that moment returning home; he was wearing a white coat and a straw hat and was loaded with sacks and cartons. I said to him, "Tell me, has the ant man been to you yet?"

"I don't know," said Reginaudo. "I've just got back, but I think he must have, because I see molasses everywhere. Claudia!"

His wife leaned out and said, "Yes, yes, he'll come to the Casa Laureri too, but don't expect him to do very much!"

As if I was expecting anything at all! I asked, "But who sent this man?"

"Who sent him?" repeated Reginaudo. "He's the man from the Argentine Ant Control Corporation, their representative who comes and puts molasses all over the gardens and houses. Those little plates over there, do you see them?"

My wife said, "Poisoned molasses . . ." and gave a little laugh as if she expected trouble.

"Does it kill them?" These questions of mine were just a deprecating joke. I knew it all already. Every now and then everything would seem on the point of clearing up, then complications would begin all over again.

Signor Reginaudo shook his head as if I'd said something improper. "Oh no . . . just minute doses of poison, you understand. Ants love sugary molasses. The worker ants take it back to the nest and feed the queens with these little doses of poison, so that sooner or later they're supposed to die from poisoning."

I did not want to ask if sooner or later they really did die. I realized that Signor Reginaudo was informing me of this proceeding in the tone of one who personally holds a different view but feels that he should give an objective and respectful account of official opinion. His wife, however, with the habitual intolerance of women, was quite open about showing her aversion to the molasses system and interrupted her husband's remarks with little malicious laughs and ironic comments; this attitude of hers must have seemed to him out of place or too open, for he tried by his voice and manner to attenuate her defeatism, though not actually contradicting her entirely — perhaps because in private he said the same things, or worse — by making little compensating remarks such as "Come now, you exaggerate, Claudia. It's certainly not very effective, but it may help . . . Then, they do it for nothing. One must wait a year or two before judging."

"A year or two? They've been putting that stuff down for twenty years, and every year the ants multiply."

Signor Reginaudo, rather than contradicting her, preferred to turn the conversation to other services performed by the corporation, and he told me about the boxes of manure which the ant man put in the gardens for the queens to go and lay their eggs in, and how they then came and took them away to burn.

I realized that Signor Reginaudo's tone was the best to use in explaining matters to my wife, who is suspicious and pessimistic by nature, and when I got back home I reported what our neighbor had said, taking care not to praise the system as in any way miraculous or speedy, but also avoiding Signora Claudia's ironic comments. My wife is one of those women who, when she goes by train, for example, thinks that the timetable, the makeup of the train, the requests of the ticket collectors, are all stupid and ill planned, without any possible justification but to be accepted with submissive rancor; so though she considered this business of molasses to be absurd and ridiculous, she made ready for the visit of the ant man (who, I gathered, was called Signor Baudino), intending to make no protest or useless request for help.

The man entered our plot of land without asking permission, and we found ourselves face-to-face while we were still talking about him, which caused rather an unpleasant embarrassment. He was a little man of about fifty, in a worn, faded black suit, with rather a drunkard's face, and hair that was still dark, parted like a child's. Half-closed lids, a rather greasy little smile, reddish skin around his eyes and at the sides of his nose, prepared us for the intonations of a clucking, rather priestlike voice with a strong lilt of dialect. A nervous tic made the wrinkles pulsate at the corner of his mouth and nose.

If I describe Signor Baudino in such detail, it's to try to define the strange impression that he made on us; but was it strange, really? For it seemed to us that we'd have picked him out among thousands as the ant man. He had large, hairy hands; in one he held a sort of coffeepot and in the other a pile of little earthenware plates. He told us about the molasses he had to put down, and his voice betrayed a lazy indifference to the job; even the soft and dragging way he had of pronouncing the word "molasses" showed both disdain for the straits we were in and the complete lack of faith with which he carried out his task. I noticed that my wife was displaying exemplary calm as she showed him the main places where the ants passed. For myself, seeing him move so hesitantly, repeating again and again those few gestures of filling the dishes one after the other, nearly made me lose my patience. Watching him like that, I realized why he had made such a strange impression on me at first sight: he looked like an ant. It's difficult to tell exactly why, but he certainly did; perhaps it was because of the dull black of his clothes and hair, perhaps because of the proportions of that squat body of his, or the trembling at the corners of his mouth corresponding to the continuous quiver of antennae and claws. There was, however, one characteristic of the ant which he did not have, and that was their continuous busy movement. Signor Baudino moved slowly and awkwardly, as he now began daubing the house in an aimless way with a brush dipped in molasses.

As I followed the man's movements with increasing irritation I noticed that my wife was no longer with me; I looked around and saw her in a corner of the garden where the hedge of the Reginaudos' little house joined that of the Braunis'. Leaning over their respective hedges were Signora Claudia and Signora Aglaura, deep in talk, with my wife standing in the middle listening. Signor Baudino was now working on the yard at the back of the house, where he could mess around as much as he liked without having to be watched, so I went up to the women and heard Signora Brauni holding forth to the accompaniment of sharp angular gestures.

"He's come to give the ants a tonic, that man has—a tonic, not poison at all!"

Signora Reginaudo now chimed in, rather mellifluously. "What will the employees of the corporation do when there are no more ants? So what can you expect of them, my dear signora?"

"They just fatten the ants, that's what they do!" concluded Signora Aglaura angrily.

My wife stood listening quietly, as both the neighbors' remarks were addressed to her, but the way in which she was dilating her nostrils and curling her lips told me how furious she was at the deceit she was being forced to put up with. And I too, I must say, found myself very near believing that this was more than women's gossip.

"And what about the boxes of manure for the eggs?" went on Signora Reginaudo. "They take them away, but do you think they'll burn them? Of course not!"

"Claudia, Claudia!" I heard her husband calling. Obviously these indiscreet remarks of his wife's made him feel uneasy. Signora Reginaudo left us with an "Excuse me" in which vibrated a note of disdain for her husband's conventionality, while I thought I heard a kind of sardonic laugh echoing back from over the other hedge, where I caught sight of Captain Brauni walking up the graveled paths and correcting the slant of his traps. One of the earthenware dishes just filled by Signor Baudino lay overturned and smashed at his feet by a kick which might have been accidental or intended.

I don't know what my wife had brewing inside her against the ant man as we were returning toward the house; probably at that moment I should have done nothing to stop her, and might even have supported her. But on glancing around the outside and inside of the house, we realized that Signor Baudino had disappeared, and I remembered hearing our gate creaking and shutting as we came along. He must have gone that moment without saying goodbye, leaving behind him those bowls of sticky, reddish molasses, which spread an unpleasant sweet smell, completely different from that of the ants but somehow linked to it, I could not say how.

Since our son was sleeping, we thought that now was the moment to go up and see Signora Mauro. We had to go and visit her, not only as a duty call but to ask her for the key of a certain storeroom. The real reasons, though, why we were making this call so soon were to remonstrate with her for having rented us a place invaded with ants without warning us in any way, and chiefly to find out how our landlady defended herself against this scourge.

Signora Mauro's villa had a big garden running up the slope under tall palms with yellowed fanlike leaves. A winding path led to the house, which was all glass verandas and dormer windows, with a rusty weathercock turning creakily on its hinge on top of the roof, far less responsive to the wind than the palm leaves, which waved and rustled at every gust.

My wife and I climbed the path and gazed down from the balustrade at the little house where we lived and which was still unfamiliar to us, at our patch of uncultivated land and the Reginaudos' garden looking like a warehouse yard, at the Braunis' garden looking as regular as a cemetery. And standing up there we could forget that all those places were black with ants; now we could see how they might have been without that menace, which none of us could get away from even for an instant. At this distance it looked almost like a paradise, but the more we gazed down, the more we pitied our life there, as if living in that wretched narrow valley we could never get away from our wretched narrow problems.

Signora Mauro was very old, thin, and tall. She received us in half darkness, sitting on a high-backed chair by a little table which opened to hold sewing things and writing materials. She was dressed in black, except for a white mannish collar; her thin face was lightly powdered and her hair drawn severely back. She immediately handed us the key she had promised us the day before but did not ask if we were all right, and this, it seemed to us, was a sign that she was already expecting our complaints.

"But the ants that there are down there, Signora . . ." said my wife in a tone which this time I wished had been less humble and resigned. Although she can be quite hard and often even aggressive, my wife is seized by shyness every now and then, and seeing her at these moments always makes me feel uncomfortable too.

I came to her support and, assuming a tone full of resentment, said, "You've rented us a house, Signora, which if I'd known about all those ants, I must tell you frankly . . ." and stopped there, thinking that I'd been clear enough.

The signora did not even raise her eyes. "The house has been unoccupied for a long time," she said. "It's understandable that there are a few Argentine ants in it—they get wherever . . . wherever things aren't properly cleaned. You"—she turned to me—"kept me waiting for four months before giving me a reply. If you'd taken the place immediately, there wouldn't be any ants by now."

We looked at the room, almost in darkness because of the half-closed blinds and curtains, at the high walls covered with antique tapestry, at the dark, inlaid furniture with the silver vases and teapots gleaming on top, and it seemed to us that this darkness and these heavy hangings served to hide the presence of streams of ants which must certainly be running through the old house from foundations to roof.

"And here," said my wife, in an insinuating, almost ironic tone, "you haven't any ants?"

Signora Mauro drew in her lips. "No," she said curtly; and then, as if she felt she was not being believed, explained, "Here we keep everything clean and shining as a mirror. As soon as any ants enter the garden, we realize it and deal with them at once."

"How?" my wife and I quickly asked in one voice, feeling only hope and curiosity now.

"Oh," said the signora, shrugging her shoulders, "we chase them away, chase them away with brooms." At that moment her expression of studied impassiveness was shaken as if by a spasm of physical pain, and we saw that as she sat, she suddenly moved her weight to another side of the chair and arched in her waist. Had it not contradicted her affirmations, I'd have said that an Argentine ant was passing under her clothes and had just given her a bite; one or perhaps several ants were surely crawling up her body and making her itch, for in spite of her efforts not to move from the chair, it was obvious that she was unable to remain calm and composed as before—she sat there tensely, while her face showed signs of sharper and sharper suffering.

"But that bit of land in front of us is black with 'em," I said hurriedly, "and however clean we keep the house, they come from the garden in their thousands."

"Of course," said the signora, her thin hand closing over the arm of the chair, "of course it's rough uncultivated ground that makes the ants increase so; I intended to put the land in order four months ago. You made me wait, and now the damage is done. It's not only damaged you but everyone else around, because the ants breed . . ."

"Don't they breed up here too?" asked my wife, almost smiling.

"No, not here!" said Signora Mauro, going pale; then, still holding her right arm against the side of the chair, she began making a little rotating movement of the shoulder and rubbing her elbow against her ribs.

It occurred to me that the darkness, the ornaments, the size of the room, and her proud spirit were this woman's defenses against the ants, the reason why she was stronger than we were in the face of them, but that everything we saw around us, beginning with her sitting there, was covered with ants even more pitiless than ours; some kind of African termite, perhaps, which destroyed everything and left only the husks, so that all that remained of this house were tapestries and curtains almost in powder, all on the point of crumbling into bits before her eyes.

"We really came to ask you if you could give us some advice on how to get rid of the pests," said my wife, who was now completely self-possessed.

"Keep the house clean and dig away at the ground. There's no other remedy. Work, just work," and she got to her feet, the sudden decision to say goodbye to us coinciding with an instinctive start, as if she could keep still no longer. Then she composed herself and a shadow of relief passed over her pale face.

We went down through the garden, and my wife said, "Anyway, let's hope the baby hasn't waked up." I too was thinking of the baby. Even before we reached the house we heard him crying. We ran, took him in our arms, and tried to quiet him, but he went on crying shrilly. An ant had got into his ear; we could not understand at first why he cried so desperately without any apparent reason. My wife had said at once, "It must be an ant!" but I could not understand why he went on crying so, as we could find no ants on him or any signs of bites or irritation, and we'd undressed and carefully inspected him. We found some in the basket, however; I'd done my very best to isolate it properly, but we had overlooked the ant man's molasses—one of the clumsy streaks made by Signor Baudino seemed to have been put down on purpose to attract the insects up from the floor to the child's cot.

What with the baby's tears and my wife's cries, we had attracted all the neighboring women to the house: Signora Reginaudo, who was really very kind and sweet, Signora Brauni, who, I must say, did everything she could to help us, and other women I'd never seen before. They all gave ceaseless advice: to pour warm oil in his ear, make him hold his mouth open, blow his nose, and I don't know what else. They screamed and shouted and ended by giving us more trouble than help, although they'd been a certain comfort at first; and the more they fussed around our baby, the more bitter we all felt against the ant man. My wife had blamed and cursed him to the four winds of heaven; and the neighbors all agreed with her that the man deserved all that was coming to him, and that he was doing all he could to help the ants increase so as not to lose his job, and that he was perfectly capable of having done this on purpose, because now he was always on the side of the ants and not on that of human beings. Exaggeration, of course, but in all this excitement, with the baby crying, I agreed too, and if I'd laid hands on Signor Baudino then, I couldn't say what I'd have done to him either.

The warm oil got the ant out; the baby, half stunned with crying, took up a celluloid toy, waved it about, sucked it, and decided to forget us. I too felt the need to be on my own and relax my nerves, but the women were still continuing their diatribe against Baudino, and they told my wife that he could probably be found in an enclosure nearby, where he had his warehouse. My wife exclaimed, "Ah, I'll go and see him, yes, go and see him and give him what he deserves!"

Then they formed a small procession, with my wife at the head and I, naturally, beside her, without giving any opinion on the usefulness of the undertaking, and other women who had incited my wife following and sometimes overtaking her to show her the way. Signora Claudia offered to hold the baby and waved to us from the gate; I realized later that Signora Aglaura was not with us either, although she had declared herself to be one of Baudino's most violent enemies, and that we were accompanied by a little group of women we had not seen before. We went along a sort of alley, flanked by wooden hovels, chicken coops, and vegetable gardens half full of trash. One or two of the women, in spite of all they'd said, stopped when they got to their own homes, stood on the threshold excitedly pointing out our direction, then retired inside, calling to the dirty children playing on the ground, or disappeared to feed the chickens. Only a couple of women followed us as far as Baudino's enclosure; but when the door opened after heavy knocks by my wife, we found that she and I were the only ones to go in, though we felt ourselves followed by the other women's eyes from windows or chicken coops; they seemed to be continuing to incite us, but in very low voices and without showing themselves at all.

The ant man was in the middle of his warehouse, a shack three-quarters destroyed, to whose one surviving wooden wall was tacked a yellow notice with letters a foot and a half long: ARGENTINE ANT CONTROL CORPORATION. Lying all around were piles of those dishes for molasses and tins and bottles of every description, all in a sort of trash heap full of bits of paper with fish remains and other refuse, so that it immediately occurred to one that this was the source of all the ants of the area. Signor Baudino stood in front of us, half smiling in an irritating questioning way, showing the gaps in his teeth.

"You," my wife attacked him, recovering herself after a moment of hesitation. "You should be ashamed of yourself! Why d'you come to our house and dirty everything and let the baby get an ant in his ear with your molasses?"

She had her fists under his face, and Signor Baudino, without ceasing to give that decayed-looking smile of his, made the movements of a wild animal trying to keep its escape open, at the same time shrugging his shoulders and glancing and winking around to me, since there was no one else in sight, as if to say, "She's bats." But his voice only uttered generalities and soft denials like "No . . . No . . . Of course not."

"Why does everyone say that you give the ants a tonic instead of poisoning them?" shouted my wife, so he slipped out the door into the road with my wife following him and screaming abuse. Now the shrugging and winking of Signor Baudino were addressed to the women of the surrounding hovels, and it seemed to me that they were playing some kind of double game, agreeing to be witnesses for him that my wife was insulting him, and yet when my wife looked at them they incited her, with sharp little jerks of the head and movements of the brooms, to attack the ant man. I did not intervene; what could I have done? I certainly did not want to lay hands on the little man, as my wife's fury with him was already roused enough; nor could I try to moderate it, as I did not want to defend Baudino. At last my wife in another burst of anger cried, "You've done my baby harm!" grasped him by his collar, and shook him hard.

I was just about to throw myself on them and separate them, but without touching her, he twisted around with movements that were becoming more and more antlike, until he managed to break away. Then he went off with a clumsy, running step, stopped, pulled himself together, and went on again, still shrugging his shoulders and muttering phrases like "But what behavior . . . But who . . ." and making a gesture as if to say "She's crazy" to the people in the nearby hovels. From those people, the moment my wife threw herself on him, there rose an indistinct but confused mutter, which stopped as soon as the man freed himself, then started up again in phrases not so much of protest and threat as of complaint and almost of supplication or sympathy, shouted out as if they were proud proclamations. "The ants are eating us alive . . . Ants in the bed, ants in the dishes, ants every day, ants every night. We've little enough to eat anyway and have to feed them too . . ."

I had taken my wife by the arm. She was still shaking

her fist every now and again and shouting, "That's not the last of it! We know who is swindling whom! We know whom to thank!" and other threatening phrases which did not echo back, as the windows and doors of the hovels on our path closed again, and the inhabitants returned to their wretched lives with the ants.

So it was a sad return, as could have been foreseen. But what had particularly disappointed me was the way those women had behaved. I swore I'd never go around complaining about ants again in my life. I longed to shut myself up in silent tortured pride like Signora Mauro—but she was rich and we were poor. I had not yet found any solution to how we could go on living in these parts, and it seemed to me that none of the people here, who seemed so superior a short time ago, had found it, or were even on the way to finding it either.

We reached home; the baby was sucking his toy. My wife sat down on a chair. I looked at the ant-infested field and hedges, and beyond them at the cloud of insect powder rising from Signor Reginaudo's garden, and to the right there was the shady silence of the captain's garden, with that continuous dripping of his victims. This was my new home. I took my wife and child and said, "Let's go for a walk, let's go down to the sea."

It was evening. We went along alleys and streets of steps. The sun beat down on a sharp corner of the old town, on gray, porous stone, with lime-washed cornices to the windows and roofs green with moss. The town opened like

a fan, undulating over slopes and hills, and the space between was full of limpid air, copper-colored at this hour.
Our child was turning around in amazement at everything,
and we had to pretend to take part in his marveling; it was
a way of bringing us together, of reminding us of the mild
flavor that life has at moments, and of reconciling us to the
passing days.

We met old women balancing great baskets resting on
head pads, walking rigidly with straight backs and lowered eyes; and in a nuns' garden a group of sewing girls
ran along a railing to see a toad in a basin and said, "How
awful!"; and behind an iron gate, under the wisteria, some
young girls dressed in white were throwing a beach ball
to and fro with a blind man; and a half-naked youth with
a beard and hair down to his shoulders was gathering
prickly pears from an old cactus with a forked stick; and
sad and spectacled children were making soap bubbles at
the window of a rich house; it was the hour when the bell
sounded in the old folks' home and they began climbing
up the steps, one behind the other with their sticks, their
straw hats on their heads, each talking to himself; and then
there were two telephone workers, and one was holding
a ladder and saying to the other on the pole, "Come on
down, time's up, we'll finish the job tomorrow."

And so we reached the port and the sea. There were also
a line of palm trees and some stone benches. My wife and
I sat down and the baby was quiet. My wife said, "There

are no ants here." I replied, "And there's a fresh wind—it's pleasant."

The sea rose and fell against the rocks of the mole, making the fishing boats sway, and dark-skinned men were filling them with red nets and lobster pots for the evening's fishing. The water was calm, with just a slight continual change of color, blue and black, darker farthest away. I thought of the expanses of water like this, of the infinite grains of soft sand down there at the bottom of the sea where the currents leave white shells washed clean by the waves.

Smog

That was a time when I didn't give a damn about anything, the period when I came to settle in this city. "Settle" is the wrong term. I had no desire to be settled in any sense; I wanted everything around me to remain flowing, temporary, because I felt it was the only way to save my inner stability, though what that consisted of, I couldn't have said. So when, after a whole series of recommendations, I was offered the job as managing editor of the magazine *Purification*, I came here to the city and looked for a place to live.

To a young man who has just got off the train, the city —as everyone must know—seems like one big station: no matter how much he walks about, the streets are still squalid, garages, warehouses, cafés with zinc counters, trucks discharging stinking gas in his face as he constantly shifts his suitcase from hand to hand, as he feels his hands swell and become dirty, his underwear stick to him, his nerves grow taut, and everything he sees is nerve-racking, piecemeal. I found a suitable furnished room in one of those very streets; beside the door of the building there were two clusters of signs, bits of shoebox hung there on lengths of string, with the information that a room was for rent written in a rough hand, the tax stamps stuck in one corner. As I stopped to shift the suitcase again, I saw the signs and went into the building. At each stairway, on each landing there were a couple of ladies who rented rooms. I rang the bell on the second floor, stairway C.

The room was commonplace, a bit dark because it opened on a courtyard, through a French window; that was how I was to come in, along a landing with a rusty railing. The room, in other words, was independent of the rest of the apartment, but to reach it I had to unlock a series of gates; the landlady, Signorina Margariti, was deaf and rightly feared thieves. There was no bath; the toilet was off the landing, in a kind of wooden shed; in the room there was a basin with running water, with no hot-water heater. But after all, what could I expect? The price was right, or rather, it was the only possible price, because I couldn't spend more and I couldn't hope to find anything cheaper; besides, it was only temporary and I wanted to make that quite clear to myself.

"Yes, all right, I'll take it," I said to Signorina Margariti, who thought I had asked if the room was cold; she showed me the stove. With that, I had seen everything and I wanted to leave my luggage there and go out. But first I went to the basin and put my hands under the faucet; ever since I had arrived I had been anxious to wash them, but I only rinsed them hastily because I didn't feel like opening my suitcase to look for my soap.

"Oh, why didn't you tell me? I'll bring a towel right away!" Signorina Margariti said; she ran into the other room and came back with a freshly ironed towel, which she placed on the footboard of the bed. I dashed a little water on my face, to freshen up—I felt irritatingly unclean —then I rubbed my face with the towel. That act finally made the landlady realize I meant to take the room. "Ah, you're going to take it! Good. You must want to change, to unpack; make yourself right at home, here's the wardrobe, give me your overcoat!"

I didn't let her slip the overcoat off my back; I wanted to go out at once. My only immediate need, as I tried to tell her, was some shelves; I was expecting a case of books, the little library I had managed to keep together in my haphazard life. It cost me some effort to make the deaf woman understand; finally she led me into the other rooms, her part of the house, to a little étagère, where she kept her work baskets and embroidery patterns; she told me she would clear it and put it in my room. I went out.

Purification was the organ of an institute, where I was to report, to learn my duties. A new job, an unfamiliar city —had I been younger or had I expected more of life, these would have pleased and stimulated me; but not now, now I could see only the grayness, the poverty that surrounded me, and I could only plunge into it as if I actually liked it, because it confirmed my belief that life could be nothing else. I purposely chose to walk in the most narrow, anonymous, unimportant streets, though I could easily have gone along those with fashionable shop windows and smart cafés; but I didn't want to miss the careworn expression on the faces of the passersby, the shabby look of the cheap restaurants, the stagnant little stores, and even certain sounds which belong to narrow streets: the streetcars, the braking of pickup trucks, the sizzling of welders in the little workshops in the courtyards: all because that wear, that exterior clashing, kept me from attaching too much importance to the wear, the clash that I carried within myself.

But to reach the institute I was obliged at one point to enter an entirely different neighborhood, elegant, shaded, old-fashioned, its side streets almost free of vehicles and its main avenues so spacious that traffic could flow past without noise or jams. It was autumn; some of the trees were golden. The sidewalk did not flank walls, buildings, but fences with hedges beyond them, flowerbeds, gravel walks, constructions that lay somewhere between the palazzo and the villa, ornate in their architecture. Now I felt lost in a different way, because I could no longer find, as I had done before, things in which I recognized myself, in which I could read the future. (Not that I believe in signs, but when you're nervous, in a new place, everything you see is a sign.)

So I was a bit disoriented when I entered the institute offices, different from the way I had imagined them, because they were the salons of an aristocratic palazzo, with mirrors and consoles and marble fireplaces and hangings and carpets (though the actual furniture was the usual kind for a modern office, and the lighting was the latest sort, with neon tubes). In other words, I was embarrassed then at having taken such an ugly, dark room, especially when I was led into the office of the president, Commendatore Cordà, who promptly greeted me with exaggerated expansiveness, treating me as an equal not only in social and business importance — which in itself was a hard position for me to maintain — but also as his equal in knowledge of and interest in the problems which concerned the institute and *Purification*. To tell the truth, I had believed it was all some kind of trick, something to mention with a wink; I had accepted the job just as a last resort, and now I had to act as if I had never thought of anything else in my whole life.

Commendatore Cordà was a man of about fifty, youthful in appearance, with a black mustache, a member of that generation, in other words, who despite everything still look youthful and wear a black mustache, the kind of man with whom I have absolutely nothing in common. Everything about him, his talk, his appearance — he wore an impeccable gray suit and a dazzlingly white shirt — his gestures — he moved one hand with his cigarette between his fingers — suggested efficiency, ease, optimism, broad-mindedness. He showed me the numbers of *Puri-fication* that had appeared so far, put out by himself (who was its editor in chief) and the institute's press officer, Signor Avandero (he introduced me to him: one of those characters who talk as if their words were typewritten). There were only a few very skimpy issues, and you could see that they weren't the work of professionals. With the little I knew about magazines, I found a way to tell him — making no criticisms, obviously — how I would do it, the typographical changes I would make. I fell in with his tone, practical, confident in results, and I was pleased to see that we understood each other. Pleased, because the more efficient and optimistic I acted, the more I thought of that wretched furnished room, those squalid streets, that sense of rust and slime I felt on my skin, my not caring a damn about anything, and I seemed to be performing a trick, to be transforming, before the very eyes of Commendatore Cordà and Signor Avandero, all their technical-industrial efficiency into a pile of crumbs, and they were unaware of it, and Cordà kept nodding enthusiastically.

"Fine. Yes, absolutely, tomorrow, you and I agree, and meanwhile," Cordà said to me, "just to bring you up to date . . ." And he insisted on giving me the proceedings of their latest convention to read. "Here." He took me over to some shelves where the mimeographed copies of all the speeches were arranged in so many stacks. "You see? Take this one, and this other one. Do you already have this? Here, count them and see if they're all there." And as he spoke, he picked up those papers, and at that moment I noticed how they raised a little cloud of dust, and I saw the prints of his fingers outlined on their surface, which he had barely touched. Now the commendatore, in picking up those papers, tried to give them a little shake, but just a slight one, as if he didn't want to admit they were dusty, and he also blew on them gently. He was careful not to put his fingers on the first page of each speech, but if he just grazed one with the tip of a fingernail, he left a little white streak over what seemed a gray background, since the paper was covered with a very fine veil of dust. Nevertheless, his fingers obviously became soiled, and he tried to clean them by bending the tips to his palm and rubbing them, but he only dirtied his whole hand with dust. Then instinctively he dropped his hands to the sides of his gray flannel trousers, caught himself just in time, raised them again, and so we both stood there, our fingertips in midair, handing speeches back and forth, taking them delicately by the margins as if they were nettle leaves, and meanwhile we went on smiling, nodding smugly, and saying, "Oh yes, a very interesting convention! Oh yes, an excellent endeavor!" but I noticed that the commendatore became more and more nervous and insecure, and he couldn't look into my triumphant eyes, into my triumphant and desperate gaze, desperate because everything confirmed the fact that it was all exactly as I had believed it would be.

. . .

It took me some time to fall asleep. The room, which had seemed so quiet, at night filled with sounds that I learned gradually to decipher. Sometimes I could hear a voice distorted by a loudspeaker, giving brief, incomprehensible commands; if I had dozed off, I would wake up thinking I was in a train, because the timbre and the cadence were those of the station loudspeakers, as during the night they rise to the surface of the traveler's restless sleep. When my ear had become accustomed to them, I managed to grasp the words: "Two ravioli with tomato sauce . . ." the voice said. "Grilled steak . . . Lamb chop . . ." My room was over the kitchen of the Urbano Rattazzi beer hall, which served hot meals even after midnight; from the counter, the waiters transmitted the orders to the cooks, snapping out the words over an intercom. In the wake of those messages, a confused sound of voices came up to me, and at times the harmonizing chorus of a party. But it was a good place to eat in, somewhat expensive, with a clientele that was not vulgar; the nights were rare when some drunk cut up and overturned tables laden with glasses. As I lay in bed, the sounds of others' wakefulness reached me, muffled, without gusto or color, as if through a fog; the voice over the loudspeaker—"Side dish of French fries . . . Where's that ravioli?"—had a nasal, resigned melancholy.

At about half past two the Urbano Rattazzi beer hall pulled down its metal blinds; the waiters, turning up the collars of their topcoats over the Tyrolean jackets of their uniform, came out of the kitchen door and crossed the courtyard, chatting. At about three a metallic clanking invaded the courtyard: the kitchen workers were dragging out the heavy, empty beer drums, tipping them on their rims and rolling them along, banging one against the other; then the men began rinsing them out. They took their time, since they were no doubt paid by the hour, and they worked carelessly, whistling and making a great racket with those zinc drums, for a couple of hours. At about six, the beer truck came to bring the full drums and collect the empties; but already in the main room of the Urbano Rattazzi the sound of the polishers had begun, the machines that cleaned the floors for the day that was about to begin.

In moments of silence, in the heart of the night, next door, in Signorina Margariti's room, an intense talking would suddenly burst forth, mingled with little explosions of laughter, questions and answers, all in the same falsetto female voice; the deaf woman couldn't distinguish the act of thinking from the act of speaking aloud, and at all hours of the day, or even when she woke up late at night, whenever she became involved in a thought, a memory, a regret, she started talking to herself, distributing the dialogue among various speakers. Luckily her soliloquies, in their intensity, were incomprehensible; and yet they filled one with the uneasiness of sharing personal indiscretions.

During the day, when I went into the kitchen to ask her for some hot water to shave with (she couldn't hear

gone into my room to take the shirt, the cat had followed her without her noticing him, and she must have shut him up inside and the animal had jumped up on the dresser to release his anger at being locked in.

I had only three shirts, and I was constantly giving them to her to wash because—perhaps it was the still disordered life I led, with the office to be straightened out—after half a day my shirt was already dirty. I was often forced to go to the office with the cat's prints on my collar.

Sometimes I found his prints also on the pillowcase. He had probably remained shut inside after having followed Signorina Margariti when she came to turn down the bed in the evening.

It was hardly surprising that the cat was so dirty: you only had to put your hand on the railing of the landing to find your palm striped with black. Every time I came home, as I fumbled with the keys at four padlocks or keyholes, then stuck my fingers into the slats of the shutters to open and close the French window, I got my hands so dirty that when I came into the room I had to hold them in the air, to avoid leaving prints, while I went straight to the basin.

Once my hands were washed and dried I immediately felt better, as if I had regained the use of them, and I began touching and shifting those few objects around me. Signorina Margariti, I must say, kept the room fairly clean; as far as dusting went, she dusted every day; but there were times when, if I put my hand in certain places she couldn't reach (she was very short and had short arms too), I drew it out all velvety with dust and I had to go back to the basin and wash immediately.

My books constituted my most serious problem: I had arranged them on the étagère, and they were the only things that gave me the impression this room was mine; the office left me plenty of free time, and I would gladly have spent some hours in my room, reading. But books collect God knows how much dust: I would choose one from the shelf, but then before opening it I had to rub it all over with a rag, even along the tops of the pages, and then I had to give it a good banging: a cloud of dust rose from it. Afterward I washed my hands again and finally flung myself down on the bed to read. But as I leafed through the book, it became hopeless; I could feel that film of dust on my fingertips, becoming thicker, softer all the time, and it spoiled my pleasure in reading. I got up, went back to the basin, rinsed my hands once more, but now I felt that my shirt was also dusty, and my suit. I would have resumed reading, but now my hands were clean and I didn't like to dirty them again. So I decided to go out.

Naturally, all the operations of leaving—the shutters, the railing, the locks—reduced my hands to a worse state than ever, but I had to leave them as they were until I reached the office. At the office, the moment I arrived I ran to the toilet to wash them; the office towel, however, was black with finger marks; as I began to dry my hands, I was already dirtying them again.

I spent my first working days at the institute putting my desk in order. In fact, the desk assigned me was covered with correspondence, documents, files, old newspapers; until then it had obviously been a kind of clearinghouse where anything with no proper place of its own was put. My first impulse was to make a clean sweep, but then I saw there was material that could be useful for the magazine, and other things of some interest which I decided to examine at my leisure. In short, I finally removed nothing from the desk and actually added a lot of things, but not in disorder: on the contrary, I tried to keep everything tidy. Naturally, the papers that had been there before were very dusty and infected the new papers with their dirt. And since I set great store by my neatness, I had given orders to the cleaning woman not to touch anything, so each day a little more dust settled on the papers, especially on the writing materials—the stationery, the envelopes, and so on—which soon looked old and soiled and were irksome to touch.

And in the drawers it was the same story. There dusty papers from decades past were stratified, evidence of the desk's long career through various offices, public and private. No matter what I did at that desk, after a few minutes I felt impelled to go wash my hands.

My colleague Signor Avandero, on the contrary, kept his hands—delicate little hands, but with a certain nervous hardness—always clean, well groomed, the nails polished, uniformly clipped.

"Excuse me for asking, but," I tried saying to him, "don't you find, after you've been here a while, I mean . . . have you noticed how one's hands become dirty?"

"No doubt," Avandero answered, with his usual composed manner, "you have touched some object or paper that wasn't perfectly dusted. If you'll allow me to give you a word of advice, it's always a good idea to keep the top of one's desk completely clear."

In fact, Avandero's desk was clear, clean, shining, with only the file he was dealing with at that moment and the ballpoint pen he held in his hand. "It's a habit," he added, "that the president feels is very important." In fact, Commendatore Cordà had said the same thing to me: the executive who keeps his desk completely clear is a man who never lets matters pile up, who starts every problem on the road to its solution. But Cordà was never in the office, and when he was there he stayed a quarter of an hour, had great graphs and statistical charts brought in to him, gave rapid, vague orders to his subordinates, assigned the various duties to one or the other without bothering about the degree of difficulty of each assignment, rapidly dictated a few letters to the stenographer, signed the outgoing correspondence, and was off.

Not Avandero, though. Avandero stayed in the office

morning and afternoon, he created an impression of working very hard and of giving the stenographers and the typists a lot to do, but he managed never to keep a sheet of paper on his desk more than ten minutes. I simply couldn't stomach this business; I began to keep an eye on him, and I noticed that these papers, though they didn't stay long on his desk, were soon bogged down somewhere else. Once I caught him when, not knowing what to do with some letters he was holding, he had approached my desk (I had stepped out to wash my hands a moment) and was placing them there, hiding them under a file. Afterward he quickly took his handkerchief from his breast pocket, wiped his hands, and went back to his place, where the ballpoint pen lay parallel to an immaculate sheet of paper.

I could have gone in at once and put him in an awkward spot. But I was content with having seen him; it was enough for me to know how things worked.

Since I entered my room from the landing, the rest of Signorina Margariti's apartment remained unexplored territory to me. The signorina lived alone, renting two rooms on the courtyard, mine and another next to it. I knew nothing of the other tenant except his heavy tread late at night and early in the morning (he was a police sergeant, I learned, and was never to be seen during the day). The rest of the apartment, which must have been rather vast, was all the landlady's.

Sometimes I was obliged to go look for her because she was wanted on the telephone; she couldn't hear it ring, so in the end I went and answered. Holding the receiver to her ear, however, she could hear fairly well, and long phone conversations with the other ladies of the parish sodality were her pastime. "Telephone! Signorina Margariti! You're wanted on the telephone!" I would shout, pointlessly, through the apartment, knocking, even more pointlessly, at the doors. As I made these rounds, I got to know a series of living rooms, parlors, pantries, all cluttered with old-fashioned, pretentious furniture, with floor lamps and bric-à-brac, pictures and statues and calendars; the rooms were all in order, polished, gleaming with wax, with snowy-white lace antimacassars on the armchairs, and without even a speck of dust.

At the end of one of these rooms I would finally discover Signorina Margariti, busy waxing the parquet floor or rubbing the furniture, wearing a faded wrapper and a kerchief around her head. I would point in the direction of the telephone, with violent gestures; the deaf woman would run and grasp the receiver, beginning another of her endless chats, in tones not unlike those of her conversations with the cat.

Going back to my room then, seeing the basin shelf or the lampshade with an inch of dust, I would be seized by a great anger: that woman spent the whole day keeping her rooms as shiny as a mirror and she wouldn't even wave a dustcloth over my place. I went back, determined to make a scene, with gestures and grimaces; and I found her in the kitchen, and this kitchen was kept even worse than my room: the oilcloth on the table all worn and stained, dirty cups on top of the cupboard, the floor tiles cracked and blackened. And I was speechless, because I knew the kitchen was the only place in the whole house where that woman really lived, and the rest, the richly adorned rooms constantly swept and waxed, were a kind of work of art on which she lavished her dreams of beauty, and to cultivate the perfection of those rooms she was self-condemned not to live in them, never to enter them as mistress of the house but only as cleaning woman, spending the rest of her day amid grease and dust.

Purification came out every two weeks and carried as a subtitle "of the Air from Smoke, from Chemical Exhaust, and from the Products of Combustion." The magazine was the official organ of the IPUAIC, the Institute for the Purification of the Urban Atmosphere in Industrial Centers. The IPUAIC was affiliated with similar associations in other countries, which sent us their bulletins and their pamphlets. Often international conventions were held, especially to discuss the serious problem of smog.

I had never concerned myself with questions of this sort, but I knew that putting out a magazine in a specialized field is not as hard as it seems. You follow the foreign reviews, you have certain articles translated, and with them and a subscription to a clipping agency you can quickly compile a news column; then there are those two or three technical contributors who never fail to send in a little article; also the institute, no matter how inactive it is, always has some communication or agenda to be printed in bold type; and there is the advertiser who asks you to publish, as an article, the description of his latest patented device. Then when a convention is held, you can devote at least one whole issue to it, from beginning to end, and you will still have papers and reports left over to run in the following issues, whenever you have two or three columns you don't know how to fill.

The editorial as a rule was written by the president. But Commendatore Cordà, always extremely busy (he was chairman of the board of a number of industries, and he could only devote his odd free moments to the institute), began asking me to draft it, incorporating the ideas that he described to me with vigor and clarity. I would then submit my draft to him on his return. He traveled a great deal, our president, because his factories were scattered more or less throughout the country, but of all his activities, the presidency of the IPUAIC, a purely honorary position, was the one, he told me, which gave him the greatest satisfaction, "because," as he explained, "it's a battle for an ideal."

As far as I was concerned, I had no ideals, nor did I want

to have any; I only wanted to write an article he would like, to keep my job, which was no better or worse than another, and to continue my life, no better or worse than any other possible life. I knew Cordà's opinions ("If everyone followed our example, atmospheric purity would already be . . .") and his favorite expressions ("We are not utopians, mind you, we are practical men who . . ."), and I would write the article just as he wished, word for word. What else could I write? What I thought with my own mind? That would produce a fine article, all right! A fine optimistic vision of a functional, productive world! But I had only to turn my mood inside out (which wasn't hard for me, because it was like attacking myself) to summon the impetus necessary for an inspired editorial by our president.

"We are now on the threshold of a solution to the problem of volatile wastes," I wrote, "a solution which will be more quickly achieved" — and I could already see the president's satisfied look — "as the active inspiration given technology by private initiative" — at this point Cordà would raise one hand, to underline my words — "is implemented by intelligent action on the part of the government, always so prompt . . ."

I read this piece aloud to Signor Avandero. Resting his neat little hands on a white sheet of paper in the center of his desk, Avandero looked at me with his usual inexpressive politeness.

"Well? Don't you like it?" I asked him.

"Oh, yes, yes indeed," he hastened to say.

"Listen to the ending: 'To answer the catastrophic predictions from some quarters concerning industrial civilization, we once more affirm that there will not be (nor has there ever been) any contradiction between an economy in free, natural expansion and the hygiene necessary to the human organism'"—from time to time I glanced at Avandero, but he didn't raise his eyes from that white sheet of paper—"'between the smoke of our productive factories and the green of our incomparable natural beauty.' Well, what do you say to that?"

Avandero stared at me for a moment with his dull eyes, his lips pursed. "I'll tell you: your article does express very well what might be called the substance of our institute's final aim, yes, the goal toward which all its efforts are directed."

"Hmm . . ." I grumbled. I must confess that from a punctilious character like my colleague I expected a less tortuous approval.

I presented the article to Commendatore Cordà on his arrival a couple of days later. He read it with care, in my presence. He finished reading, put the pages in order, and seemed about to reread it from the beginning, but he only said, "Good." He thought for a moment, then repeated, "Good." Another pause, and then: "You're young." He warded off an objection I had no intention of making. "No, that's not a criticism, believe me. You are young, you have faith, you look far ahead. However, if I may say so, the situation is serious, yes, more serious than your article would lead the reader to believe. Let's speak frankly: the danger of air pollution in the big cities is huge, we have the analyses, the situation is grave. And precisely because it is grave, we are here to solve it. If we don't solve it, our cities too will be suffocated by smog."

He had risen and was pacing back and forth. "We aren't hiding the difficulties from ourselves. We aren't like the others, especially those who are in a position which should force them to think about this, and who instead don't give a damn. Or worse: try to block our efforts."

He stood squarely in front of me, lowered his voice. "Because you are young, perhaps you believe everybody agrees with us. But they don't. We are only a handful. Attacked from all sides, that's the truth of it. All sides. And yet we won't give up. We speak out. We act. We will solve the problem. This is what I would like to feel more strongly in your article, you understand?"

I understood perfectly. My insistent pretense of holding opinions contrary to my own had carried me away, but now I would be able to give the article just the right emphasis. I was to show it to the president again in three days' time. I rewrote from beginning to end. In the first two thirds of it I drew a grim picture of the cities of Europe devoured by smog, and in the final third I opposed this with the image of an exemplary city, our own, clean, rich in oxygen, where a rational complex of sources of production went hand in hand with . . . et cetera.

To concentrate better, I wrote the article at home, lying on my bed. A shaft of sunlight fell obliquely into the deep courtyard, entered through the panes, and I saw it cut across the air of my room with a myriad of impalpable particles. The counterpane must be impregnated with them; in a little while, I felt, I would be covered by a blackish layer, like the slats of the blind, like the railing of the balcony.

When I read the new draft to Signor Avandero, I had the impression he didn't dislike it. "This contrast between the situation in our cities and that in others," he said, "which you no doubt expressed according to our president's instructions, has really come off quite well."

"No, no, the president didn't mention that to me, it was my own idea," I said, a bit annoyed despite myself because my colleague didn't believe me capable of any initiative.

Cordà's reaction, on the other hand, took me by surprise. He laid the typescript on the desk and shook his head. "We still don't understand each other," he said at once. He began to give me figures on the city's industrial production, the coal, the fuel oil consumed daily, the traffic of vehicles with combustion engines. Then he went on to meteorological data, and in every case he made a summary comparison with the larger cities of northern Europe. "We are a great, foggy industrial city, you realize; therefore smog exists here too, we have no less smog than anywhere else.

It is impossible to declare, as rival cities here in our own country try to do, that we have less smog than foreign cities. You can write this quite clearly in the article, you *must* write it! We are one of the cities where the problem of air pollution is most serious, but at the same time we are the city where most is being done to counteract the situation! At the same time, you understand?"

I understood, and I also understood that he and I would never understand each other. Those blackened facades of the houses, those dulled panes of glass, those windowsills on which you couldn't lean, those human faces almost erased, that haze which now, as autumn advanced, lost its humid, bad-weather stink and became a kind of quality of all objects, as if each person and each thing had less shape every day, less meaning or value — everything that was for me the substance of a general wretchedness, for men like him was surely the sign of wealth, supremacy, power, and also of danger, destruction, and tragedy, a way of feeling filled — suspended there — with a heroic grandeur.

I wrote the article a third time. It was all right at last. Only the ending ("Thus we are face-to-face with a terrible problem, affecting the destiny of society. Will we solve it?") caused him to raise an objection.

"Isn't that a bit too uncertain?" he asked. "Won't it discourage our readers?"

The simplest thing was to remove the question mark and shift the pronoun. "We will solve it." Just like that, without any exclamation point: calm self-confidence.

"But doesn't that make it seem too easy? As if it were just a routine matter?"

We agreed to repeat the words. Once with the question mark and once without. "Will we solve it? We will solve it."

But didn't this seem to postpone the solution to a vague future time? We tried putting it in the present tense. "Are we solving it? We are solving it." But this didn't have the right ring.

Writing an article always proceeds in the same way. You begin by changing a comma, and then you have to change a word, then the word order of a sentence, and then it all collapses. We argued for half an hour. I suggested using different tenses for the question and the answer: "Will we solve it? We are solving it." The president was enthusiastic, and from that day on his faith in my talents never wavered.

One night the telephone woke me, the special, insistent ring of a long-distance call. I turned on the light: it was almost three o'clock. Even before making up my mind to get out of bed, rush into the hall, and grope for the receiver in the dark, even before that, at the first jolt in my sleep, I already knew it was Claudia.

Her voice now gushed from the receiver and it seemed to come from another planet; with my eyes barely open I had a sensation of sparks, dazzle, which were instead the shifting tones of her unceasing voice, that dramatic excitement she always put into everything she said, and which now arrived even here, at the end of the squalid hall in Signorina Margariti's apartment. I realized that I had never doubted Claudia would find me; on the contrary, I had been expecting nothing else for all this time.

She didn't bother to ask what I had been doing in the meanwhile, or how I had ended up there, nor did she explain how she had traced me. She had heaps of things to tell me, extremely detailed things, and yet somehow vague, as her talk always was, things that took place in environments unknown and unknowable to me.

"I need you, quickly, right away. Take the first train."

"Well, I have a job here. The institute . . ."

"Ah, perhaps you've run into Senator ——. Tell him—"

"No, no, I'm just the—"

"Darling, you will leave right away, won't you?"

How could I tell her I was speaking from a place full of dust, where the blinds' slats were covered with a gritty black grime and there were cat's prints on my collar, and this was the only possible world for me, while hers, her world, could exist for me, or seem to exist, only through an optical illusion? She wouldn't even have listened; she was too accustomed to seeing everything from above, and the wretched circumstances that formed the texture of my life naturally escaped her. What was her whole relationship with me if not the outcome of this superior distraction of hers, thanks to which she had never managed to realize I was a modest provincial newspaperman without a future, without ambitions? And she went on treating me as if I were part of high society, the world of aristocrats, magnates, and famous artists, where she had always moved and where, in one of those chance encounters that occur at the beach, I had been introduced to her one summer. She didn't want to admit it, because that would mean admitting she had made a mistake, so she went on attributing talents to me, authority, tastes I was far from possessing; but my real, fundamental identity was a mere detail, and in mere details she did not want to be contradicted.

Now her voice was becoming tender, affectionate: this was the moment that—without even confessing it to myself—I had been waiting for, because it was only in moments of amorous abandon that everything separating us disappeared and we discovered we were just two people, and it didn't matter who we were. We had barely embarked on an exchange of amorous words when behind me a light came on beyond a glass door, and I could hear a grim cough. It was the door of my fellow tenant, the police sergeant, right there, beside the telephone. I promptly lowered my voice. I resumed the interrupted sentence, but now that I knew I was overheard, a natural reserve made me tone down my loving expressions until they were reduced to a murmuring of neutral phrases, almost unintelligible. The light in the next room went off, but from the other end of the wire protests began: "What did you say? Speak louder! Is that all you have to tell me?"

"But I'm not alone."

"What? Who's with you?"

"No, listen, you'll wake up the tenants, it's late."

By now she was in a fury; she didn't want explanations, she wanted a reaction from me, a sign of warmth on my side, something that would burn up the distance between us. But my answers had become cautious, whining, soothing. "No, Claudia, you see, I . . . Don't say that, I swear, I beg you, Claudia, I . . ." In the sergeant's room the light came on again. My love talk became a mumble, my lips pressed to the receiver.

In the courtyard the kitchen workers were rolling the empty beer drums. Signorina Margariti, in the darkness of her room, began chatting, punctuating her words with brief bursts of laughter, as if she had visitors. The fellow tenant uttered a southern curse. I was barefoot, standing on the tiles of the hall, and from the other end of the wire Claudia's passionate voice held out her hands to me, and I was trying to run toward her with my stammering, but each time we were about to cast a bridge between us, it crumbled to bits a moment later, and the impact of reality crushed and denied all our words of love, one by one.

After that first time, the telephone took to ringing at the oddest hours of the day and night, and Claudia's voice, tawny and speckled, leaped into the narrow hall with the heedless spring of a leopard who doesn't know he is throwing himself into a trap, and since he doesn't know, he manages, with a second leap, as he came, to find the path out again, and he hasn't realized anything. And I, torn between suffering and love, joy and cruelty, saw her mingling with this scene of ugliness and desolation, with the loudspeaker of the Urbano Rattazzi which blurted out "Noodle soup," with the dirty bowls in Signorina Margariti's sink, and I felt that by now even Claudia's image must be stained by it all. But no, it ran off, along the wire, intact, aware of nothing, and each time I was left alone with the void of her absence.

Sometimes Claudia was gay, carefree, she laughed, said senseless things to tease me, and in the end I shared in her gaiety, but then the courtyard, the dust, saddened me all the more because I had been tempted to believe life could be different. At other times, instead, Claudia was gripped by a feverish anxiety, and this anxiety then was added to the appearance of the place where I lived, to my work as managing editor of *Purification*, and I couldn't rid myself of it, I lived in the expectation of another, more dramatic call which would waken me in the heart of the night, and when I finally did hear her voice again, surprisingly different, gay or languid, as if she couldn't even remember the torment of the night before, rather than liberated, I felt bewildered, lost.

"What did you say? You're calling from Taormina?"

"Yes, I'm down here with some friends, it's lovely, come right away, catch the next plane!"

Claudia always called from different cities, and each time, whether she was in a state of anxiety or of exuberance, she insisted that I join her at once, to share that mood with her. Each time I started to give her a careful explanation of why it was absolutely impossible for me to travel, but I couldn't continue because Claudia, not listening to me, had already shifted to another subject, usually a harangue against me, or else an unpredictable hymn of praise for some casual expression of mine which she found abominable or adorable.

When the allotted time of the call was up and the day or night operator said, "Three minutes. Do you wish to continue?" Claudia would shout, "When are you arriving, then?" as if it were all agreed. I would stammer some answer, and we ended by postponing final arrangements to another call she would make to me or I was to make to her. I knew that in the meanwhile Claudia would change all her plans and the urgency of my trip would come up again, surely, but in different circumstances, which would then justify further postponements; and yet a kind of remorse lingered in me, because the impossibility of my joining her was not so absolute—I could ask for an advance on my next month's salary and a leave of three or four days with some pretext; these hesitations gnawed at me.

Signorina Margariti heard nothing. If, crossing the hall, she saw me at the telephone, she greeted me with a nod, unaware of the storms raging within me. But not the fellow tenant. From his room he heard everything, and he was obliged to apply his policeman's intuition every time the phone's ring made me jump. Luckily, he was hardly ever in the house, and therefore some of my telephone conversations even managed to be self-confident, nonchalant, and, depending on Claudia's humor, we could create an atmosphere of amorous exchange where every word took on a warmth, an intimacy, an inner meaning. On other occasions, however, she was in the best of moods and I was instead blocked, I answered only in monosyllables, with reticent, evasive phrases: the sergeant was behind his door, a few feet from me; once he opened it a crack, stuck out his dark, mustachioed face, and examined me. He was a little man, I must say, who in other circumstances wouldn't have made the least impression on me, but there, late at night, seeing each other face-to-face for the first time, in that lodging house for poor wretches, I making and receiving amorous long-distance calls of half an hour, he just coming off duty, both of us in our pajamas, we undeniably hated each other.

Often Claudia's conversation included famous names, the people she saw regularly. First of all, I don't know anybody; secondly, I can't bear attracting attention; so if I absolutely had to answer her, I tried not to mention any names, I used paraphrases, and she couldn't understand why and it made her angry. Politics too is something I've always steered clear of, precisely because I don't like making myself conspicuous; and now, besides, I was working for a government-sponsored institute and I had made it a rule to know nothing of either party; and Claudia—God knows what got into her one evening—asked me about certain members of Parliament. I had to give her some kind of answer, then and there, with the sergeant behind the door. "The first one . . . the first name you mentioned, of course . . ."

"Who? Whom do you mean?"

"That one, yes, the big one, no, smaller . . ."

In other words, I loved her. And I was unhappy. But how could she have understood this unhappiness of mine? There are those who condemn themselves to the most gray, mediocre life because they have suffered some grief, some misfortune; but there are also those who do the same thing because their good fortune is greater than they feel they can sustain.

I took my meals in certain fixed-price restaurants, which in this city are all run by Tuscan families, all of them related among themselves, and the waitresses are all girls from a town called Altopascio, and they spend their youth here, but with the thought of Altopascio constantly in their minds, and they don't mingle with the rest of the city; in the evening they go out with boys from Altopascio, who work here in the kitchens of the restaurants or perhaps in factories, but still sticking close to the restaurants as if they were outlying districts of their village; and these girls and these boys marry and some go back to Altopascio, others stay here to work in their relatives' or their fellow townsmen's restaurants, saving up until one day they can open a restaurant of their own.

The people who eat in those restaurants are what you would expect: apart from travelers, who change all the time, the habitual customers are unmarried white-collar workers, even some spinster typists, and a few students or soldiers. After a while these customers get to know one another and they chat from table to table, and at a certain point they eat at the same table, groups of people who at first didn't know one another and then ended up by falling into the habit of always eating together.

They all joked, too, with the Tuscan waitresses, good-natured jokes, obviously; they asked about the girls' boyfriends, they exchanged witticisms, and when there was nothing else to talk about they started on television, saying who was nice and who wasn't among the faces they had seen in the latest programs.

But not me, I never said anything except my order, which for that matter was always the same: spaghetti with butter, boiled beef, and greens, because I was on a diet; and I never called the girls by name even though by then I too had learned their names, but I preferred to go on saying "Signorina" so as not to create an impression of familiarity: I had happened upon that restaurant by chance, I was just a random customer, perhaps I would continue going there every day for God knows how long, but I wanted to feel as if I were passing through, here today and somewhere else tomorrow, otherwise the place would get on my nerves.

Not that they weren't likable. On the contrary: both the staff and the clientele were good, pleasant people, and I enjoyed that cordial atmosphere around me; in fact, if it hadn't existed, I would probably have felt something was lacking, but still I preferred to look on, without taking part in it. I avoided conversing with the other customers, not even greeting them, because as everyone knows, it's easy enough to strike up an acquaintance, but then you're involved; somebody says, "What's on this evening?" and you end up all together watching television or going to the movies, and after that evening you're caught up in a group of people who mean nothing to you, and you have to tell them your business and listen to theirs.

I tried to sit down at a table by myself; I would open the morning or evening paper (I bought it on my way to the office and took a glance at the headlines then, but I waited to read it until I was at the restaurant), and then I read through it from beginning to end. The paper was of great use to me when I couldn't find a seat by myself and had to sit down at a table where there was already someone else; I plunged into my reading and nobody said a word to me. But I always tried to find a free table, and for this reason I was careful to put off as late as possible the hour of my meals, so I turned up there when most of the customers had already left.

There was the disadvantage of the crumbs. Often I had to sit down at a table where another customer had just got up and left the table covered with crumbs, so I avoided looking down until the waitress came to clear away the dirty dishes and glasses, sweeping up all the remains into the cloth and changing it. At times this task was done hastily and between the top cloth and the bottom one there were bread crumbs, and they distressed me.

The best thing, at lunchtime for example, was to discover the hour when the waitresses, thinking that by then no more customers would be coming, clean up everything properly and prepare the tables for the evening; then the whole family — owners, waitresses, cooks, dishwashers — set one big table and finally sit down to eat, themselves. At that moment I would go in, saying, "Oh, perhaps I'm too late. Can you give me something to eat?"

"Why, of course! Sit down wherever you like! Lisa, serve the gentleman."

I sat down at one of those lovely clean tables, a cook went back into the kitchen, I read the paper, I ate calmly, I listened to the others laughing at their table, joking and telling stories of Altopascio. Between one dish and the next I would have to wait perhaps a quarter of an hour, because the waitresses were sitting there eating and chatting, and I would finally make up my mind to say, "An orange, please, Signorina." And they would say, "Yes sir! Anna, you go. Oh, Lisa!" But I liked it that way; I was happy.

I finished eating, finished reading the paper, and went

out with the paper rolled up in my hand. I went home, I climbed up to my room, threw the paper on the bed, washed my hands. Signorina Margariti kept watch to see when I came in and when I left, because the moment I was outside she came into my room to take the newspaper. She didn't dare ask me for it, so she took it away in secret and secretly she put it back on the bed before I came home again. She seemed to be ashamed of this, as if of a somehow frivolous curiosity; in fact she read only one thing, the obituaries.

Once when I came in and found her with the paper in her hand, she was deeply embarrassed and felt obliged to explain: "I borrow it every now and then to see who's dead, you know, forgive me, but, sometimes, you know, I have acquaintances among the dead . . ."

Thanks to this idea of postponing mealtimes, for example by going to the movies on certain evenings, I came out of the film late, my head a bit giddy, to find a dense darkness shrouding the neon signs, an autumnal mist, which drained the city of dimensions. I looked at the time, I told myself there probably was nothing left to eat in those little restaurants, or in any case I was off my usual schedule and I wouldn't be able to get back to it again, so I decided to have a quick bite standing at the counter in the Urbano Rattazzi beer hall, just below where I lived.

Entering the place from the street was not just a passage

from darkness to light: the very consistency of the world changed. Outside, all was shapeless, uncertain, dispersed, and here it was full of solid forms, of volumes with a thickness, a weight, brightly colored surfaces, the red of the ham they were slicing at the counter, the green of the waiters' Tyrolean jackets, the gold of the beer. The place was full of people, and I, who in the streets was accustomed to look on passersby as faceless shadows and to consider myself another faceless shadow among so many, rediscovered here all of a sudden a forest of male and female faces, as brightly colored as fruit, each different from the rest and all unknown. For a moment I hoped still to retain my own ghostly invisibility in their midst, then I realized that I too had become like them, a form so precise that even the mirrors reflected it, with the stubble of beard that had grown since morning, and there was no possible refuge; even the smoke which drifted in a thick cloud to the ceiling from all the lighted cigarettes in the place was a thing apart with its outline and its thickness and didn't modify the substance of the other things.

I made my way to the counter, which was always very crowded, turning my back on the room full of laughter and words from each table, and as soon as a stool became free I sat down on it, trying to attract the waiter's attention so he would set before me the square cardboard coaster, a mug of beer, and the menu. I had trouble making them notice me, here at the Urbano Rattazzi, over which I kept vigil night after night, whose every hour, every jolt I knew, and the noise in which my voice was lost was the same I heard rise every evening up along the rusty iron railings.

"Gnocchi with butter, please," I said, and finally the waiter behind the counter heard me and went to the microphone to declare, "One gnocchi with butter!" and I thought of how that cadenced shout emerged from the loudspeaker in the kitchen, and I felt as if I were simultaneously here at the counter and up there, lying on my bed in my room, and I tried to break up in my mind and muffle the words that constantly crisscrossed among the groups of jolly people eating and drinking and the clink of glasses and cutlery until I could recognize the noise of all my evenings.

Transparently, through the lines and colors of this part of the world, I was beginning to discern the features of its reverse, of which I felt I was the only inhabitant. But perhaps the true reverse was here, brightly lighted and full of open eyes, whereas the side that counted in every way was the shadowy part, and the Urbano Rattazzi beer hall existed only so you could hear that distorted voice in the darkness, "One gnocchi with butter!" and the clank of the metal drums, and so the street's mist might be pierced by the sign's halo, by the square of misted panes against which vague human forms were outlined.

One morning I was wakened by a call from Claudia, but this wasn't long distance; she was in the city, at the station, she had just that moment arrived and was calling me because in getting out of the sleeping car she had lost one of the many cases that comprised her luggage.

I got there barely in time to see her coming out of the station, at the head of a procession of porters. Her smile had none of that agitation she had transmitted to me by her phone call a few minutes before. She was very beautiful and elegant; each time I saw her I was amazed to see I had forgotten what she was like. Now she suddenly pronounced herself enthusiastic about this city and she approved my idea of coming to live here. The sky was leaden; Claudia praised the light, the streets' colors.

She took a suite in a grand hotel. For me to go into the lobby, address the desk clerk, have myself announced by phone, follow the bellboy to the elevator, caused endless uneasiness and dismay. I was deeply moved that Claudia, because of certain business matters of hers but in reality perhaps to see me, had come to spend a few days here: moved and embarrassed, as the abyss between her way of life and mine yawned before me.

And yet I managed to get along fairly well during that busy morning and even to turn up briefly at the office to draw an advance on my next paycheck, foreseeing the exceptional days that lay ahead of me. There was the problem of where to take her to eat: I had little experience of deluxe restaurants or special regional places. As a start, I had the idea of taking her up to one of the surrounding hills.

I hired a taxi. I realized now that in that city, where nobody earning above a certain figure was without a car (even my colleague Avandero had one), I had none, and anyway I wouldn't have known how to drive one. It had never mattered to me in the least, but in Claudia's presence I was ashamed. Claudia, on the other hand, found everything quite natural, because, she said, a car in my hands would surely spell disaster; to my great annoyance she loudly made light of my practical ability and based her admiration of me on other talents, though there was no telling what they were.

So we took a taxi; we hit on a rickety car driven by an old man. I tried to make a joke of how flotsam, wreckage, inevitably comes to life around me, but Claudia wasn't upset by the ugliness of the taxi, as if these things couldn't touch her, and I didn't know whether to be relieved or to feel more than ever abandoned to my fate.

We climbed up to the green backdrop of hills that girdles the city to the east. The day had cleared into a gilded autumnal light, and the colors of the countryside too were turning gold. I embraced Claudia in that taxi; if I let myself give way to the love she felt for me, perhaps that green-and-gold life would also yield to me, the life that, in blurred images (to embrace her, I had removed my eyeglasses), ran by at either side of the road.

Before going to the little restaurant, I told the elderly driver to take us somewhere to look at the view, up higher. We got out of the car. Claudia, with a huge black hat, spun around, making the folds of her skirt swell out. I darted here and there, pointing out to her the whitish crest of the Alps that emerged from the sky (I mentioned the names of the mountains at random, since I couldn't recognize them) and, on this side, the broken and intermittent outline of the hill with villages and roads and rivers, and down below, the city like a network of tiny scales, opaque or glistening, meticulously aligned. A sense of vastness had seized me; I don't know whether it was Claudia's hat and skirt or the view. The air, though this was autumn, was fairly clear and unpolluted, but it was streaked by the most diverse kinds of condensation: thick mists at the base of the mountains, wisps of fog over the rivers, chains of clouds, stirred variously by the wind. We were there leaning over the low wall: I, with my arm around her waist, looking at the countless aspects of the landscape, suddenly gripped by a need to analyze, already dissatisfied with myself because I didn't command sufficiently the nomenclature of the places and the natural phenomena; she ready instead to translate sensations into sudden gusts of love, into effusions, remarks that had nothing to do with any of this. At this point I saw the thing. I grabbed Claudia by the wrist, clasping it hard. "Look! Look down there!"

"What is it?"

"Down there! Look! It's moving!"

"But what is it? What do you see?"

How could I tell her? There were other clouds or mists

which, according to how the humidity condenses in the cold layers of air, are gray or bluish or whitish or even black, and they weren't so different from this one, except for its uncertain color, I couldn't say whether more brownish or bituminous; but the difference was rather in a shadow of this color, which seemed to become more intense first at the edges, then in the center. It was, in short, a shadow of dirt, soiling everything and changing—and in this too it was different from the other clouds—its very consistency, because it was heavy, not clearly dispelled from the earth, from the speckled expanse of the city over which it flowed slowly, gradually erasing it on one side and revealing it on the other, but trailing a wake, like slightly dirty strands, which had no end.

"It's smog!" I shouted at Claudia. "You see that? It's a cloud of smog!"

But she wasn't listening to me, she was attracted by something she had seen flying, a flight of birds; and I stayed there, looking for the first time, from outside, at the cloud that surrounded me every hour, at the cloud I inhabited and that inhabited me, and I knew that in all the variegated world around me, this was the only thing that mattered to me.

That evening I took Claudia to supper at the Urbano Rattazzi beer hall, because except for my cheap restaurants I knew no other place and I was afraid of ending up somewhere too expensive. Entering the Urbano Rattazzi with a girl like Claudia was a new experience: the waiters in their Tyrolean jackets all sprang to attention, they gave us a good table, they rolled over the trolleys with the specialties. I tried to act the nonchalant escort, but at the same time I felt I had been recognized as the tenant of the furnished room over the courtyard, the customer who had quick meals on a stool at the counter. This state of mind made me clumsy, my conversation was dull, and soon Claudia became angry with me. We fell into an intense quarrel; our voices were drowned by the noise of the beer hall, but we had trained on us not only the eyes of the waiters, prompt to obey Claudia's slightest sign, but also those of the other customers, their curiosity aroused by this beautiful, elegant, imposing woman in the company of such a meek-looking man. And I realized that the words of our argument were followed by everyone, also because Claudia, in her unconcern for the people around her, made no effort to disguise her feelings. I felt they were all waiting only for the moment when Claudia, infuriated, would get up and leave me there alone, making me once more the anonymous man I had always been, the man nobody notices any more than one would notice a spot of damp on the wall.

Instead, as always, the quarrel was followed by a tender, amorous understanding; we had reached the end of the meal and Claudia, knowing I lived nearby, said, "I'll come up to your place."

Now I had taken her to the Urbano Rattazzi because it was the only restaurant I knew of that sort, not because it was near my room; in fact, I was on pins and needles at the very thought that she might form some idea of the house where I lived just by glancing at the doorway of the building, and I had relied chiefly on her flightiness.

Instead she wanted to go up there. Telling her about the room, I exaggerated its squalor, to turn the whole event into something grotesque. But as she went up and crossed the landing, she noticed only the good aspects: the ancient and rather noble architecture of the building, the functional way in which those old apartments were laid out. We went in, and she said, "Why, what are you talking about? The room is wonderful. What more do you want?"

I turned at once to the basin, before helping her off with her coat, because as usual I had soiled my hands. But not she; she moved around, her hands fluttering like feathers among the dusty furnishings.

The room was soon invaded by those alien objects: her hat with its little veil, her fox stole, velvet dress, organdy slip, satin shoes, silk stockings. I tried to hang everything up in the wardrobe, put things in the drawers, because I thought that if they stayed out they would soon be covered with traces of soot.

Now Claudia's white body was lying on the bed, on that

bed from which, if I hit it, a cloud of dust would rise, and she reached out with one hand to the shelf next to it and took a book. "Be careful, it's dusty!" But she had already opened it and was leafing through it; then she dropped it to the floor. I was looking at her breasts, still those of a young girl, the pink, pointed tips, and I was seized with torment at the thought that some dust from the book's pages might have fallen on them, and I extended my hand to touch them lightly in a gesture resembling a caress but intended really to remove from them the bit of dust I thought had settled there.

Instead her skin was smooth, cool, undefiled; and as I saw in the lamp's cone of light a little shower of dust specks floating in the air, soon to be deposited also on Claudia, I threw myself upon her in an embrace which was chiefly a way of covering her, of taking all the dust upon myself so that she would be safe from it.

After she had left (a bit disappointed and bored with my company, despite her unshakable determination to cast on others a light that was all her own), I flung myself into my editorial work with redoubled energy, partly because Claudia's visit had made me miss many hours in the office and I was behind with the preparation of the next number, and also because the subject the biweekly *Purification* dealt with no longer seemed so alien to me as it had at the beginning.

The editorial was still unwritten, but this time Commendatore Cordà had left me no instructions. "You handle it. Be careful, however." I began to write one of the usual diatribes, but gradually, as one word led to the next, I found myself describing how I had seen the cloud of smog rubbing over the city, how life went on inside that cloud, and the facades of the old houses, all jutting surfaces and hollows where a black deposit thickened, and the facades of the modern houses, smooth, monochrome, squared off, on which little by little dark, vague shadows grew, as on the office workers' white collars, which never stayed clean more than half a day. And I wrote that, true, there were still people who lived outside the cloud of smog, and perhaps there always would be, people who could pass through the cloud and stop right in its midst and then come out, without the tiniest puff of smoke or bit of soot touching their bodies, disturbing their different pace, their otherworldly beauty, but what mattered was everything that was inside that smog, not what lay outside it: only by immersing oneself in the heart of the cloud, breathing the foggy air of these mornings (winter was already erasing the streets in a formless mist), could one reach the bottom of the truth and perhaps be free of it. My words were all an argument with Claudia; I realized this at once and tore up the article without even having Avandero read it.

Signor Avandero was somebody I hadn't yet fathomed. One Monday morning I came into the office, and what did I find? Avandero with a suntan! Yes, instead of his usual

face the color of boiled fish, his skin was something between red and brown, with a few marks of burning on his
forehead and his cheeks.

"What's happened to you?" I asked (calling him *tu*, as we
had been addressing each other recently).

"I've been skiing. The first snowfall. Perfect, nice and
dry. Why don't you come too, next Sunday?"

From that day on, Avandero made me his confidant,
sharing with me his passion for skiing. Confidant, I say,
because in discussing it with me he was expressing something more than a passion for a technical skill, a geomet-
rical precision of movements, a functional equipment, a
landscape reduced to a pure white page; he, the impeccable and obsequious employee, put into his words a secret
protest against his work, a polemical attitude he revealed
in little chuckles, as if of superiority, and in little malicious
hints: "Ah, yes, that's *purification*, all right! I leave the smog
to the rest of you." Then he promptly corrected himself,
saying, "I'm joking, of course." But I had realized that he,
apparently so loyal, was another one who didn't believe in
the institute or the ideas of Commendatore Cordà.

One Saturday afternoon I ran into him, Avandero, all
decked out for skiing, with a visored cap like a blackbird's
beak, heading for a large bus already assailed by a crowd of
men and women skiers. He greeted me with his smug little
manner: "Are you staying in the city?"

"Yes, I am. What's the use of going away? Tomorrow
night you'll already be back in the soup again."

He frowned beneath his blackbird's visor. "What's the city for, then, except to get out of on Saturday and Sunday?" And he hurried to the bus, because he wanted to suggest a new way of arranging the skis on the top.

For Avandero, as for hundreds and thousands of other people who slaved all week at gray jobs just to be able to run off on Sunday, the city was a lost world, a mill grinding out the means to escape it for those few hours and then return from country excursions, from trout fishing, and then from the sea, and from the mountains in summer, from the snapshots. The story of his life — which, as I saw him regularly, I began to reconstruct year by year — was the story of his means of transportation: first a motorbike, then a scooter, then a proper motorcycle, now his cheap car, and the years of the future were already designated by visions of cars more and more spacious, faster and faster.

The new number of *Purification* should already have gone to press, but Commendatore Cordà hadn't yet seen the proofs. I was expecting him that day at the IPUAIC, but he didn't show up, and it was almost evening when he telephoned for me to come to him at his office at the Wafd, to bring him the proofs there because he couldn't get away. In fact, he would send his car and driver to pick me up.

The Wafd was a factory of which Cordà was managing director. The huge automobile, with me huddled in one corner, my hands and the folder of proofs on my knees, carried me through unfamiliar outskirts, drove along a blind wall, entered, saluted by watchmen, through a broad gateway, and deposited me at the foot of the stairway to the directors' offices.

Commendatore Cordà was at his desk, surrounded by a group of executives, examining certain accounts or production plans spread out on enormous sheets of paper, which spilled over the sides of the desk. "Just one minute, please," he said to me. "I'll be right with you."

I looked beyond his shoulder: the wall behind him was a single pane of glass, a very wide window that dominated the whole expanse of the plant. In the foggy evening only a few shadows emerged; in the foreground there was the outline of a chain hoist which carried up huge buckets of — I believe — iron tailings. You could see the row of metal receptacles rise in a series of jerks, with a slight swaying that seemed to alter a bit the outline of the pile of mineral, and I thought I saw a thick cloud rise from it into the air and settle on the glass of the commendatore's office.

At that moment he gave orders for the lights to be turned on; suddenly against the outside darkness the glass seemed covered by a tiny frosting, surely composed of iron particles, glistening like the stardust of a galaxy. The pattern of shadows outside was broken up; the lines of the smokestacks in the distance became more distinct, each crowned by a red puff, and over these flames, in contrast, the black, inky streak was accentuated as it invaded the whole sky and you could see incandescent specks rise and whirl within it.

Cordà was now examining with me the *Purification* proofs, and immediately entering the different field of enthusiasms, receiving the mental stimulation of his position as president of the IPUAIC, he discussed the articles in our bulletin with me and with the Wafd executives. And though I had so often, in the offices of the institute, given free rein to my natural dependent's antagonism, mentally declaring myself on the side of the smog, the smog's secret agent who had infiltrated the enemy's headquarters, I now realized how senseless my game was, because Cordà himself was the smog's master; it was he who blew it out constantly over the city, and the IPUAIC was a creature of the smog, born of the need to give those working to produce the smog some hope of a life that was not all smog, and yet at the same time to celebrate its power.

Cordà, pleased with the issue, insisted on taking me home in the car. It was a night of thick fog. The driver proceeded slowly, because beyond the faint headlights you couldn't see a thing. The president, carried away by one of his bursts of general optimism, was outlining the plans of the city of the future, with garden districts, factories surrounded by flowerbeds and pools of clear water, installations of rockets that would sweep the sky clear of the smoke from the stacks. And he pointed into the void outside, beyond the windows, as if the things he was imagining were already there; I listened to him, perhaps frightened or perhaps in admiration, I couldn't say, discovering how the clever captain of industry coexisted in him with the visionary, and how each needed the other.

At a certain point I thought I recognized my neighborhood. "Stop here, please. This is where I get out," I said to the driver. I thanked Cordà, said goodnight, and got out of the car. When it had driven off, I realized I had been mistaken. I was in an unfamiliar district, and I could see nothing of my surroundings.

At the restaurant I went on having my meals alone, sheltered behind my newspaper. And I noticed that there was another customer who behaved as I did. Sometimes, when no other places were free, we ended up at the same table, facing each other with our unfolded papers. We read different ones: mine was the newspaper everybody read, the most important in the city; surely I had no reason to attract attention, to look different from the others, by reading a different paper, or to seem (if I had read the paper of the stranger at my table) a man with strong political ideas. I had always given political opinions and parties a wide berth, but there at the restaurant table, on certain evenings when I put the newspaper down, my fellow diner said, "May I?" motioning to it, and offering me his own: "If you'd like to have a look at this one . . ."

And so I glanced at his paper, which was, you might

say, the reverse of mine, not only because it supported opposing ideas, but because it dealt with things that didn't even exist for the other paper: workers who had been discharged, mechanics whose hands had been caught in their machinery (it also published the photographs of these men), charts with the figures of welfare payments, and so on. But above all, the more my paper tried to be witty in the writing of its articles and to attract the reader with amusing minor events, for example the divorce cases of pretty girls, the more this other paper used expressions that were always the same, repetitious, drab, with headlines that emphasized the negative side of things. Even the printing of the paper was drab, cramped, monotonous. And I found myself thinking, Why, I like it!

I tried to explain this impression to my casual companion, naturally taking care not to comment on individual news items or opinions (he had already begun by asking me what I thought of a certain report from Asia) and trying at the same time to play down the negative aspect of my view, because he seemed to me the sort of man who doesn't accept criticisms of his position and I had no intention of launching an argument.

Instead he seemed to be following his own train of thought, where my opinion of his paper must have been superfluous or out of place. "You know," he said, "this paper still isn't the way it should be. It isn't the paper I'd like it to be."

He was a short but well-proportioned young man, dark,

with carefully combed curly hair, his face still a boy's, pale, pink-cheeked, with regular, refined features, long black lashes, a reserved, almost haughty manner. He dressed with rather fastidious care. "There's still too much vagueness, a lack of precision," he went on, "especially in what concerns *our* affairs. The paper still resembles the others too much. The kind of paper I mean should be mostly written by its readers. It should try to give scientifically exact information about everything that goes on in the world of production."

"You're a technical expert in some factory, are you?" I asked.

"Skilled worker."

We introduced ourselves. His name was Omar Basaluzzi. When he learned that I worked for the IPUAIC, he became very much interested and asked me for some data to use in a report he was preparing. I suggested some publications to him (things in the public domain, as a matter of fact; I wasn't giving away any office secrets, as I remarked to him, just in case, with a little smile). He took out a notebook and methodically wrote down the information, as if he were compiling a bibliography.

"I'm interested in statistical studies," he said, "a field where our organization is far behind." We put on our overcoats, ready to leave. Basaluzzi had a rather sporty coat, elegantly cut, and a little cap of rainproof canvas. "We're very far behind," he went on, "whereas, the way I look at it, it's a fundamental field."

"Does your work leave you time for these studies?" I asked him.

"I'll tell you," he said (he always answered with some hauteur, in a slightly smug, ex cathedra manner), "it's all a question of method. I work eight hours a day in the factory, and then there's hardly an evening when I don't have some meeting to go to, even on Sunday. But you have to know how to organize your work. I've formed some study groups among the young people in our plant . . ."

"Are there many . . . like yourself?"

"Very few. Fewer all the time. One by one, they're getting rid of us. One fine day you'll see here"—and he pointed to the newspaper—"my own picture, with the headline 'Another worker discharged in reprisal.'"

We were walking in the cold of the night; I was huddled in my coat, the collar turned up; Omar Basaluzzi proceeded calmly, talking, his head erect, a little cloud of steam emerging from his finely drawn lips, and every now and then he took his hand from his pocket to underline a point in his talk, and then he stopped, as if he couldn't go ahead until that point had been clearly established.

I was no longer following what he said; I was thinking that a man like Omar Basaluzzi didn't try to evade all the smoky gray around us but to transform it into a moral value, an inner criterion.

"The smog . . ." I said.

"Smog? Yes, I know Cordà wants to play the modern industrialist—purify the atmosphere. Go tell that to his workers! He surely won't be the one to purify it. It's a question of social structure . . . If we manage to change that, we will also solve the smog problem. We, not they."

He invited me to go with him to a meeting of union representatives from the different plants of the city. I sat at the back of a smoky room. Omar Basaluzzi took a seat at the table on the dais with some other men, all older than he. The room wasn't heated; we kept our hats and coats on.

One by one, the men who were to speak stood up and took their place beside the table; all of them addressed the public in the same way: anonymous, unadorned, with formulas for beginning their speech and for linking the arguments which must have been part of some rule, because they all used them. From certain murmurs in the audience I realized a polemical statement had been made, but these were veiled polemics, which always began by approving what had been said before. Many of those who spoke seemed to have it in for Omar Basaluzzi; the young man, seated a bit sideways at the table, had taken a tooled-leather tobacco pouch from his pocket and a stubby English pipe, which he filled with slow movements of his small hands. He smoked in cautious puffs, his eyes slightly closed, one elbow on the table, his cheek resting in his hand.

The hall had filled with smoke. One man suggested opening a little high window for a moment. A cold gust changed the air, but soon the fog began coming in from outside, and you could hardly see the opposite end of the room. From my seat I examined that crowd of backs, motionless in the cold, some with upturned collars, and the row of bundled-up forms at the table, with one man on his feet talking, as bulky as a bear, all surrounded, impregnated now by that fog, even their words, their stubbornness.

Claudia came back in February. We went to have lunch in an expensive restaurant on the river, at the end of the park. Beyond the windows we looked at the shore and the trees that, with the color of the air, composed a picture of ancient elegance.

We couldn't understand each other. We argued on the subject of beauty. "People have lost the sense of beauty," Claudia said.

"Beauty has to be constantly invented," I said.

"Beauty is always beauty; it's eternal."

"Beauty is born always from some conflict."

"What about the Greeks?"

"Well, what about them?"

"Beauty is civilization!"

"And so . . ."

"Therefore . . ."

We could have gone on like this all day and all night.

"This park, this river . . ."

(This park, this river, I thought, can only be marginal, a consolation to us for the rest; ancient beauty is powerless against new ugliness.)

"This eel . . ."

In the center of the restaurant there was a glass tank, an aquarium, and some huge eels were swimming inside it. "Look!"

Some customers were approaching, important people, a family of well-to-do gourmets: mother, father, grown daughter, adolescent son. With them was the maître d'hôtel, an enormous, corpulent man in frock coat, stiff white shirt; he was grasping the handle of a little net, the kind children use for catching butterflies. The family, serious, intent, looked at the eels; at a certain point the mother raised her hand and pointed out an eel. The maître d'hôtel dipped the net into the aquarium; with a rapid swoop he caught the animal and drew it out of the water. The eel writhed and struggled in the net. The maître d'hôtel went off toward the kitchen, holding the net with the gasping eel straight out in front of him like a lance. The family watched him go off, then they sat down at the table, to wait until the eel came back, cooked.

"Cruelty . . ."

"Civilization . . ."

"Everything is cruel . . ."

Instead of having them call a taxi, we left on foot. The lawns, the tree trunks, were swathed in that veil which rose from the river, dense, damp, here still a natural phenomenon. Claudia walked protected by her fur coat, its wide collar, her muff, her fur hat. We were the two shadowy lovers who form a part of the picture.

"Beauty . . ."

"Your beauty . . ."

"What good is it? As far as that goes . . ."

I said, "Beauty is eternal."

"Ah, now you're saying what I said before, eh?"

"No, the opposite."

"It's impossible to discuss anything with you," she said.

She moved off as if she wanted to go on by herself, along the path. A layer of fog was flowing just over the earth: the fur-covered silhouette proceeded as if it weren't touching the ground.

I saw Claudia back to her hotel that evening, and we found the lobby full of gentlemen in dinner jackets and ladies in long, low-cut dresses. It was carnival time, and a charity ball was being held in the hotel ballroom.

"How marvelous! Will you take me? I'll just run and put on an evening dress!"

I'm not the sort who goes to balls, and I felt ill at ease.

"But we don't have an invitation . . . and I'm wearing a brown suit . . ."

"I never need an invitation . . . and you're my escort."

She ran up to change. I didn't know where to turn. The place was full of girls wearing their first evening dress, powdering their faces before going into the ballroom, exchanging excited whispers. I stood in a corner, trying to imagine I was a shop clerk who had come there to deliver a package.

The elevator door opened. Claudia stepped out in a sweeping skirt, pearls on a pink bodice, a little diamond-studded mask. I couldn't play the role of clerk anymore. I went over to her.

We went in. All eyes were on her. I found a mask to put on, a kind of clown's face with a long nose. We started dancing. When Claudia twirled around, the other couples stepped back to watch her; as I'm a very bad dancer, I wanted to stay in the midst of the crowd, so there was a kind of hide-and-seek. Claudia complained that I wasn't the least bit jolly, that I didn't know how to enjoy myself.

At the end of one dance, as we were going back to our table, we passed a group of ladies and gentlemen standing on the dance floor. "Oh!" There I was, face-to-face with Commendatore Cordà. He was in full dress, with a little orange paper hat on his head. I had to stop and say hello to him. "Why, it *is* you, then! I thought so, but I wasn't sure," he said, but he was looking at Claudia, and I realized he meant he would never have expected to see me with a woman like her, I looking the same as usual, in the suit I wore to the office.

I had to make the introductions; Cordà kissed Claudia's hand, introduced her to the other older men who were with him, and Claudia, absent as always and superior, paid no attention to the names (as I was saying to myself, "My

God! Is that who he is?" because they were all big shots in industry). Then Cordà introduced me: "And this is the managing editor of our periodical, you know, *Purification*, the paper I put out . . ." I realized they were all a bit intimidated by Claudia, and they were talking nonsense. So then I felt less timid myself.

I also realized something else was about to happen, namely that Cordà could hardly wait to ask Claudia to dance. I said, "Well then, we'll see you later . . ." I waved expansive goodbyes and led Claudia back to the dance floor as she said, "Wait a minute, you don't know how to dance to this, can't you hear the music?"

All I could hear or feel was that, in some way not yet clear even to those men, I had spoiled their evening when I appeared at Claudia's side, and this was the only satisfaction I could derive from the ball. *"Cha cha cha,"* I sang softly, pretending to dance with steps I didn't know how to make, holding Claudia only lightly by the hand so that she could move on her own.

It was carnival time; why shouldn't I have some fun? The little toy trumpets blared, fluttering their long fringes; handfuls of confetti pattered like crumbling mortar on the backs of the tailcoats and on the bare shoulders of the women, it slipped inside the low-cut gowns and the men's collars; and from chandelier to floor, where they collected in limp piles pushed about by the shuffling of the dancers, streamers unrolled like strips of bare fibers or like wires left hanging among collapsed walls in a general destruction.

"You can accept the ugly world the way it is because you know you have to destroy it," I said to Omar Basaluzzi. I spoke partly to provoke him; otherwise it was no fun.

"Just a moment," Omar said, setting down the little cup of coffee he had been raising to his lips. "We never say it has to get worse before it can get better. We want to improve things . . . No reformism, and no extremism. We . . ."

I was following my train of thought, he his. Ever since that time in the park with Claudia, I had been looking for a new image of the world which would give a meaning to our grayness, which would compensate for all the beauty that we were losing, or would save it. "A new face for the world."

The worker unzipped a black leather briefcase and took out an illustrated weekly. "You see?" There was a series of photographs. An Asiatic race, with fur caps and boots, blissfully going to fish in a river. In another photograph there was that same race, going to school; a teacher was pointing out, on a sheet, the letters of an incomprehensible alphabet. Another illustration showed a feast day and they all wore dragon heads, and in the middle, among the dragons, a tractor was advancing with a man's portrait over it. At the end there were two men, still in fur caps, operating a power lathe.

"You see? This is it," he said, "the other face of the world."

I looked at Basaluzzi. "You people don't wear fur caps, you don't fish for sturgeon, you don't play with dragons."

"What of it?"

"So your group doesn't resemble those people in any way, except for this"—and I pointed to the lathe—"which you already have."

"No, no, it'll be the same here as there, because it's man's conscience that will change, for us as it has for them, we'll be new inside ourselves, even before we are new outside," Basaluzzi said, and he went on leafing through the magazine. On another page there were photographs of blast furnaces and of workers with goggles over their eyes and fierce expressions. "Oh, there'll be problems then too, you mustn't think that overnight . . ." he said. "For quite a while it'll be hard: production . . . But a big step forward will have been made . . . Certain things won't happen as they do now," and he started speaking of the same things he always talked about, the problems that concerned him day in and day out.

I realized that for him, whether or not that new dawn ever came mattered less than one might think, because what counted for him was the line of his life, which was not to change.

"There'll always be trouble, of course . . . It won't be an earthly paradise . . . We're not saints, after all . . ."

Would the saints change their lives if they knew heaven didn't exist?

"They fired me last week," Omar Basaluzzi said.

"And now what?"

"I'm doing union work. Maybe next autumn one of the bosses will retire."

He was on his way to the Wafd, where there had been a violent demonstration that morning. "Want to come with me?"

"Eh! That's the one place I mustn't be seen. You understand why."

"I mustn't be seen there either. I'd get the comrades in trouble. We'll watch from a café nearby."

I went with him. Through the windows of a little café we saw the workers coming off their shift walk through the gates, wheeling their bicycles or crowding toward the streetcars, their faces already prepared for sleep. Some of them, obviously forewarned, came into the café and went at once to Omar, and so a little group was formed, which went off to one side to talk.

I understood nothing of their grievances, and I was trying to discover what was different between the faces of the countless men who swarmed through the gates surely thinking of nothing but their family and Sunday and these others who had stopped with Omar, the stubborn ones, the tough ones. And I could find no mark that distinguished them: the same aged or prematurely old faces, product of the same life; the difference was inside.

And then I studied the faces and the words of the latter group to see if I could distinguish the ones whose actions were based on the thought "The day will come . . ." and those for whom, as for Omar, whether the day really came or not didn't matter. And I saw they couldn't be distinguished, because perhaps they all belonged to the second category, even those few whose impatience or ready speech might make them seem to be in the first category.

And then I didn't know what to look at so I looked at the sky. It was an early spring day, and over the houses of the outskirts the sky was luminous, blue, clear; however, if I looked at it carefully, I could see a kind of shadow, a smudge, as if on an old, yellowed snapshot, like the marks you see through a spectroscope. Not even the fine season would cleanse the sky.

Omar Basaluzzi had put on a pair of dark glasses with thick frames and he continued talking in the midst of those men, precise, expert, proud, a bit nasal.

In *Purification* I published a news item I had found in a foreign paper concerning pollution of the air by atomic radiation. It was in small type and Commendatore Cordà didn't notice it in the galleys, but he read it when the paper was printed and he then sent for me.

"My God, I have to keep an eye on every little thing; I ought to have a hundred eyes, not two!" he said. "What came over you? What made you publish that piece? This isn't the sort of thing our institute should bother with. Not by a long shot! And then, without a word to me! On such a delicate question! Now they'll say we've started printing propaganda!"

I answered with a few words of defense: "Well, sir, since it was a question of air pollution . . . I'm sorry, I thought . . ."

I had already taken my leave when Cordà called me back. "See here, do you really believe in this danger of radioactivity? I mean, do you really think it's so serious?"

I remembered certain data from a scientific congress, and I repeated the information to him. Cordà listened to me, nodding, but irked.

"Hmph, what awful times we have to live in, my friend!" he blurted out at one point, and he was again the Cordà I knew so well. "It's the risk we have to run. There's no turning back the clock, because big things are at stake, my boy, big things!"

He bowed his head for a few moments. "We, in our field," he went on, "not wanting to overestimate the role we play, of course, still . . . we make our contribution, we're equal to the situation."

"That's certain, sir. I'm absolutely convinced of that." We looked at each other, a bit embarrassed, a bit hypocritical. The cloud of smog now seemed to have grown smaller, a tiny little puff, a cirrus, compared to the looming atomic mushroom.

I left Commendatore Cordà after a few more vague, affirmative words, and once again it wasn't clear whether his real battle was fought for or against the cloud.

After that, I avoided any mention of atomic explosions or radioactivity in the headlines, but in each number I tried to slip some information on the subject into the columns devoted to technical news, and even into certain articles; in the midst of the data on the percentages of coal or fuel oil in the urban atmosphere and their physiological consequences, I added analogous data and examples drawn from zones affected by atomic fallout. Neither Cordà nor anyone else mentioned these to me again, but this silence, rather than pleasing me, confirmed my suspicion that absolutely nobody read *Purification*.

I had a file where I kept all the material concerning nuclear radiation, because as I read through the papers with an eye trained to select usable news items and articles, I always found something on that subject and I saved it. A clipping service too, to which the institute had subscribed, sent us more and more clippings about atomic bombs, while those about smog grew fewer all the time.

So every day my eye fell upon statistics of terrible diseases, stories about fishermen overtaken in the middle of the ocean by lethal clouds, guinea pigs born with two heads after some experiments with uranium. I raised my eyes to the window. It was late June, but summer hadn't yet begun: the weather was oppressive, the days were smothered in a gloomy haze, during the afternoon hours the city was immersed in a light like the end of the world, and the passersby seemed shadows photographed on the ground after the body had flown away.

The normal order of the seasons seemed changed; intense cyclones coursed over Europe, the beginning of summer was marked by days heavily charged with electricity, then by weeks of rain, by sudden heat waves and sudden resurgences of March-like cold. The papers denied that these atmospheric disorders could be in any way connected with the effects of the bombs; only a few solitary scientists seemed to sustain this notion (and, for that matter, it was hard to discover if they were trustworthy) and, with them, the anonymous voice of the man in the street, always ready, of course, to give credence to the most disparate ideas.

Even I became irritated when I heard Signorina Margariti talking foolishly about the atomic bomb, warning me to take my umbrella to the office that morning. But to be sure, when I opened the blinds, at the livid sight of the courtyard, which in that false luminosity seemed a network of stripes and spots, I was tempted to draw back, as if a discharge of invisible particles were being released from the sky at that very moment.

This burden of unsaid things transformed them into superstition, influenced the banal talk about the weather, once considered the most harmless subject of conversation. Now people avoided mentioning the weather, or if they had to say it was raining or it had cleared they were filled with a kind of shame, as if some obscure responsibility of ours were being kept quiet. Signor Avandero, who lived through the weekdays in preparation for his Sunday excursion, had assumed a false indifference toward the weather; it seemed totally hypocritical to me, and servile.

I put out a number of *Purification* in which there wasn't one article that didn't speak of radioactivity. Even this time I had no trouble. It wasn't true, however, that nobody read the paper; people read it, all right, but by now they had become inured to such things, and even if you wrote that the end of the human race was at hand, nobody paid any attention.

The big weeklies also published reports that should have made you shudder, but people now seemed to believe only in the colored photographs of smiling girls on the cover. One of these weeklies came out with a photograph of Claudia on its cover; she was wearing a bathing suit and was making a turn on water skis. With four thumbtacks I pinned it on the wall of my furnished room.

Every morning and every afternoon I continued to go to that neighborhood of quiet avenues where my office was located, and sometimes I recalled the autumn day when I had gone there for the first time, when in everything I saw I had looked for a sign, and nothing had seemed sufficiently gray and squalid to suit the way I felt. Even now my gaze looked only for signs; I had never been able to see anything else. Signs of what? Signs that referred one to the other, into infinity.

At times I happened to encounter a mule-drawn cart: a two-wheeled cart going down an avenue, laden with sacks. Or else I found it waiting outside the door of a building, the mule between the shafts, his head low, and on top of the pile of sacks a little girl.

Then I realized that there wasn't only one of these carts going around that section; there were several of them. I couldn't say just when I began to notice this; you see so many things without paying attention to them; maybe these things you see have an effect on you but you aren't aware of it; and then you begin to connect one thing with the other and suddenly it all takes on meaning. The sight of those carts, without my consciously thinking of them, had a soothing effect on me, because an unusual encounter, as with a rustic cart in the midst of a city that is all automobiles, is enough to remind you that the world is never all one thing.

And so I began to pay attention to them: a little girl with pigtails sat on top of the white mountain of sacks reading a comic book, then a heavy man came from the door of the building with a couple of sacks and put those too on the cart, turned the handle of the brake and said "Gee" to the mule, and they went off, the little girl still up there, still reading. And then they stopped at another doorway; the man unloaded some sacks from the cart and carried them inside.

Farther ahead, in the opposite lane of the avenue, there was another cart, with an old man at the reins, and a woman who went up and down the front steps of the buildings with huge bundles on her head.

I began to notice that on the days when I saw the carts I was happier, more confident, and those days were always Mondays: so I learned that Monday is the day when the laundrymen go through the city with their carts, bringing back the clean laundry and taking away the dirty.

Now that I knew about it, the sight of the laundry carts no longer escaped me: all I had to do was see one as I went to work in the morning, and I would say to myself, "Why, of course, it's Monday!" and immediately afterward another would appear, following a different route, with a dog barking after it, and then another going off in the distance so I could see only its load from behind, the sacks with yellow-and-white stripes.

Coming home from the office, I took the streetcar through other streets, noisier and more crowded, but even there the traffic had to stop at a crossing as the long-spoked wheels of a laundry cart rolled by. I glanced into a side street, and by the sidewalk I saw the mule with bundles of laundry that a man in a straw hat was unloading.

That day I took a much longer route than usual to come home, still encountering the laundrymen. I realized that for the city this was a kind of feast day, because everyone was happy to give away the clothes soiled by the smoke and to wear again the whiteness of fresh linen, even if only for a short while.

The following Monday I decided to follow the laundry carts to see where they went afterward, once they had made their deliveries and picked up their work. I walked for a while at random, because I first followed one cart, then another, until at a certain point I realized that they were all finally going in the same direction, there were certain streets where they all passed eventually, and when they met or lined up one after the other they hailed one another with calm greetings and jokes. And so I went on following them, losing them, over a long stretch, until I was tired, but before leaving them I had learned that there was a village of laundries: the men were all from an outlying town called Barca Bertulla.

One day in the afternoon I went there. I crossed a bridge over a river and was virtually in the country; the highways were flanked still by a row of houses, but immediately behind them all was green. You couldn't see the laundries. Shady pergolas surrounded the wine shops along the canals interrupted by locks. I went on, casting my gaze beyond each farmyard gate and along each path. Little by little I left the built-up area behind, and now rows of poplars grew along the road, marking the banks of the frequent canals. And there in the background, beyond the poplars, I saw a meadow of white sails: laundry hung out to dry.

I turned into a path. Broad meadows were crisscrossed

with lines at eye level, and on these lines, piece after piece, was hung the laundry of the whole city, the linen still wet and shapeless, every item the same, with wrinkles the cloth made in the sun, and in each meadow this whiteness of long lines of washing was repeated. (Other meadows were bare, but they too were crossed by parallel lines, like vineyards without vines.)

I wandered through the fields white with hanging laundry, and I suddenly wheeled about at a burst of laughter. On the shore of a canal, above one of the locks, there was the ledge of a pool, and over it, high above me, their sleeves rolled up, in dresses of every color, were the red faces of the washerwomen, who laughed and chattered, the young ones' breasts bobbing up and down inside their blouses, and the old, fat women with kerchiefs on their heads; and they moved their round arms back and forth in the suds and they wrung out the twisted sheets with an angular movement of the elbows. In their midst the men in straw hats were unloading baskets in separate piles, or were also working with the square coarse soap, or else beating the wet cloth with wooden paddles.

By now I had seen, and I had nothing to say, no reason to pry. I turned back. At the edge of the highway a little grass was growing, and I was careful to walk there, so as not to get my shoes dusty and to keep clear of the passing trucks. Between the fields, the hedgerows, and the poplars, I continued to follow with my eyes the washing pools, the signs on certain low buildings—STEAM LAUNDRY, LAUNDRY CO-

303

OPERATIVE OF BARCA BERTULLA — the fields where the women passed with baskets as if harvesting grapes and picked the dry linen from the lines, and the countryside in the sun gave forth its greenness amid that white, and the water flowed away swollen with bluish bubbles. It wasn't much, but for me, seeking only images to retain in my eyes, perhaps it was enough.

About the Author

ITALO CALVINO's superb storytelling gifts earned him international renown and a reputation as "one of the world's best fabulists" (*New York Times Book Review*). He is the author of numerous works of fiction, as well as essays, criticism, and literary anthologies. Born in Cuba in 1923, Calvino was raised in Italy, where he lived most of his life. At the time of his death, in Siena in 1985, he was the most translated contemporary Italian writer.